FORGOTTENNESS

FORGOTTENNESS

a novel

Tanja Maljartschuk

*Translated from Ukrainian by
Zenia Tompkins*

Liveright Publishing Corporation

*A Division of W. W. Norton & Company
Independent Publishers Since 1923*

The publication of this book has been made possible in part by a Translation-in-Progress Grant of the Peterson Literary Fund at BCU Foundation (Toronto, Canada).

Originally published in the Ukrainian language under the title "Забуття"
© 2016 Tanja Maljartschuk
All rights reserved
© 2019, 2022, Verlag Kiepenheuer & Witsch, Köln
Translation © 2024 by Liveright Publishing Corporation,
A Division of W. W. Norton & Company, Inc.

Printed in the United States of America

Manufacturing by Lakeside Book Company
Book design by Beth Steidle
Production manager: Julia Druskin

ISBN 978-1-324-09322-0 (pbk)

Liveright Publishing Corporation, 500 Fifth Avenue, New York, N.Y. 10110
www.wwnorton.com

W. W. Norton & Company Ltd., 15 Carlisle Street, London W1D 3BS

1 2 3 4 5 6 7 8 9 0

For Michael.

Contents

FORGOTTENNESS

I.

IN THE BELLY OF THE BLUE WHALE

(Us)

THE MOST DIFFICULT THING TO EXPLAIN—even to myself—is why him? Where did this story of ours come from? Who are we to one another?

No one, I reply.

We've never met. (Our meeting was physically impossible.) We aren't relatives, we aren't fellow countrymen, we aren't even of the same nationality. He was Polish, and I'm Ukrainian. He was an intellectual, a philosopher active in politics, a poet with a place in history. I'm just a person who manipulates words and ideas, with no real profession; I can write, or I can remain silent. Our lives were too disparate to comfortably fit into a shared narrative, if not for my irrational stubbornness.

I'VE PULLED TOGETHER THREE POINTS where our lives intersected, two in space and one in time. That's the best I've been able to do. There simply are no more. Here is the first one: He once spent a few days in my hometown. World War I had just ended. He was an envoy of the Ukrainian State and had an important engagement there. I, likewise, spent a few hours in his native village. I went there purposely. A villager with an old-fashioned mustache by the name of Petro, who now looks after his family estate, showed me around gladly but did ask, "So, who is he to you? Why are you interested? For an average tourist, you know too much."

I replied that, well, I was just interested. Simply because. That it was hard to explain. Peter nodded that he understood. He squeezed my hand with his own coarse, callused one. I didn't admit that there was a third thing that united us, a strange coincidence that I had noticed quite recently and was cherishing as if it were the ultimate justification of my obsession. Our lives had intersected once in time as well. We were born on the same day, both on April 17, only he exactly a hundred years before me.

I now find myself thinking about time often and tell everyone that only with time does a sense of time come. That the further in time you go, the more palpable it becomes. The longer you live, the more of it there is. And all the other times—those in which I haven't lived, but which I know existed—grow over the little grain of my individual time, stratify it, encrust it. That's why it always seems as though I've lived interminably long and that the end should be arriving at any moment.

THE END, IN FACT, had arrived: my heart started going into my throat. That's how I described the sudden panic attacks, that feeling of being consumed by a tremendous fright, when my heart, the central organ of my body, suddenly thundered and crept up to my throat, threatening to leap out onto the floor. I tried to describe my bouts with words (they're my defense, my army; I am, after all, a woman of letters), but the words raveled apart, as if someone were cooking them, stirring them sporadically with a wooden spoon. Words no longer meant anything. The end that I was experiencing, the end of all times within me, couldn't be described the way I used to, the way I expected to. New words were needed, a new truth, and the search for them grabbed hold of my entire mind.

OVER THE COURSE of my past "literary career," which entailed all of six slight books, I always worked on a computer. I never wrote by hand and, quite frankly, don't know how to, so when the need arose, I painstakingly traced out scribbles and, for lack of practice, made a slew of mistakes. My computer, by contrast, felt like a weaving loom. In the past, I seemed to type on it as though weaving a rug, and I'd strive to make the text as colorful as possible. Now the process of writing reminds me more of playing a piano. I'm making music. I press the keys adeptly; I rhythmically lean my torso forward; when the music tires, my fingers halt midair and then obediently drop down to the keyboard, forcing the needed letters to sound. Whereas in the past, when I wrote, I was weaving a colorful life path, these days I'm composing the inexorable music of the end, a requiem for my own self. That doesn't mean that I'll die tomorrow—not at all. Having survived and accepted one's own end, it's possible to still live as long as one pleases.

THE FEELING OF MY HEART in my throat used to be so unbearable, especially in the beginning, that I would've thrown myself out the window had I been able to move in the moment: anything to stop the palpitations, the pain in my chest and temples, the shortness of breath, the dizziness, the nausea. Though it wasn't the physical suffering that was truly unbearable, but the distortion of reality, my new perception of it—as if I were looking at life from the far side, the one from which there is no longer any return. It was the complete horror that we, the living, imagine death to be. Simultaneously, I was experiencing the loss (or the primordial absence?) of the slightest sense of meaning—the foundational one, the one from which everything begins. The question, "What for?" eclipsed all the rest. The "who am I" wasn't important, just the "what for." The "when" and "how" didn't matter either, only the "why."

And so, at one such instance, while suffering from abysmal uselessness, I suddenly began to think about time as the thing that unites an endless rosary of senseless events; and also about the fact that only in the sequence of these events is there meaning; and that it's not God, not love, not beauty, not the greatness of intellect that determines this world, but only time—the flow of time and the glimmering of human life within it.

Human life is its sustenance. Time consumes everything living by the ton, like a gigantic blue whale consumes microscopic plankton, milling and chewing it into a homogeneous mass, so that one life disappears without a trace, giving another, the next life, a chance. Yet it wasn't the disappearance that grieved me the most, but the tracelessness of it. I thought to myself: I've already got one foot there, out in complete forgottenness. The process of my inevitable disappearance was initiated at the moment of my birth. And the longer I live, the more I vanish. My feelings and my emotions vanish, my pain and my joy; the places I've seen vanish, and the people I've met. My memories vanish, as do my thoughts. My conception of the world vanishes. My body vanishes, more and more every day. The world within me and around me vanishes, leaving no trace, and I can do nothing to safeguard it.

IT WAS IN THE WAKE of this revelation that I took to reading old newspapers in large quantities. The fragility of human life in the face of the omnipotence of time can be felt most in the dusty pages of daily newspapers. There, these lives were still important. The headlines abounded with the dreams and fears of entire nations, discussions were conducted, scandals exploded, rebuttals were published, pharmacies and bookstores and travel agencies placed their ads, someone was collecting donations for war-crippled country-men, someone else was announcing a literary soiree, and on the final page there were always one or two mediocre poems with patriotic themes, for the soul, until suddenly, poof!—and this gurgling time of the present had become the past, the mouth of the blue whale was already open and was beginning to gulp it all down, the editor sorrowfully shared that due to a lack of funding the newspaper was halting circulation, "but not for good!" And not a single issue more. The end. Time had prevailed. The blue whale was swimming away.

That's what happened with the first Ukrainian newspaper, *Dilo* (*Deed*), which was published from 1880 to 1939 in Lviv. In 1939, a centuries-long history of this city came to a close. The Red Army's entry into Lviv that year initiated a new—Soviet—era, the particular predilection of which was the killing of the past and a ban on memory.

That's what also happened with the other large Ukrainian newspaper, *Rada* (*Council*), which was published daily in Kyiv from 1906 to 1914. The publisher, Yevhen Chykalenko, had been forced to contribute considerable funds from his own pocket so that the newspaper would continue to exist because no one subscribed to it. The First World War addressed this problem in a definitive manner, and Yevhen Chykalenko breathed a sigh of relief because his conscience wouldn't have permitted him to shut down the newspaper himself. He said that a newspaper was like a flag: if it was flying, that meant Ukraine was still in existence.

But the fate of the newspaper *Svoboda* (*Liberty*), which the Ukrainian community in America began to publish in New York back in 1893 and still publishes to this day, was entirely different. This newspaper became my favorite not because it was the best, but because it saw everything and forgot nothing. One hundred and twenty uninterrupted years. Six generations of people united by one chronology. The murder of Franz Ferdinand in Sarajevo and the fall of the Soviet Union, or events on Ukrainian lands, like the fire in Husiatyn in 1893 and the Bolekhiv butcher Anton, who in 1934 cut off his own mother's head with an ax. Or, for another example, the June 20, 1931, issue, which reported in its pages that the gangster Al Capone had been arrested in Chicago.

I mulled over this information for a moment, attempting to imagine what was going on in another part of the world that same year, in the villages of my grandmothers and grandfathers, for instance, but the only thing that kept popping into my mind was that the women in those Ukrainian villages didn't wear underwear because they simply didn't have any, and routinely, when the need arose, had to sit at home so that no one would see the ritual blood trickling down their calves.

Only later did my attention migrate to the big black uppercase letters on the front page, which only an unscrupulous reader could have skipped past in favor of the arrest of a Chicago gangster. Three words in total, stamped in black ink. It was impossible to not see them. An eerie chill swept down my back. I reread the headline over and over until I stopped feeling anything. Over and over:

VIACHESLAV LYPYNSKYI DEAD

At the time, I didn't know who he was or how he had died. But the death of this man must have been of considerable importance to someone in the Ukrainian diaspora if *Svoboda* was reporting it on the front page, neglecting the fates of Al Capone and his New York counterpart Dutch Schultz, who would also be thrown in jail days later. The announcement that the Russian writer Maxim Gorky had been admitted into the ranks of the Communist Party likewise didn't outweigh the death notification in importance, nor did the suicide of the wife of the Rabbi of Vilnius, the cause of which was apparently a "nervous disorder." In this issue of *Svoboda*, nothing was more important than the death of Viacheslav Lypynskyi. In contrast to the hapless wife of the rabbi, whose name went altogether unreported, Lypynskyi's name needed no explanation, otherwise he wouldn't have been written about in the spot typically reserved for some sort of global catastrophe, such as, say, the devastating 1906 earthquake in San Francisco.

I read the obituary below the black headline. An eminent historian and a prominent politician. He had left instructions to have his heart pierced after his death because he feared being buried alive. The heart puncture was performed in the Austrian sanatorium Wienerwald, the same one where the little-known writer Franz Kafka had unsuccessfully undergone treatment a few years earlier. Lypynskyi's daughter Ewa and his brother Stanisław served as witnesses to the procedure.

AT THAT SAME TIME, in June 1931, my paternal grandfather had just turned five years old. His mother, my great-grandmother, who didn't own any horses, used to harness herself to a plow in order to till up a hectare of land, and signed her name with an *X*. Their homeland, Ukraine—or more precisely, Eastern Halychyna—was still a part of Poland then.

My maternal grandmother was also alive already. Her mother, another great-grandmother of mine, had the best voice in her parts, but few got the chance to enjoy it because she died immediately after giving birth to her daughter. Her widower, a once-prosperous grain farmer, left his daughter on the steps of an orphanage and himself died of starvation in 1933. Their homeland—Malorossiia or "Little Russia," the Greater Ukraine that straddled the Dnipro River, the original Ukrainian Soviet Socialist Republic—was de facto a part of Russia. Though can a land that kills really be called a "homeland"? I don't know. I had ended up right in the belly of the blue whale. Swallowed whole, I still had the chance to resuscitate my story. Mine and his, Viacheslav Lypynskyi's. My story through his story. I needed only to pretend that no one's heart had been pierced and that it was still beating. Just now, in my throat.

II.

INHALE, EXHALE

(Him)

ACTUALLY, THE ENTIRETY of the Ukrainian press reported his death, though did so with some delay. Viacheslav Lypynskyi died. Lypynskyi was dead. What a loss. Finally. Everyone knew Lypynskyi. It would be harder without him. Or easier? In any case, it would be lonelier, because he didn't let anyone get bored. Ukrainian nobility died along with him. He was a mad tubercular consumptive. A recluse. It had been years since anyone had seen him. But everyone had continued to read what he wrote. And he wrote a lot. At times, ten letters a day. Did anyone even understand his scribbles? Did anyone even grasp what it was exactly he was trying to say? He was feared because he demanded dignity from people, contending that it was their duty. Who needed that? That's precisely why no one liked him: Everyone just endured him. And sighed with relief when he died. Lypynskyi's enemies wrote laudatory obituaries. They had stockpiled drafts long before. Everyone had been waiting for his death. It's a wonder he hadn't died sooner.

———

THEY CARRIED HIM out of his home in their arms. Outside, a car waited to take him to the sanatorium.

"Will I see all this again?" he asked himself, glancing around.

"You'll see it. You've lived through worse," replied Lypynskyi's housekeeper Fräulein Yulia Rosenfeld. He was speaking in Ukrainian, she in German. Their interactions after many shared years were perfectly tuned. She understood him better than anyone else alive, knowing how to assess the state of his health on a given day solely by the depth and rate of his breathing. Analyzing Lypynskyi's breathing was a fixation of hers—a hobby the housekeeper had managed to polish to perfection alongside the housework, the washing of his clothes, and the shining of shoes that Lypynskyi hadn't worn in years.

Everyone called the fräulein Fin Yulí. Older than her employer by five years, never wed, a now gray-blond, she was not one to mince words, but was also fair and loving. It was she who would often say, "Where are you rushing to? Breathe slower. O-o-one, two. Inha-a-ale, exhale."

Lypynskyi would wave her off with exasperation. "I'm glad to still be breathing at all. Let me be."

Inha-a-ale, exhale. Inha-a-ale, exhale.

Lypynskyi would try to calm his lungs—that is, the part of them that (so he thought) hadn't become entirely perforated yet. Then Fin Yulí would open the windows wide, and the cold mountain wind would burst into the tidy room with a large bed in the middle. This bed had long served as Lypynskyi's office. Snow-covered alpine peaks were visible from the window. Lypynskyi would close his eyes and breathe. O-o-one, two. Inha-a-ale, exhale. Two hours, three hours. As if rocking in a cradle stretched between two mountaintops over a deep valley. Bit by bit, his mustache, still fully black, would grow covered with hoarfrost.

———

LYPYNSKYI'S DAUGHTER EWA was standing in the yard. She had made a special trip from Kraków after learning about the heart attack. It happened in late May: the doctor took six hours to arrive because horrible weather had enveloped the mountains and turbid waters filled with uprooted saplings were streaming from the highlands in stormy torrents, eroding even the main roads, to say nothing of the mountain paths. Lypynskyi had been very nervous. Fin Yulí stood at the window while he, like a child, asked every few minutes, "Is he here yet?"

"Not yet, but soon."

"In my condition," he exclaimed, "I can't afford to wait this long for a doctor."

It was decided after that he would go to the sanatorium. Lypynskyi sold his archive to Andrii Sheptytskyi, the metropolitan archbishop of the Ukrainian Greek Catholic Church, so as to pay for the costly stay in Wienerwald. For the entire archive, which consisted of letters, manuscripts, notes, unpublished articles, and related materials, he received a few hundred dollars. That should suffice for the first while.

Viacheslav Lypynskyi had been preparing for death since childhood, but precisely then, as it stood right next to him in the forty-ninth year of his life, he began to resist it with all his might. He didn't want to die. He would mutter under his breath, "Just a few years more," when he thought that no one was watching him. It would be good to finish writing a few more articles, to see a few more people, to do a few more things. To destroy his political enemies, of which Lypynskyi had a fair number. To spend a few days with his daughter. Perhaps go with her to the sea as he once had with her mother? It was just a shame that breezes did him such harm. Breezes and mistrals were his nemeses. Wind in its various forms—that's what destroyed Lypynskyi. He was able to distinguish them by scent. Based on the wind's scent, he knew the time of day. The wind that blows at five in the morning smells different from the one that replaces it at six. That scent is sharper, somewhat fresher, like morning soap. It was the winds that had directed him his entire life, in the very end making him a hostage of a certain small country in which, after the collapse of the Austro-Hungarian Empire, no one would have lived of their own volition. The cold northwestern mistrals drove him out of Geneva, where he had spent a year studying sociology; then, together with the mighty western winds, they chased him out of Vienna, where, for almost a year, he had been an ambassador of the Ukrainian State headed by Hetman Pavlo Skoropadskyi; and the mistrals later became the reason for his departure from Berlin, where, convinced that an "enlightened monarchy" was the only viable form of political governance for Ukraine, Lypynskyi was attempting to mitigate court intrigues and remind the exiled candidate for the post of Ukrainian monarch to maintain his honor, like a true hetman. Geneva, Vienna, Berlin. Listening to his lungs, the doctors would shake their heads every time and advise leaving. The winds expelled him from his life and condemned him to eternal imprisonment in those at once beautiful and detestable foothills of the Austrian Alps. The hamlet of Badegg, Post Office Tobelbad, Styria. Three kilometers to the railway station, a half hour by train to Graz, five hours by train to Vienna.

The house in Badegg, or, as he himself called it, *das Sterbehaus*, "the death house," hadn't cost much at all—a total of fifty-five hundred shillings, or eight hundred dollars—but for Lypynskyi, who had long made do on twenty dollars a month, even this sum was sky-high. A certain philanthropist from Canada helped, as did Lypynskyi's younger brother Stanisław. In exchange for his brother's aid, Lypynskyi renounced any claims whatsoever to their parents' estate in Ukraine, in the village Zaturtsi, not far from Lutsk. Stanisław, a successful agricultural selectionist, lived there now, where he mostly bred new types of wheat and potatoes. Their older brother Wlodzimierz was a doctor who lived in Lutsk, where he had been the first in the city to own an automobile. Though the Lypynski family—or rather, it would be more correct to say the Lipiński family—weren't people of great means. They were middling Polish noblemen who kept afloat thanks only to good education and sensible estate management.

STANISŁAW ALSO CAME TO THE STERBEHAUS in Badegg when he heard about the heart attack. He had lost his shape somewhat, had acquired a paunch, and the features of his face had softened—as typically happens with happily married good souls, which he, no doubt, was.

Carrying Lypynskyi out of the house in his arms, he gently admonished him. "I told you, Wacław, that buying a house in this kind of backwater isn't worth it. Why couldn't you come stay with us in Zaturtsi? There's enough room there, the nature is beautiful, there are barely any winds. Maria and the children would've been glad to have you. You know how they love you . . ."

"Don't call me Wacław," Lypynskyi rasped in response. His brother and daughter were speaking in Polish, Lypynskyi in Ukrainian.

THIS PHRASE, "DON'T CALL ME WACŁAW," had become Lypynskyi's go-to weapon back when he was nineteen. He had just returned from the Kyiv Preparatory School to Zaturtsi for winter vacation. The whole family was gathered around the dinner table. Lypynskyi listened to their reports of local news in silence. The school uniform suited him particularly well, highlighting his slim but somewhat hunched and almost frail silhouette. His hair, thick and black as tar, was combed back prep-school-style.

"Wacław, how are your studies going?" his mother Klara Lipińska asked at last. Everyone looked at him, and the longer the silence lasted, the more their interest grew. Stanisław, Wlodzimierz, and their sister Wanda gazed intently. Only their father, Kazimierz Lipiński, with his characteristic insouciance, continued daintily eating the holiday cutlet. Lypynskyi timidly cleared his throat.

"Wacław?" Klara was still waiting for an answer. That's when Lypynskyi first shot out his new weapon—the socially unacceptable one that he would later take out of its holster frequently to protect himself.

"Don't call me Wacław. I'm Viacheslav."

His father nearly choked on the cutlet. His mother squealed. His brothers and sister exchanged silent glances. To make things worse, Lypynskyi was talking in Ukrainian, a language—though it wasn't even a language, just a rural dialect, a hodgepodge of Polish and Russian—the Lipiński family had never heard emerge from the lips of an educated person, only from the local poor.

"Did something happen that we should know about?" Klara Lipińska asked, trying with all her might to remain calm. She was a small woman but an authoritative one.

"I consider myself Ukrainian," the newly minted Viacheslav rejoined quietly, almost inaudibly. His confidence was gradually dissipating. His stoop was becoming ever more noticeable.

Finally, Klara Lipińska erupted. "What kind of Ukrainian are you? You're a Pole, son! All of us are Poles, from our great-grandfathers on down!"

Lypynskyi's head hung in silence. It was evident that he wasn't in agreement, that he wasn't planning to budge, but he didn't have enough of an argument for an effective rebuff yet. This was what he always did in situations like this: he'd keep quiet, to brace himself to field the oncoming attack. Klara Lipińska knew this trait better than anyone and was now shaking with enfeebled rage. He had always been like that—unreliable, weak, emotionally fragile—and now, for the love of God, he had definitively gone mad.

At that the celebratory dinner ended. Everyone dispersed to their own corners, scowling. And that night, an unusually large amount of snow fell. Lypynskyi, lying in his room and staring at the ceiling, was scared that the roof would cave under such a load, and that he'd be buried under a white snowdrift, as if lying covered by a mound of soil in a freshly dug grave. Years later, he would at times find himself gripped by the sensation that he was lying at the very bottom of some sort of pit, where it was cold and lonely, and from down there, from deep down inside, the pit seemed even deeper than it really was, infinitely deep, as if there were no bottom at all, just an eternal fall downward, and Lypynskyi would raise his arms upward in desperation to catch on to something, anything, some sort of invisible handrail, to steady himself.

HIS DECISION, UPON GRADUATING from the Kyiv Preparatory School, to study agriculture at a university in Kraków somewhat reduced the tension in the family. Even though, at the time, land cultivation interested Lypynskyi no more than ladies' hat trends, for a young man of his pedigree and financial means, agricultural education was a very rational choice: landowners had to know what to do with their hectares. And where else should a young Pole study, if not in Kraków? *He'll outgrow it*, hoped Klara Lipińska. *Wacław is a smart boy. He's just rebelling.*

HIS BROTHER STANISŁAW burst out laughing when he heard the familiar and already long-belabored, "Don't call me Wacław."

"You're right," he said. "A respectable Wacław never did actually come of you."

Now, in 1931, the philosophical and ideological conflicts between them had lost their acuteness. Stanisław, in calling his brother Wacław, did so intentionally, for fun, just to annoy him. Now that everything had already transpired, all the wars over and all the battles lost, names no longer mattered. There was no more cause for arguments. All that remained were perforations in the lungs.

O-o-one, two. Inha-a-ale, exhale.

They climbed into the car. Fin Yulí was going to the sanatorium too; Lypynskyi couldn't imagine his stay there without her. Just as she had at home, she was supposed to adjust his pillows, make arrangements with the doctors, read newspapers aloud, serve him water at night, and place her hand on his forehead while uttering the words, "Everything's all right. There's no fever." She was supposed to listen to his patchy breathing and determine whether Lypynskyi was still alive. At times, he himself would doubt it, and then it would suffice to glance at Fin Yulí, and the housekeeper would reassuringly nod her head as if to say, *Don't fret, you're alive.*

The driver started the engine. It was seven in the morning. The trip would take four to five hours. On the wooden stairs of the house, Lypynskyi's secretary of many years, Savur-Tsyprianovych—his loyal dog—was left standing. He waved his hand in farewell. A short red-mustached man of roughly the same age as Lypynskyi. Hailing from somewhere around Kyiv, though no one will find details about his place of birth in any encyclopedia. A ghost of a man. A shadow of a man.

TSYPRIANOVYCH HAD LIVED with Lypynskyi for the preceding eleven years after fleeing Kyiv, which had been seized by the Bolsheviks yet again, by freight train to Vienna. There he knew only one address—Hotel Bristol on Kärntner Ring 1—and the fact that the Ukrainian ambassador resided there. He had arrived and positioned himself in the lobby next to the window; the porter measured the newcomer distrustfully from head to toe.

"I'm here for Envoy Lypynskyi," announced Tsyprianovych, but the porter shook his head.

"The envoy has relinquished his position and is in the process of moving to new quarters. He's actually very ill. Give him some peace, for once."

Tsyprianovych was at a loss. He didn't have anywhere else to go. The porter repeated the same thing over and over: "Leave him in peace. Go on. There's nothing worth waiting for here. You all flock to him like flies to carrion."

"Then who's the Ukrainian envoy now?" Tsyprianovych asked in despair.

The porter exploded, "How should I know, good man? As if I'm the one to ask!"

At that moment, Lypynskyi had descended into the foyer: groomed pointed whiskers, a meticulously combed head of black hair, and large eyes, surprisingly animated on such a withered body. A carriage was waiting for Lypynskyi at the entrance, which was supposed to drive him to a sanatorium in Baden for treatment. Fin Yulí was giving instructions to the cabman.

"Herr Lypynskyi—" Tsyprianovych called out to him, then fearfully broke off because he didn't know what to say next.

Lypynskyi stopped short and glanced inquisitively at Tsyprianovych.

"Tell me where I should go, Mr. Lypynskyi."

"And who are you?"

"Mykhailo Petrovych Savur-Tsyprianovych."

"I already told him that there's nothing worth waiting for here," the porter interjected.

Lypynskyi was seized by a coughing fit. Fin Yulí extended a white kerchief monogrammed in red with *W. Lipiński.*

"And what are your skills?" Lypynskyi asked unexpectedly.

"I'm a secretary," Tsyprianovych mumbled despondently. "I worked in the administration of the Directorate of Ukraine, in the office of the Ministry of Education. We were evacuated from Kyiv a month ago."

"What languages do you know?"

"German, as you can see, and French and Russian."

"And do you know Ukrainian?"

"That's my native tongue."

"Come visit me in the sanatorium in Baden in a month. If we can reach an agreement, you'll be my secretary. I'm looking for one right now."

Tsyprianovych thanked him. His eyes welled with dog tears of devotion, but he brushed them away with the sleeves of his frayed frock coat. From the doorway, Lypynskyi added, "Do you have somewhere to stay?"

"I don't, Mr. Ambassador."

"I'm no longer an ambassador. Address me as you would anyone else from Ukraine, by my first name and patronymic—Viacheslav Kazymyrovych." He whispered something to the porter, then walked out of the hotel and climbed into the carriage.

"You're lucky," the porter grunted before instructing Tsyprianovych to follow him. "He's a good man, so everyone takes advantage of him. I would chase the likes of you off to hell. Flocking here like flies to carrion . . ."

A month later, after agreeing on the terms of his employment, Tsyprianovych took up his new position. His responsibilities were diverse. Besides his regular duties as a secretary, he performed the more labor-intensive tasks around the house in Badegg, fetched the doctor in the event of an emergency (occasionally several times in a single night), and transported guests from the gate to the house in a dray. On Lypynskyi's behalf, Tsyprianovych also corresponded with those Lypynskyi himself found wearisome. He composed his responses on the basis of previously written letters; he didn't have the right to arbitrarily improvise, no matter how tempting it was. He met with Lypynskyi's old friends in Vienna, queried them about their present lives, and then relayed everything in detail to his master. Sometimes he would fib a little, embellish things; other times he would fail to mention someone's death. Tsyprianovych's wages consisted of two dollars a month plus food and a roof over his head. Now and then Lypynskyi offered him additional bonuses, but Tsyprianovych usually declined them, aware that Lypynskyi didn't have enough money for treatments. Tsyprianovych was healthy; he was never in need of much. His only problem was his aching teeth. Sometimes Lypynskyi would cover the cost of a dentist in town for the secretary because in the rural area where they lived dentistry was performed by an ordinary doctor who knew only that teeth stopped hurting if you pulled them out.

Their mornings, set aside for work, looked like this: Fin Yulí would enter the room and open the window wide so that Lypynskyi could begin his respiratory regimen. His so-called "air therapy." Tsyprianovych would inquire matter-of-factly, "Are you going to write yourself today, or dictate?"

His query was pointless. It had been a long time since Lypynskyi had picked up a pencil. No one could make out his scribbles afterward, not even he himself.

"Dictate," would come in response, and Tsyprianovych would carry into the bedroom his idol, his deity—his typewriter. He was prepared to die for it. It nourished him wholesomely and completely like a cow in Halychyna nourishes its peasants. He would place it reverently on the table, then sit down next to it and knead his hands ritualistically.

"I'm ready, Viacheslav Kazymyrovych. How many letters today?"

"One. But make two copies. And I beg you, Tsyprianovych, don't twist around what I say. Don't correct what you think are my mistakes. Write what I dictate."

"But the word 'commendable' is written with two *m*'s. Anyone you ask will confirm that for you."

Lypynskyi waved him off, agitated at being corrected.

"Then write as you know how. To hell with you. You'll do it your own way all the same. My friends have told me many a time already that your typed letters differ from my handwritten ones and that sometimes they don't recognize me in my own correspondence."

Tsyprianovych had learned to not react to these kinds of attacks. Over his years of service, he softheartedly forgave Lypynskyi his linguistic quirks, which no respectable secretary would have tolerated. "Hooliganish," for example. Why, what kind of word is that? What does it even mean? "Hooliganish danger"—and make of it what you will! Or "selfstatelessness." That's both a joke and a sin! But Tsyprianovych tolerated it and, his teeth clenched, typed even greater nonsense.

"To Ivan Krevetskyi." Lypynskyi gave the name of the recipient and waited while the secretary rapped out the standard heading on the typewriter: Badegg, Post Office Tobelbad, Austria. A snowstorm was blowing in through the window; bit by bit, Lypynskyi's mustache and eyebrows were growing white.

Inha-a-ale, exhale.

"*Esteemed and Dear Mister Ivan!*" he began to dictate slowly. "*On the occasion of the Christmas holidays and the New Year, I send You heartfelt wishes for all the best in the coming year. I thank you for your wishes and for remembering me. There is only one wish of yours I cannot understand: For a return to my native land? By whom and for what am I needed in this native land?*"

Tsyprianovych's typing slowed. He was getting cold.

"No, I maintain hope that in the end God the Merciful will at least relieve me of any contact with the Ukrainian populace, to whom I gave everything I had and who thanked me with the gravest insult that can exist for an honest man. Not a single voice stood in my defense when the froth that now grows into moss on the wreckage and spreads befell me. Moss with a double *s."*

"I know how to spell 'moss.'" Tsyprianovych was piqued. "You don't need to tell me, Viacheslav Kazymyrovych."

"Forgive me, forgive me. I'm doing it out of habit. I'm continuing. *My Ukraine has perished. I have nothing and no one to return to.* Signed: *He who is dead to the deceased."*

"He who is dead to the deceased? What kind of signature is that? You're still alive."

"Just write what I say."

Tsyprianovych gave in, narrating aloud what he was typing. "*He who is dead to the deceased.* Dated: *December 30.* Should I write the Rusyn *Detsember* or the more properly Ukrainian *Hruden?"*

"Write *Detsember."*

"*Detsember 30. With the utmost respect, Your Lypynskyi."*

Afterward, Lypynskyi asked to be left alone. From the corridor, Tsyprianovych could hear him crying.

STANDING ON THE STEPS of the Sterbehaus and seeing off the car packed up for the sanatorium, Tsyprianovych had no idea that he was seeing his master for the last time. Otherwise, he would have somehow prepared himself. Perhaps he would have embraced him. They never embraced, only bickered, though they respected and depended on each other. One time, after a routine "orthographic" argument, Tsyprianovych got so angry that he resigned and pointedly went to Vienna to look for another job. After spending two weeks at their mutual friend Zhuk's and never receiving the apologetic letter from Lypynskyi he was waiting for, he returned. Lypynskyi wordlessly accepted him back. He had, in fact, written a letter of apology but hadn't known what address to send it to.

There's one photograph of them together. Lypynskyi in his predictable dressing gown with a cane in his hands, Tsyprianovych in a double-breasted baize shirt in a slanted plaid; the colors aren't visible because the photograph is black-and-white. They're sitting shoulder to shoulder in front of the house in Badegg. Someone else's children, possibly Stanisław's, are in the background. It looks to be warm outside. The terrace is filled with blooming flowerpots. Both men are diminished in size, thinned from age, and narrow in the shoulders. Lypynskyi is gazing into the lens, Tsyprianovych somewhere off to the side. Lypynskyi's head is egg-shaped, his nape completely bald already, his eyebrows knit. Tsyprianovych looks like a ghost of a man. No one will find details about his subsequent life in any encyclopedia. No one knows what happened to him afterward. With the death of Lypynskyi, he too died.

THE ONLY THING that Tsyprianovych left behind was a very short but detailed, almost physiological, account of the final days of his master's life. A magazine in Lviv published it a year after Lypynskyi's death. Tsyprianovych reports that the final journey to the sanatorium went well: Lypynskyi was cheery and hopeful. At the sanatorium, he was immediately given an injection of camphor. The following day, after a thorough examination, Fin Yulí asked the doctor if there was any hope, and he, with a shake of the head, replied that Lypynskyi had come there to die. The housekeeper didn't give much credence to the words, as she had heard such prognoses before. The brother and daughter, after lengthy conversations with the patient, departed. Lypynskyi rose only in the mornings in order to wash himself, seated. The housekeeper would read him German newspapers. The entire time, he was fully conscious. When he slept, his eyes stayed open. He kept repeating that he needed to survive for a few more years, muttered things about the sea and about salt, reminisced about his wife, whom he never again saw after the divorce in 1919. The housekeeper made arrangements to have a priest hear his confession, to which Lypynskyi agreed, but he expressed surprise, assuring her that he didn't feel all that bad. At eight in the evening, after yet another injection of camphor, he complained that he was very tired and wanted to sleep. The housekeeper adjusted the pillows. He fell asleep, again with his eyes open. His breathing was, as usual, short and rapid. Fin Yulí dozed off beside him in a chair. Around half past ten, she heard him exhale deeply. She counted to five. He didn't inhale again.

III.

KRAKÓW

(Him)

FRESHLY SHAVEN, WITH WELL-TENDED NAILS, dressed meticulously in black from head to toe, with even a black necktie: that's how he first appeared to Bohdan Lepkyi, the Ukrainian studies professor at Jagiellonian University in Kraków.

"Are you from Russia?" he asked by way of greeting. Lypynskyi confirmed. His family was Polish but from Zaturtsi, in the Volyn region of the Russian Empire.

Lypynskyi was actually studying agronomy and had wandered into Lepkyi's lecture on Ukrainian language by chance, but the class had proven very interesting. It was clear Lypynskyi spoke better Ukrainian than his peers of Ukrainian descent. The astounded Professor Lepkyi immediately invited him and another student to his home for tea.

"Thank you for the invitation. I'll come with great pleasure, Professor," he replied. "Only, please, call me Viacheslav, not Wacław."

"He's a marvel," the professor would tell everyone. "A complete marvel!"

Lepkyi had a reputation for being an exceptionally generous and upstanding person and was renowned for his hospitality. His compliant wife would wordlessly offer food and drink to their frequent guests at their apartment on Zielona Street. Many a time this apartment served as a refuge for Ukrainian "artists and litterateurs," who would arrive in Kraków without a krone in their pockets. "Suspicious Ukrainian-speaking characters" were perpetually milling around their home in hopes of, at best, a roof over their heads or, at the very least, three meals a day. Professor Lepkyi's wife took them all for vagrants. "I can't refuse a man in need of a lump of bread," Lepkyi would say to her with a proudly raised chin, all the while running deeper and deeper into debt. Such naïve generosity and such a romantic faith in selfless toil, all for the good of the idea of Ukrainianness, always repaid him a hundredfold. People instinctively clung to Lepkyi, even if they rarely listened to him. This gave him a feeling of fulfillment. Of his considerable artistic oeuvre—he wrote historical novels, composed poetry, assembled calendars, painted, published, and edited—his thankless progeny would remember only a single doleful poem: a poem about cranes that fly off to foreign lands, knowing that they'll perish on their journey back. The professor did in fact die in a foreign land, but of old age and natural causes, which for a Ukrainian of his generation and profession could be considered a great fortune.

Lepkyi's financial situation had drastically improved after he was invited to Jagiellonian University to teach Ukrainian—though the inauguration of the department became an anti-academic sensation amid the Slavists, the overwhelming majority of whom considered the Ukrainian language to be a dialect of either Russian or Polish, or both concurrently. Studying a dialect at the university level seemed nonsensical. A prohibition on the use of Ukrainian in print—or Little Ukraine's "Malorossiian regiolects," as the language as a whole was dismissively referred to—was in effect in the

Russian Empire, and the concealment of a lone Ukrainian dictionary was deemed comparable to revolutionary activity and punishable by imprisonment or exile. Routine searches had taught the custodians of Ukrainian dictionaries to pass them from hand to hand at the slightest suspicion of yet another shakedown. Aristocratic families could lose privileges for the use of Ukrainian in the home. Only a few such families, notwithstanding, spoke "the peasant tongue" despite the dangers.

The Ukrainian language wasn't prohibited here in Austria-Hungary, but even in cities like Kraków, its instruction at the university level was virtually an impossible affair because, for teaching materials, there existed only one grammar book, published ten years earlier, in 1893, and even that book was intended for high school students. Nonetheless, Professor Lepkyi managed a brilliant work-around to this situation: when he was short a grammar book, he would recite Ukrainian poetry, and when he was short on Ukrainian poetry, he would sing Ukrainian songs. Folklore and a love of everyday traditions—that was all the Ukrainian society of 1903 could boast of. Divided between two empires—the Austro-Hungarian and the Russian—the stateless Ukrainian society increasingly resembled a dust-coated stage set that someone had simply forgotten to strike. The antiquated world of Ukrainians had diminished to a shallow but warm pond in which there was no room for big fish, though frogs and tiny fry felt wonderful there. Wacław Lipiński, the young Polish agriculture student, was just such a fry. But even then it was clear to many, and in particular to Professor Lepkyi, that he was evolving into an anomaly—something completely different than Ukrainian society was prepared for.

Before long, Lypynskyi had become the professor's pet, often lingering on Zielona Street late into the night. Lepkyi's wife didn't mind at all because, in contrast to the rest of the vagrants, Lypynskyi came from a wealthy family and distinguished himself with the utmost pedantry in matters of money. He preferred to overpay rather than eat on someone else's dime. He always kissed the lady of the house's hand politely, apologizing for the late (or early, or Sunday, or long, or short) visit. Mrs. Lepka would flush. "How droll he is," she would say to her husband. "But better droll than hungry."

Typically, Kraków's Ukrainian community, which was informally headed by Professor Lepkyi, would rendezvous at the Mroziński Café in the city's Main Square. Every day the owner of the coffee shop would reserve a little table—next to the window to the right of the entrance—for the occasion; he had even agreed to order the Ukrainian-language newspaper *Dilo* from Lviv. The same discussions always took place at the table: about the lethargy of the Ukrainian community, the hopelessness of the Ukrainian situation, the illiteracy of the Ukrainian peasant, and the unscrupulousness of the Ukrainian disposition. Mroziński himself, while unobtrusively topping off his guests' cups with coffee or glasses with wine, would carefully memorize what he had heard, afterward transcribing it all verbatim onto paper and passing neat little envelopes to the agents of the secret police every week. His informant letters were nevertheless rarely read in full. A certain measured dose of underground revolutionary activity suited Kraków as it did no other town in Halychyna. It's no wonder that it was precisely here—in what was seemingly the heart of Polish pomposity—that Lipiński the student, in full view of many witnesses, transformed into Lypynskyi the activist and entered the ranks of Ukrainian community leaders. No one had summoned him there or even extended their welcome; he came of his own accord. "He's a marvel," Professor Lepkyi would repeat.

THE MONUMENT TO IVAN KOTLIAREVSKYI, the pioneer of Ukrainian literature and the father of Ukrainian light vaudeville, was to blame for everything.

It was finally erected that September 1903 in the Russian Empire, on Protopopivskyi Boulevard in Poltava, and the event had enormous and hitherto unprecedented resonance. The funds for the bust had been collected swiftly among the Ukrainian community, and the design of the bust had been executed just as swiftly, but the dedication ceremony had been postponed for many years on account of the tsarist government's categorical disapprobation of the inscription on the pedestal: "From the homeland, to its first poet Ivan Kotliarevskyi." Tsarist censorship wouldn't approve the inscription, obviously fearing that in the first poet's wake, monuments to other Ukrainians would ensue. The compound word "homeland" also sounded suspect. Well before the monument's erection, Mykola Mikhnovskyi, a Ukrainian lawyer from Kharkiv—a rash and unusually obdurate man, and author of the inflammatory pamphlet *Independent Ukraine* (who would commit suicide in 1924)—had even sent an angry letter defending the right to the ill-starred inscription to Dmitry Sipyagin, the minister of the interior of the Russian Empire. The closing words of this letter could have easily been interpreted as a threat: "The Ukrainian nation must secure independence for itself, even if all of Russia teeters! Even if rivers of blood spill! And that blood, if it spills, will fall on Your head, Mr. Minister, like a national curse, and on the heads of all our oppressors." Fortunately for Mikhnovskyi, Sipyagin didn't have a chance to provide an adequate response because he was opportunely assassinated in April 1902 by a member of the Russian militant Socialist Revolutionaries.

Despite Mikhnovskyi's daring letter, in the end it proved necessary to abandon sentimentality all the same, and the bust was underwritten with the laconic "Ivan Kotliarevskyi, 1769–1838."

FINALLY, THE TSARIST censorship approved the opening of the monument, and a date was set. In September 1903, virtually every well-known Ukrainian, including politically active university students from Kyiv, the editor-in-chief of the Lviv-based *Dilo*, composers, historians, activists from Halychyna, and representatives of the Viennese Parliament, all converged on Poltava. The monument had become a symbol of protest against the oppression of the Ukrainian people, and making the trip to Poltava was viewed as a matter of honor. Never before had the Ukrainians of both empires, the Austro-Hungarian and the Russian, declared their presence so loudly. For greater potency, Ivan Kotliarevskyi's maid was even tracked down, the 111-year-old Varvara Lelechykh, the one person still alive to have seen the poet with her own eyes.

At a loss in the face of such eager excitement, the tsarist censorship unexpectedly forbade the use of the Ukrainian language during the festivities. People were scandalized.

The evening before the celebratory gathering, in an oak forest near Poltava, the university students held a secret meeting to work out a plan of action in response to this prohibition. In a conspiratorial spirit, they sailed to the meeting in boats, and the boats were so numerous that the local Vorskla River appeared covered by a toy fleet. The hotheads called for armed action, but the majority didn't support the idea, as they were well aware that government troops across the entire Poltava Governorate had been brought into the city. Armed action would end in blood, arrests, and even greater repressions. They settled on a silent protest, which they then implemented the following day during the official reception in the city's Building of Education.

The Austro-Hungarian delegation from Halychyna was presenting first; as foreign guests subject to different censorship rules, they were permitted to speak in Ukrainian. "Honor to you, oh glorious city!" a representative of the Viennese Parliament from this delegation addressed the audience, and the jam-packed hall erupted in applause. After that the stage was occupied by a subject of the

Russian Empire, who also—albeit very quietly—began speaking in Ukrainian. Mayor Trehubov of Poltava sprang up in alarm and, pale as death, voiced a reminder that any and all remarks in Ukrainian were prohibited for Russian subjects. The audience let out a roar. The prominent Ukrainian writer Mykhailo Kotsiubynskyi, then living in Chernihiv, approached Trehubov and handed him the cover page of his speech (not the speech itself, because it was written in the prohibited language), after which he left the hall in a show of defiance: if he wasn't allowed to speak in Ukrainian, he just wouldn't speak. The rest of the speakers did the same. The spectators joined in the protest, and within a matter of minutes the hall had emptied.

Vyacheslav Plehve, the new minister of the interior of the Russian Empire and the person behind the language ban for the duration of the Poltava activities, would be killed by Russian terrorists in July 1904, less than a year after the described events—assassinated, just as his predecessor had been. Within a few months, in the fall of 1904, another terrorist group, Defense of Ukraine, would attempt to blow up a monument to the Russian author Alexander Pushkin in the nearby city of Kharkiv, but for some reason no one would interpret this crime as a precise and subtle act of retaliation for Pushkin's Ukrainian literary colleague in Poltava, Ivan Kotliarevskyi.

As news of the events in Poltava spread, the entirety of the Ukrainian world was gripped by agitation. Newspapers teemed with the recollections of eyewitnesses. Everyone who had been in Poltava talked about how unforgettable the experience was, the unprecedented solidarity they witnessed, and the feeling of tremendous inspiration with which they returned home.

ON THE OCCASION of such momentous events, Professor Lepkyi hosted a celebratory dinner at his home in late November, to which he invited his closest friends and some local Poles loyal to

Ukrainians. It was with these pro-Ukrainian Poles that an unpleasant argument arose after midnight, long after the professor's wife had gone off to bed, which the previously taciturn and placid student Lypynskyi initiated.

"This is an incredible triumph over despotism on the part of the Ukrainian community," he commented with passion, to which someone less romantic remarked that the events were likely a fluke and not the beginning of a victorious pattern.

"The Ukrainian community is a flock of naïve sheep ruled by wolves. It's feeble and helpless because it doesn't have its own leaders."

"New leaders are rising," Lypynskyi exclaimed. "We must become these leaders!"

"Don't be silly, Mr. Lypynskyi. You, as a Pole, will get handed over to the wolves first by the Ukrainian community. Or they'll eat you up themselves. Ukrainian sheep are a carnivorous lot."

Lypynskyi fell silent for a while, but when the room had grown quiet again, he unexpectedly proclaimed, "The Polish intelligentsia of Ukraine has no other alternative but to support the inevitable formation of a Ukrainian state."

The Poles present—all of ripe old age—were dumbstruck. They would have silently smiled and nodded their heads in response to similar assertions from their Ukrainian brethren, but pride didn't permit them to tolerate such a thing from the lips of one of their own.

"Young man," one began, "you're talking rubbish. May the esteemed master of this home forgive me, but for there to be a Ukrainian state, it's not enough to have one monument in a provincial town, don't you think?"

Lypynskyi seemed to be expecting this. "The monument is just the beginning. The rebirth of the Ukrainian nation is inevitable."

"So, you're a clairvoyant?"

"One need not be a clairvoyant to foresee the obvious course of events, corroborated long ago by history. Ukrainians, split between the Austro-Hungarian Kaiser and the Russian Tsar, have ended up in a situation where they must either surrender and perish as a nation or revolt. In all of history, there is no example of a nation surrendering of its own volition. The Ukrainian people are no exception and won't surrender without a fight. They lived through a similar period in the mid–seventeenth century and found the strength for a war of national liberation. That war was, incidentally, led by none other than Bohdan Khmelnytskyi, a Ukrainian Pole."

"A Ukrainian Pole? Ha! Such a concept doesn't exist."

"Then take a look at me," Lypynskyi parried. "Do I exist? Because I am a Ukrainian Pole. My language is Polish and my faith Catholic. I have renounced neither my language nor my faith, nor will I renounce them. Yet right now, in the midst of the Ukrainian nation's uprising, I feel compelled to take its side. These aren't romantic convictions, as many might think, but a matter of logic and political expediency."

"In Poland, people like you, Mr. Lypynskyi, are called renegades."

Lypynskyi jumped from his seat in vexation.

"A renegade betrays his own people, but I'm not betraying my own people, and you won't manage to convince me that I am. Was Bohdan Khmelnytskyi, the son of a Polish courtier, a renegade for initiating a political revolution of unprecedented scale against the Polish crown? Was he a renegade for serving as a catalyst for the collapse of the Polish state and the rise of the Ukrainian Cossack state in the seventeenth century? Khmelnytskyi understood, as I do now as well, the historical necessity of this. Your own people are those who live alongside you. Common *land* creates common goals—not language or religion."

The affronted Poles left without so much as a good-night. A bit of kerosene remained at the very bottom of the lamps, and an icy wind pushed its way in through the cracks in the window frames.

"You're a valiant man," said the professor in an effort to dilute the dense silence.

Lypynskyi, who had taken refuge in an armchair, remained very still, as if fearing that the world he had just constructed for himself out of nothing might turn out stillborn. For a fleeting moment it seemed he was already regretting every word he had uttered, and that he wanted nothing more than to clear off this thin, fragile ice he was standing on. He had never ventured this far before.

"I've never heard a Pole voice anything to this effect," Lepkyi said as he filled their crystal goblets with a fragrant transparent liquid. "Marille—an apricot liqueur. A gift from friends in Vienna. It's just what we need right now."

Lypynskyi pushed the goblet away. "Thank you ever so much, Professor, but I avoid strong drinks. I'm short of breath all night after them." He rose, making clear he was ready to leave. The momentary weakness had passed. Lypynskyi's face now emanated a stony coolness—a dissociation, like that of a military volunteer who, by definition, is not entitled to desertion. Putting on his coat, he said, "Thank you very much for the evening. I'll likely remember it my entire life."

"Don't resort to drastic measures, my dear friend. That's my advice to you."

Lepkyi also rose. They stood facing one another, almost equal in height, then embraced.

"You know, Professor, this 'don't resort to drastic measures' has always been rather off-putting to me. I don't doubt that you wish only the best for me, and by no means do I want to offend you with harsh words. But I speak as I think. It's not just the wicked and cowardly who resort to drastic measures. A worthy man devotes himself to a cause for whose sake he lives completely, sparing neither himself nor others."

"You're right, Mr. Lypynskyi. I beg your pardon and withdraw my advice. I wanted to ease the tension, but I see that it's necessary to closely monitor one's tongue around you. At the first sound of a falsehood, you lunge for the throat like a tiger."

Lypynskyi pulled on an astrakhan half coat, bade the professor farewell, and walked out into the frosty night. He moved like a stray who didn't belong, oblivious to the world around him.

During his three academic years in Kraków, he lived in the fairly expensive Hotel Polski next to the city arsenal that the Polish princely Czartoryski family had acquired not long before as a museum for its prodigious archives. Wherever he found himself, Lypynskyi always rented accommodations as close as possible to sources of information. His suite consisted of three rooms, one of which he requested to be lined with bookcases, to give him somewhere to stack the books he purchased.

Back at the small but luxuriant hotel, Lypynskyi sat down at his writing desk, hoping to record his impressions of the evening in a pocket notebook, but quickly abandoned this idea, jotting down only the date and, as was his custom in such instances, "I feel ill." The practice of pinning down his thoughts was something akin to an indispensable daily hygiene of the soul for him; when, for one reason or another, no thoughts arrived, he would mark the date in the little notebook and place a small black cross alongside it. This absence of thoughts Lypynskyi attributed to the advance of a disease still unknown to science. One of the many he was destined to suffer from.

He heaved a deep sigh. He didn't undress. He didn't lie down. For the first time, Kraków had bared its teeth at him. It had shoved him out into incertitude, where it was cold and lonely, and where one had to decide for oneself what was good and what was evil. No one would counsel or hearten him; on the contrary, they would ridicule and frighten him just to thwart him from finding his true self. But who was he truly? A renegade. A traitor. Kindred. Foreign. A Pole. A Ukrainian. Wacław. Viacheslav. Who was he?

Though the answer hid in the thickets of his mind, Lypynskyi already suspected that it was irrelevant. Who he was didn't matter; what mattered was who he wanted to become. He had to choose someone's side, but no matter what side he might choose, he would be a traitor all the same. Traitor—that was his new name. And the entirety of his life force would henceforth go to bearing this name with pride.

IV.

THE FIRST GOLDEN-HAIRED MAN

(Me)

TIME IS A BIG BLUE WHALE. It devours me along with all my thoughts, experiences, and memories, but I'm not enough. In order to fully satiate itself and keep functioning, it needs an endless supply of those like me—billions of minuscule, almost invisible worlds. They commingle and become its sustenance, but don't become a single big world for the blue whale. The blue whale continues to live in its own whale-space, absolute and immutable, where the need to think about something or remember anything doesn't exist.

I APPROACH REMEMBRANCE with abandon. I grow first tense, then muddled, as if I'm falling through some bottomless tunnel and there's nothing to grab hold of: my fingers scratch against the sleek surface in vain. I fall into the past. I yearn to scream, but my voice dies away in the depths of the body that I won't be able to call my own before long. Only flashes of love—not of the love others felt for me, but of the love I felt for others—occasionally illuminate the surrounding darkness.

They, the men (though I have loved not only men), were all oddly similar. All three were fair-haired, with roundish heads, though this too sounds somewhat strange since it's customary to assume that a head is always round. That's not what I think. There are heads that are so sharp or rectangular or irregularly shaped that it's simply impossible to call them round. A round head is a head that will roll if it's removed from a neck and pushed. That's what I could have done with the heads of the men that I have loved. They would have moved smoothly and with equal speed, their golden hair scintillating in the sun as they rolled.

All three had blue eyes. Only now do I realize this; I'm generally prone to not noticing the color of human eyes. I never noticed and can't recall the color of my own mother's eyes, for example, or my father's—the people whom I've seen the most in my life. Sometimes I get embarrassed, particularly around ophthalmologists who are impeccably versed in the slightest color variations in irises. I didn't pay attention to the color of the eyes of the men that I loved, but now when I think of them, I distinctly remember that blueness into which I would plunge every time I looked at them. Blue eyes suited these men. They couldn't have had any other eyes, only blue ones, the color of a cloudless sky on an ice-cold February day. These eyes emanated elation and sorrow at the same time. Melancholy. The boredom that ate away at them from inside. I disturbed their boredom only temporarily, like a gentle breeze over a bottomless mountain lake. In retaliation, I had the urge to betray my blue-eyed men with someone whose eyes would have been blackish or muddy-hued. As black as possible, as muddy as possible. In reality, I was betraying one blue-eyed man with another.

I met the first one when I was beginning my university studies. In all honesty, I was totally indifferent to my major, but I was pursuing a degree in Ukrainian studies. I would have tinkered with either chemistry or jurisprudence with the same enthusiasm because, overall, what I liked most was working out information in detail, dividing up knowledge into individual branches and moving along every branch toward its roots, as far as my strength and memory allowed. By contrast, synthetic analysis, generalization, and ascending by way of a few details to the very top of a tree for the sake of a sweeping panorama didn't come easily to me. I saw no spectacular panoramas, only bizarre and captivating minutiae, which I nonetheless learned to sort and, by means of fortuitous similarities, retain in my head.

Incidentally, my own head isn't round but egg-shaped, with an elongated jaw and protruding cheekbones. It's a good kind of skull to posthumously plant on a stake in a secret catacomb, to scare the occasional tourists with its eerie perfection.

I recall it being very important to me to remember as many details from Ukrainian Baroque literature as possible. Its artistic value wasn't all that impressive, at least for a contemporary reader's taste, but it was incredibly interesting in its historical accoutrements, in the names of forgotten and only recently rediscovered authors about whose fates nothing was known, thus nothing restricted the flights of my fancy. The refined titles of the works—generally of a spiritual and religious nature—beguiled me, a person of weak faith, with their abstruseness. And because the language they were written in was also antiquated, together there emerged a chimerical sacral abracadabra—mystical labyrinths of hidden knowledge that I very much wanted to decipher and understand but was struggling to. I made lists of authors and the titles of their works, recorded the historical events that served as their backdrop (principally religious polemics between the Orthodox and Catholics, and, later, the Ukrainian-Polish War of 1648–1657 under the leadership of Bohdan Khmelnytskyi), and studied the biographies of the professors of the Kyiv-Mohyla Academy, around which (originally as the Kyiv Fraternal School) the Ukrainian Baroque first swirled up. I reveled in the Baroque; I swooned in it. It was already then that I started to sense this irrepressible and unbearable desire to taste time, to live through something more than this one life of mine, which in and of itself wasn't all that noteworthy.

My parents, the color of whose eyes I don't recall yet whom I've always felt very close to, meddled little in the daily course of my life, particularly after I finished high school and entered university. They commemorated this stupendous event with the purchase of an incredibly expensive (for our means) computer; they brought it into my room, turned it on, marveled for a moment at its sky-blue screen, then left me alone with it, closing the door behind themselves noiselessly. From that point on, my parents appeared in my room only to bring me something to eat (my mom) or to wake me up in the morning (my dad). Beyond that, they didn't keep tabs on me, though there was nothing to keep tabs on. I dyed my short hair white, and then a reddish color, bought a bright green puffer jacket at a thrift shop, and wore it around with flared raspberry-colored velvet pants. In lectures, I always sat in the back row and didn't talk to anyone. I didn't strike up any friendships, especially after a Protestant classmate with luxuriant hair called me "unsaved," and with complete seriousness assured me that I would burn in hell because I worshipped literature but didn't believe in God himself.

AND THAT WAS when he appeared in the lecture hall. At first I didn't take any notice. It was a gloomy late autumn day, so from my back row the golden hair of the newcomer seemed lackluster, greasy, and unkempt. The man was dressed carelessly but predictably, in a cheap turtleneck sweater and a black leather jacket, which ninety-eight percent of the adult male population in my city also wore (the remaining two percent were in the process of saving up for one). I turned my gaze away to the window; I wasn't interested in what he would say. The man positioned himself behind the podium and began laying out the papers from which he intended to deliver his lecture. The students quieted down, not out of anticipation, but because that's what they always did before another routine descent into a two-hour slumber of lethargy: first they fell silent, then they fell asleep with eyes wide open, languidly reacting only to sharp rises in the lecturer's voice. The man finished laying out his papers, then he too shifted his eyes to the window. He didn't glance at us as other instructors were prone to doing, he didn't seek to pique our interest or, at the very least, draw our attention to a new subject somehow, and that struck me as odd, even somewhat arrogant. It crossed my mind that this instructor was more apathetic toward us than we were toward him. His young face exuded some sort of inhuman fatigue in which he seemed to be dissolving with no resistance, like salt in milk. Even though the hall was warm, he didn't even take off his leather jacket and finally mumbled out something that I didn't catch, something along the lines of, "Today we're going to look at the creative work of so-and-so." Who-who? I wasn't sure I wanted to know. Outside the window, an autumn wind was picking up and dying down again, swaying the withered browned leaves of the dwarf maples in the university courtyard and amplifying the chaos within me.

"*Thrênos albo Plach!*" the man behind the podium suddenly exclaimed so shrilly that the students, almost sunken in lethargy already, startled in fright and pricked up their ears. No one had understood.

"Thrênos albo Plach," the voice repeated somewhat more quietly but just as shrilly, and proceeded, "of the One, Holy, Catholic, and Apostolic Eastern Church."

This, apparently, was the title of a work. It pulsated in my head, stretched taut like a crossbow string: two of the first three uttered words I had never heard before, and their obscurity perturbed and at once lured me. It was only later that I learned that *thrênos* was, in fact, Greek for the Ukrainian *plach*, "lament," while *albo* was "or" in Polish. "A Lament, or a Lament." At the time, the title sounded like veritable magic to me—an ancient incantation that caused clouds to disperse and cows to yield three times as much milk.

The lecturer went on, attempting to re-create with his intonation the style of similar "laments," which he ultimately didn't succeed at:

> *Woe is me, poor one,*
> *Oh, woe is me, unfortunate one,*
> *In my good deeds, tattered from all sides,*
> *To my body's shame, stripped of my robes before the world!*

A chuckle rolled through the rows of students, yet his words struck me as so erotic that I blushed deeply and once more turned away to the window. I felt ensnared. A few sunrays suddenly pierced through the gloomy autumn sky and haloed the round head of the instructor. Wisps of his golden hair glimmered, and his face, filled with that inhuman fatigue, suddenly emitted an exalted sorrow—that same sorrow that pervaded all that literature that I so worshipped.

> *Nets on all sides, pits everywhere,*
> *Poisonous stings in every direction.*
> *Over there, predacious wolves,*
> *And there, enraged lions.*
> *Venomous dragons over here,*
> *And here, ferocious basilisks.*
> *I can't see which way to turn,*
> *I don't know which way to go,*
> *Whom to lean my head against, whom to ask for protection.*

After a few quotations, the lecture took on a more conventional nature: the man dictated from his notes in a monotone while the students lethargically scratched notes with their ballpoint pens, writing down every word they heard so that they, God forbid, wouldn't have to remember it. I alone sat immobile. I didn't write anything down, I just listened. The instructor came to a stop and intently surveyed the lecture hall for the first time. His eyes stumbled against my suspended gaze.

"You aren't taking notes? You know everything that well?"

I didn't immediately grasp that these words were addressed to me.

"I'm listening," I mumbled belatedly, so all my classmates in the front rows had time to glance back in consternation. Who is it that's not taking notes? That was likely the first time they noticed my existence. The back row is good for hiding from the enthusiasts who go rushing forward.

The man at the podium pretended to not hear my response. He didn't need my excuses. He wasn't asking (I comprehended this later) but reproaching, mocking, poking fun. His gibes aroused me. He would resort to them often later on, and I would delight in them. So be it that he was making fun of me then; the other seventy-some students he wasn't noticing at all. They were merely the stagehands to the theater of his daily fatigue, the stage set for his all-encompassing sorrow.

Every class thereafter, as he entered the hall in his predictable leather jacket and fraying pleather shoes, he would run his eyes furtively all the way to the back row and visibly relax when he had assured himself that I was there too. In order to be spotted more easily, I would crane my neck, ready for the next joust.

"Should I buy you a pen so that you have something to take notes with?" he would ask in greeting, smiling just barely, so that only I understood that the words were addressed to me and that he was joking.

"We have our own," some student would answer with a giggle, but he wasn't listening anymore. He'd spread out the day's stack of handwritten papers on the podium and begin. Under the escort of his somewhat high and grating voice, the seventeenth-century Ukrainian Orthodox archbishop Lazar Baranovych would burst into our lecture hall with the Catholic poet Kasjan Sakowicz, or Kyrylo Tranquillon-Stavrovetskyi, whose didactic gospel was burned publicly in the squares of Moscow in 1627 as a furious missive of the devil. Ivan Velychkovskyi, the Ukrainian John Owen, would stroll leisurely down the isles with his booklet *Zehar z Poluzeharkom*, (*The Half-Hour Clock*), handwritten in 1690, which remained unknown to his contemporaries and which wasn't discovered until two hundred years after the author's death. Before us students, Stefan Yavorskyi—a former rector of the Kyiv-Mohyla Academy and then a servant of Russian Tsar Peter I—bade a tearful farewell to his books prior to his death in 1722, the poet Klymentii Zynoviiv wove praise for all life's trades into verse, while, up beneath the cracked ceiling, countless anonym works hovered above our young heads like the spirits of unbaptized infants.

The golden-haired man didn't joke when discussing the Ukrainian Baroque. He, a resident of post-Soviet Ukraine, handled the Ukrainian Baroque like a sacred crystal chalice adorned with pearls and a gilded rim. Taking a sip of the life-giving nectar from this chalice was permitted only on high feast days. I would accept the chalice he offered as a gift and sip with reverence. Watching, he would beam with gratitude and approval.

For the longest time, we never spoke in private, we just exchanged jabs during lectures. He would prick me, then I him. One time I managed to poke him in the nose with an error, and I was very proud of myself. Revenge was swift to come. At the next lecture, when my triumph had more or less been forgotten already, he shamed me in front of everyone because, as it turned out, I knew nothing at all about eighteenth-century Europe. We took turns flaunting our knowledge, though in reality we were experiencing a mutual joy of discovery. By the will of chance, two wholly unacquainted people became valuable, even dear to each other. Life gained color and meaning. A drop of moisture had fallen on the desert. A short-lived spark had flashed in the pitch-dark gloom.

One night I was working late in the university library. It stayed open until eight p.m. It was a quarter till and the middle of February. A mound of books that I needed to at least leaf through loomed before me. The library patrons were growing fewer and fewer; the tables were emptying. In the enormous windows that spanned almost the entire wall glimmered the well-lit university yard with its frozen dwarf maples. An unease wavered in the air. All at once, thunder rolled and lightning flashed outside. Winter thunder is a very unusual phenomenon. I cowered at the premonition that the end of the world was approaching. From a celestial clap, the windowpanes let out a jangle and the library lamps flickered. It dawned on me that I had never before experienced thunder in February. I evidently voiced this thought aloud, because the golden-haired man, who was passing by with an armload of some sort of broadsheet newspapers, stopped right next to me and said, "Yes, me too."

That was the first thing that he said to me face-to-face. Yes, me too. His voice was serious and warm. I got the urge to muffle myself up in it, to become a word that he would utter.

I glanced around. Only the two of us remained in the reading room.

"What is it you're reading so late into the night?" he asked, this time encouraging a response, waiting for it expectantly. Now his interest was piqued. His interest had always been piqued, actually, but only now did he allow his interest to be revealed. I turned the books around so that he could see their spines. I was unable to speak. He leaned in to peruse the titles.

"Mikhail Bakhtin. That's good. Aleksei Losev. That's good too. You like literature."

"I'm unsaved," I squeezed out for some reason, and he laughed.

"Let's grab a drink?"

V.

SHAME

(Him)

IN 1905, WORKING-CLASS and peasant revolutionary demonstrations directed against the Tsar, the nobility, and the ruling class rocked the entire Russian Empire. Lypynskyi barely noticed them. Emotionally, he was living through other times—specifically, the Cossack revolution of 1648 under the leadership of Bohdan Khmelnytskyi, which he considered the most significant event in the history of the Ukrainian people. Everything he read and researched pertained somehow to Khmelnytskyi.

Rational enthusiasm metamorphosed into mystical revelation when Lypynskyi, by complete happenstance, stumbled upon a posthumous portrait of the wealthy Polish nobleman Mykhailo Krzyczewski—hitherto unknown, but one of the central participants of the Cossack uprising in the eastern territories of the Polish-Lithuanian Commonwealth—in the archives of the Princes Czartoryski. Krzyczewski, a colonel of the commonwealth assigned to Kyiv, switched to the side of the Ukrainian rebels at a pivotal moment and, in doing so, saved the young Cossack republic from premature vanquishment. Some two hundred and fifty years earlier, an unknown court artist had painted the portrait from his corpse, after he had died from fatal wounds in the captivity of a Lithuanian prince. In a euphoric stupor, Lypynskyi espied parallels with his own life and interpreted the discovered portrait as none other than a sign from above. Lypynskyi painted a replica of it himself and hung it in his office above his desk, alongside a photograph of his family and a likeness of Bohdan Khmelnytskyi. Now this was his personal iconostasis.

He could spend hours studying the dead face. A linen shirt peeking out from under the sheepskin coat, an ample Cossack-style *oseledets* of hair sprouting out of the crown of the smooth-shaven round skull, a contented face, and even though the eyes should have underscored his premature death, it seemed as though Krzyczewski was as alive as life itself. He was just playing blind man's bluff, and as soon as your gaze drifted away, he would break into playful laughter. Lypynskyi could have sworn that the colonel had winked at him a few times.

The Pole's sacrifice for the benefit of Ukrainian statehood moved him exceedingly. Lypynskyi found more significance in the life and death of Mykhailo Krzyczewski than anyone had or would have before or after him.

IN THE MIDST of his growing fascination, a new historical lecture series, open to the general public, was announced at the university. Still an enrolled student, Lypynskyi was one of the first to submit his name to be a speaker. History enthused him above all else. Lypynskyi saw nothing in this passion that would have contradicted his chosen profession. History and agriculture had, so he believed, a common object of study—roots. History was the theoretical preparation for the practical utilization of the earth. In order to understand the earth's properties and nature, it was necessary to know who had walked upon it and what they had yearned for. The end goal of history was to trace the earth's roots to their smallest offshoots and to investigate the particularities of their growth, the causes of their decay, and the miracle of their rebirth. The dying off of one root and the triumph of another. Lypynskyi hoped to get a quick overview of the theory, so that he could move on to the daily working of the land with a calm heart. To pay tribute to the land, in order to then be able to utilize that land.

The lectures were being held for just a few days in the main hall of the Collegium Novum and proved rather popular in the spring social program of Kraków's fashionable elite. The audience that gathered was diverse—from university students and instructors, to doctors and city officials accompanied by their dolled-up wives. For the best lecture, the presenter would receive a monetary award and the opportunity to speak at the annual history conference in Vienna, which was considered a great honor in and of itself.

Backstage, Lypynskyi was quite nervous. He felt light-headed, his eyes were clouded over, his ears were plugged, and he had lost his voice. When he panicked right before walking out to the podium, overwhelmed by the urge to flee, Mykola Shemet, his university friend, clutched him by the vest and said, "Imagine that all these people in the hall are naked. Completely stark-naked. Recent studies by British doctors have shown that this approach helps alleviate stage fright. The audience is naked, so it can't be scary."

Whether moved by these words or his own reserves of inner strength, he set off toward the podium, where he pronounced: "The participation of the Polish gentry in the Ukrainian–Polish War of 1648–49. . . ."

The audience let out a contented murmur at the mention of Poland's noble class, the *szlachta*. It didn't yet suspect what was to come.

Lypynskyi continued, unrushed: "For us citizens of the twentieth century, who blindly believe in the creative omnipotence of parliamentary speeches and reverently bow our heads before the potency of journalistic pens, who view the development of society through the prism of literary moods or construct the future of the state on an increase in, say, the output of dairy products—to us, the Ukrainian nation's voluntary blood sacrifice in the seventeenth century to secure its own freedom may seem incomprehensible. In strength and scale, the Ukrainian uprising of 1648–49 surpassed anything Europe had previously seen. The might demonstrated by the Ukrainian people in their rebellion against Polish and Lithuanian rule had a subsequent radical influence on the fates of two neighboring states, the Polish-Lithuanian Commonwealth and the Tsardom of Muscovy, being the beginning of the end for Poland and the beginning of intensified development and growth for Moscow. Contemporary historians, who are subservient in their ideology to Poland or Moscow, forget about objective judgment in their assessment of this period of, above all"—and here Lypynskyi paused briefly—"Ukrainian history."

The listeners fell silent, perplexed. The coupling of the words "Ukrainian" and "history" had never been heard in these walls.

"The participation of the *szlachta* in the Cossack Uprising can no longer be subject to doubt," Lypynskyi said from the podium. "The noble-born Polish insurgents, who supported the Cossacks and Ukrainian peasantry against Poland, their own hereditary homeland, included families with recognizable names, such as the Vyhovski, the Krekhovetski, the Hulianytski, the Iskrytski, and the Fedkovychi. Mykhailo Krzyczewski, previously a loyal son of the Polish crown, indeed switched to Khmelnytskyi's side and converted from Catholicism to Orthodoxy. It was then that he renounced his Catholic name, Stanisław, and took the Orthodox Mykhailo. This was an exceptional event for those times. That's why the Khmelnytskyi period can no longer be treated as an uprising of the poor against the rich, as Polish historiography likes to do in order to devalue it and mask its true essence. The participation of the ruling class transformed a 'revolt of the underlings' from a social phenomenon into a political one, from a Rusyn rebellion into a liberation movement for the creation of an independent Ukrainian state. Therein lies its greatest value."

Lypynskyi took a gulp of air and read on eagerly, like a witness who only has a few minutes to tell the whole truth on the stand. "Was Krzyczewski a Judas and a renegade, as he was still depicted by Polish masters on court tapestries multiple centuries later? At a time when the *szlachta* was creating the Polish state and, conversely, the Polish state was creating the *szlachta*, for the Ukrainian people, not having their own statehood meant the loss of their own aristocracy for the benefit of another state. The old Ukrainian family line of the Krychevski—namely, Mykhailo Krzyczewski's—is the best example of this. Contemporaries considered Mykhailo Krzyczewski a Pole and marveled at how he could sacrifice royal favor and his material fortune, which flowed from this favor, on a quest for an impalpable idea—that of Ukrainian statehood. But that entire generation of *szlachta* members, which rediscovered its true roots in Ukrainian soil and stood up in battle for the opportunity at independence, proved that sometimes impalpable ideas are more important than royal material fortune. Their actions merit not condemnation, but praise and the highest respect. It's plain to see what happened to their children after so many years of Ukrainian statelessness: the *szlachta* in the eastern Ukrainian lands, on the left bank of the Dnipro, is almost completely Russified, and the *szlachta* in the western Ukrainian lands, on the right bank, is Polonized. The class from which a state of Ukraine could have grown was instead coopted for the building up of Ukraine's neighbors. But be that as it may, this sacrifice didn't prove to be in vain. Because if Ukrainians do in fact exist as a nation now, as I believe they do, it is only owing to the Khmelnytskyi period. There hasn't been a more important moment in the life of the Ukrainian people than the great Revolution of 1648–49."

When Lypynskyi concluded, the audience sat in stunned silence. The speaker dug his fingers into the sheets of paper on the podium, which were already crumpled and spattered with drops of sweat, while his entire body trembled.

A young woman rose in one of the back rows. It was so quiet that Lypynskyi could hear the menacing rustle of her skirts.

"Shame!" exclaimed the woman, and at that moment their eyes met.

The woman was looking at him with majesty and scorn simultaneously; Lypynskyi had received similar looks from his mother.

"Shame! Shame!" the woman exclaimed again and again, until the audience came back to its senses and joined in as well.

"Take this buffoon away!"

"Who gave him the right to present?"

"Traitor! Shame!"

An unbelievable racket erupted in the hall. Lypynskyi abandoned the podium in a rush, running out into the street, feeling barely alive. A spring downpour pelted him, and the air smelled of something sweet and seductive, something still unknown.

"Don't worry about it," his university friend comforted him later as they strolled through the meadows of Błonia Park. "With that kind of a lecture, you weren't expecting to receive applause, were you?"

"I did as you told me to, my friend," Lypynskyi replied, distracted and flushed. "I pictured them all naked."

RUMORS ABOUT THE SHAMING of Wacław Lipiński, the son of Klara and Kazimierz, bearers of Poland's noble Brodzic coat of arms, spread with lightning speed. His mother wrote him an incensed letter ordering him to come home immediately. Lypynskyi obeyed and was back in Zaturtsi by Easter.

The family estate now reminded him of a prison, whose guards had stocked up on whips and couldn't wait for the public flogging. His brothers taunted him. His father attempted to make light of the situation. Klara Lipińska initially burst into a tirade, then burst into tears. Having released herself of these principal emotions, she devoted the entire ensuing period to lecturing Lypynskyi as he sulked in silence.

When it came time for Lypynskyi to leave, his younger brother, Stanisław, with whom he had a close relationship, simply nodded his head sorrowfully in farewell. He was finishing his preparatory studies at the Kyiv Polytechnic Institute and was supposed to move to Kraków as well the following year. But at the final moment, as Lypynskyi awaited his driver on the porch, Stanisław said in passing that he actually preferred the university in Leipzig and would enroll there instead.

"Did Mother decide that? So that you don't fall under my bad influence in Kraków?"

Stanisław hesitated.

"Mother has nothing to do with it. It's my decision. I want to learn German."

Lypynskyi left without another word to his brother. Klara Lipińska, warming her feet next to the fireplace, exuded such dramatic sighs that everyone in the house could hear: "I don't know what will become of all this."

Lypynskyi didn't know either. The impertinent face of that woman in the audience surfaced in his mind again and again, thin and sharp, as if a painter had forgotten to round the lines in the frenzy of creation. "Shame, shame!" the woman cried unceasingly. She was a fiend, nothing more. Since their public exchange, she hadn't left Lypynskyi in peace for more than a moment. Green-eyed, her hair dark blond and straight, her voice ruthless.

Kazimiera Szumińska—that was her name. A student in the agriculture department, two years his junior, which is why their paths hadn't crossed till then. Though there were so few women in the university that only a bookworm like him could have not noticed one of them.

NOW, HOWEVER, EVERYTHING WAS DIFFERENT. Kazimiera began to appear to Lypynskyi constantly, wherever he was: the university hallways were filled with Kazimiera, the streets of Kraków were filled with Kazimiera, his thoughts were filled with Kazimiera. Kazimiera was everywhere.

Lypynskyi couldn't last more than a minute in the library archives because he knew he had no chance of seeing her there. He studied her class schedule and would hover near the lecture hall from which she might exit. And when she did exit, like some medieval Polish princess under the escort of frivolous suitors, Lypynskyi would freeze, accepting her crushing glance with gratitude, like a mercifully tossed bone. After that, he would remain in that very spot for a long time, not having the strength to take even a step, until the university janitors would ask him to move aside in order to sweep up his dignity, splattered against the wooden floor.

The Szumiński family were impoverished aristocrats. A widow and two daughters of marriageable age, all three famous for their sharp tongues and petulant dispositions. They owned a building not far from the train station, occupying a spacious apartment on the second floor and renting out the rest. The building had long needed repair, but Mrs. Szumińska didn't have the funds because her husband, before his sudden death at age forty-two, had come up with the wise idea of investing the family savings in some senseless invention that was supposed to register earthquakes. This gadget looked like a plain old vase with incomprehensible hooks that stuck out every which way. Mrs. Szumińska received one such vase by mail following her husband's death, accompanied by a confidential letter informing her that the inventor had unfortunately been mistaken in his calculations and was now enthusiastically working on a new project, namely, glasses that would shine at night, and should Mrs. Szumińska be interested in an investment, he was ready to name the fantastical glasses in her honor. Mrs. Szumińska proved uninterested. She placed the "earthquake vase" in a prominent spot in the living room as a memento of her husband's stupidity.

A disdain toward the opposite sex was hereditary in this home—something Lypynskyi couldn't have known.

Kazimiera Szumińska quickly intuited his feelings and began resorting to cruel mockery in public. Every biting word of hers found its way to Lypynskyi.

"Lypynskyi has fallen head over heels in love with an Erinys," his classmates would assess and recommend various salons with attractive Kraków prostitutes, hinting that his love was merely a consequence of a dearth of female warmth. Lypynskyi had never experienced anything like this, so he wasn't sure if what he was feeling was love. If love was fear, devastating longing, nausea, obsession, then yes, he was in love. But why then was love so exalted? Why was it imbued with the meaning of life and treated like a cult, when, instead, it should be treated as a disease? In Lypynskyi's view, that's what it was, a disease filled with suffering. An extremely dangerous one. An incurable one.

Difficult times befell him. He barely slept, completely stopped eating, and wasted away to beyond recognition. Professor Lepkyi invited him over for tea a few times, but he spent the entire visits silently examining the cup in his hands and the little Hutsul rug from the Carpathian Mountains beneath his feet. Professor Lepkyi's wife tried to feed him *borshch*, but Lypynskyi declined, saying that he digested beets poorly.

With the passage of time, the unbearable desire to cross paths with Kazimiera transformed into an aching wound that just wouldn't heal. He was tormented when he didn't see her, but was even more tormented when their gazes would meet and she would swiftly walk past, projecting disdain with the entirety of her elegant being. That's why he no longer sought her out, trying instead to console himself with the little things—with just the simple thought that she was somewhere close by, possibly in the next hall over, sitting at a desk, cheekily correcting the aging professors. She was intelligent; no one doubted it. Her large green eyes radiated a lively interest in everything they saw before them. Other than Lypynskyi, of course. When he was standing before her, her eyes blazed like two red-hot coal embers, promising to turn into ash at the slightest approach.

Lypynskyi was convinced that this was damnation. He prayed often. When someone would try to cheer him up, he would listen in silence. "Viacheslav, this girl isn't worth such torment," they'd tell him. "Go back to the libraries, that's where you belong, you're going to become a great man."

ALARMING NEWS FROM RUSSIA was reaching Kraków. The peasants and workers were revolting and, where they could, burning the estates of landowners; high school students were striking; soldiers were refusing to carry out orders. A premonition of freedom tinged with chaos hung in the air. The Russian government finally lifted the ban on the Ukrainian language, and in November 1905, in the city of Lubny in the Poltava region, Mykola Shemet, who had briefly studied with Lypynskyi at Jagiellonian University, began to publish the first Ukrainian newspaper in the Russian-controlled part of Ukraine with his brothers Serhii and Volodymyr. Lypynskyi suggested the name *Khliborob*, or *Grain Farmer*, and Shemet agreed.

LYPYNSKYI'S CUSTOMARY STYLE of dressing in all black now suited him as never before. He was wearing his mourning dress. Some part of him was dying in grave torment, and no one could do anything to help other than send for the clergy to sing a funeral service when the time arrived.

And at last, the time arrived.

Lypynskyi had worked out which of Kraków's myriad churches the Szumiński family likely attended and began going there on occasion. After the conclusion of one Sunday mass, when people had begun to slowly file out, he hesitated at the exit, searching for her with his eyes. Kazimiera suddenly appeared right before him but didn't walk past him as usual. She stopped and deftly blocked his escape. The trap had closed: Lypynskyi had nowhere to run. Kazimiera sneered, "Take a look at the Pole who cares more about the Rusyns than his own state!"

Lypynskyi ignored her actual words, just watched her mouth move. He knew what Kazimiera was capable of.

"Why, Mr. Lypynskyi, are you in a Catholic church? Go pray to the God of the Orthodox serfs."

Her face, so harsh and merciless, seemed to him the dearest in the entire world; despite its angular severity, hers was the gentlest and most alluring of all faces. Lypynskyi teetered, losing his balance for a moment. He understood that one more step, and the boundary would be crossed beyond which any and all love between them would become impossible. He whispered, dropping his defenses, "Ms. Szumińska has forgotten that there is but one God, for everyone."

A crowd of gaping mouths had already gathered around—cold-blooded extras who would serve as witnesses to the long-awaited execution of the convict.

"Not at all, Mr. Lypynskyi! The people who talk about one God are those who don't believe in any! And we already heard about the particulars of your ungodly faith at the spring lectures at the university. Such talk is blasphemy."

"What did I say there that was so ungodly? That every nation, including the Ukrainian one, will fight for the right to self-determination? As it has already done on more than one occasion? Is that not what I said?"

"The Ukrainian nation has no past because there is no such nation. And you, Mr. Lypynskyi, are now, whether consciously or unconsciously, playing into the hands of the enemies of the Polish state."

"I will remind you, miss, that Poland was partitioned among its neighbors a long time ago. There is no Polish state, just as there is no Ukrainian nation."

Kazimiera gave a snort and Lypynskyi lapsed into a strange, almost paralytic calm. This calm spilled through his body, demanding the termination of their joust and complete acquiescence, even if it were to cost parts of his anatomy. That's how animals save themselves from an iron trap in the woods, by gnawing off the ensnared paw.

"Ms. Szumińska is now, whether consciously or unconsciously, playing into those improvident Polish patriots who, dreaming of a Greater Poland, ignore the aspirations of Ukrainians—or Rusyns, as you call them—to be independent. When the time comes, Ukrainians will catch the Poles by surprise when they go up against them because people like you, dear lady, are perpetually belaboring that the Ukrainian nation doesn't exist. So which of us is the bigger traitor? Which of us harms Poland more: I with my truth or you with your lies?"

He straightened up. He felt numb, almost dead. The clergy could be sent for to sing a funeral service. In fact, one of them did show up, the church's Roman Catholic *ksiądz*. "A house of God is not the place for such discussions," he said, and, with a peaceable gesture, led everyone outside.

At the exit, Lypynskyi and Kazimiera brushed shoulders and recoiled as if scalded. A moment later, she had dissolved into the crowd, and the last thing that Lypynskyi saw was her chin, raised upward and pointed like an alpine prickle. That prickly and upraised face promised to hate him as long as the world kept spinning, perhaps even after it stopped. This was the end. Lypynskyi sighed, relieved and exhausted, and headed off in the opposite direction.

He decided to visit the Kraków prostitutes the following day and did so with an uncharacteristic malevolence. In the embrace of a voluptuous stranger, Lypynskyi made his peace. He wouldn't think about Kazimiera anymore.

But she would think about him.

VI.

KAZIMIERA

(Him)

LYPYNSKYI SPENT THE WINTER seemingly dazed, almost as if in a light blissful haze. He didn't think about anything, he didn't feel anything; he just mechanically read through everything he could find in the field of sociology—a new and not-yet-recognized science that had suddenly grabbed his attention.

Nearly every evening all winter long, he would go walking at Błonia Park. The meadow would be blanketed in fog, thick and luscious like a sheep's wool, so Lypynskyi could see no farther than a step ahead of him. Now and then strangers would glide out of the fog—aimless wanderers just like him. He had to tread very carefully and sometimes halt abruptly to avoid knocking foreheads with them. Lypynskyi would walk all the way to Oleandry Street, beyond Kraków, then cross a little bridge over the Rudawa River. Lone swans, which for some reason lingered in the winter more and more often, would glimmer on the dark water.

Lypynskyi felt protected in these fogs, where his longing for the unattainable melted away without a trace.

———

BLOODY ROUNDUPS BEGAN in Russia. Anyone could get shot on suspicion of ties to the anti-tsarist rebels yearning for reform. Against the backdrop of the government's brutal reaction to the protests, the establishment of the Duma in August 1905 and the Tsar's manifesto promising democratic freedoms in October swiftly lost any potentially everlasting significance. The fourth issue of *Khliborob*, the Shemet brothers' first Ukrainian-language newspaper in the empire, with an estimated circulation of five thousand, was confiscated in December, and the censors wouldn't even allow the fifth issue to be printed. In lieu of a New Year's postcard, Mykola Shemet sent Lypynskyi a short letter in which he requested that he not write him from Austria-Hungary for some time because letters from abroad were being compromised by Russian authorities. He ended with the sentence, "If you only knew, dear Viacheslav, how often I think of you these days."

IT WAS APRIL 1906. Spring kept refusing to arrive, even though the sun had shone in recent weeks. Black and lifeless trees jutted out of the frozen ground; only the credulous grass bloomed with tiny daisies here and there. Lost in his thoughts, Lypynskyi walked through Błonia Park at an amble, all in black.

"It's worth carrying an umbrella in this sort of weather," a female voice rang out nearby, unexpectedly pulling him out of his reverie. Lypynskyi immediately knew who that voice—at once melodious and shrill—belonged to.

He raised his head dispassionately. "Ms. Szumińska? There has yet to be weather that would make me carry an umbrella. I have a particular dislike to that form of luxury, for some reason."

"In that case, enjoy being drenched." She was standing in front of Lypynskyi, and for the first time her thin face was emanating something other than hatred. What was it? Cockiness? Defiance? A playful rage? An old yearning stirred in him like a three-headed serpent emerging from a grueling battle—dazed, but still alive. The first droplets of cold rain fell on his forehead. At a loss, Lypynskyi glanced up at the clouded sky, hoping for some much-needed advice from whoever was sitting up there: Should he run away at full tilt or stay and risk his life at the hands of this woman? Kazimiera let out a merry laugh. She wasn't alone, but with two girlfriends. She wore a simple dress, fitted all the way down, and an English drape-cut coat. A polar-fox collar hung around her neck. Her face too looked like a fox's.

"Unfortunately, Mr. Lypynskyi, we're of no help at all to you because we have one umbrella for the three of us. But if you like, you can accompany us to the city. We're such interesting company that you won't mind getting drenched to the bone."

All three of them laughed again. Kazimiera began to leisurely move onward, giving Lypynskyi a few seconds for contemplation. His body made the decision for him faster than he had time to collect himself, and he docilely traipsed after them.

So, that was how it was going to be: in matters concerning Kazimiera, his body would win out over his mind.

Then aloud he said, "To what do I owe the unexpected change in your demeanor? I remember the last time we met Ms. Szumińska more resembled a provoked panther ready to pounce—in a house of God, no less."

"I must admit, Mr. Lypynskyi, your coarse words in the church didn't leave me indifferent. At first I was truly very angry, but now that the anger has passed, I'm tempted to get to know you better. You strike me as a direct and honest person. I very much value these two qualities, even if they belong to an enemy of mine."

A piercing wind was lashing his face mercilessly, but Lypynskyi didn't notice. Kazimiera was chattering to him so amicably, just a step away, as if an entire year of mutual animosity hadn't happened at all. As if they had just met and Kazimiera had never humiliated Lypynskyi in front of a half thousand witnesses, never ridiculed him, hadn't walked past him so many times, hadn't turned up her nose at him, hadn't shot through him with those huge green eyes.

"I haven't changed my position regarding the Ukrainian question, my dear lady."

"Call me Kazimiera."

"And you can call me Viacheslav."

"Call you what?" She laughed again. Under the little bridge across the Rudawa River, a lone swan hissed vigilantly.

"Isn't your name Wacław?"

"In Polish it's Wacław, in Ukrainian it's Viacheslav."

"So long as we're on Polish land, Mr. Lypynskyi, I'm going to call you Wacław and nothing else."

Lypynskyi didn't respond. His name was the least of what he sacrificed that evening.

THE FOLLOWING SUNDAY, he was invited to the Szumiński's for afternoon tea. For the entirety of his visit, Kazimiera's mother sat morosely in the living room, not once intruding on the conversation, though she did ask if Lypynskyi was by any chance an inventor, because there were a lot of swashbucklers among inventors.

"My dream is to work with the land, my esteemed lady," he replied. "I'm currently finishing my studies in agronomy and still intend to attend lectures in philosophy and sociology. Sociology is a new but very promising field. After completing my studies, I'll return to Russia, where I grew up. I have an inheritance there, my uncle Adam Rokicki's estate, not far from Uman, perhaps you know of it."

"I don't," Mrs. Szumińska muttered, but any hostility had vanished from her face, leaving only dissatisfaction. "Have you read about the tragedy that happened in San Francisco? The earthquake? So many houses collapsed! Thousands of people died! Just imagine! That's what you need to study—how to save cities from such atrocities, not philosophy. You need to look to the future, young man."

In the female realm of the Szumiński family, unexpected guests weren't liked. Guests weren't liked in general. If a continental fracture more massive than the one in San Francisco weren't forming inside Lypynskyi right then and there, he wouldn't have lasted more than half a minute in their home.

In the epicenter of his own personal earthquake, Kazimiera stood smiling at him. Cheerful, witty, smart. She was clearly flirting, but in the way that women do to compute the ambit of a man's feelings and the amount of pride that the wretch is willing to forgo for the sake of those feelings. Just a few months before, Lypynskyi would have easily given away his soul to have her merely glance in his direction. But now, stupefied by the unexpected gift of her attention and her smile, he simply watched in confusion as a stranger in his body surrendered to the mercy of the conqueress without the least bit of resistance. Word after word, laugh after laugh, joke after joke, Kazimiera occupied his impregnable fortresses swiftly and deftly, boldly setting foot on his lands that were overgrown with thickets. The blissful haze didn't disperse but, conversely, grew so dense, like a fog, that Lypynskyi felt its dulcet warmth on his skin. His eyes, which were blinded anyway, closed in the gentle languor, and now and then he was enveloped by a fear that perhaps he was sleeping and all of this was just a perfidious dream. Perhaps, not having obtained what it desired from reality, his mind had simply dreamt up a woman for itself, one terribly similar to Kazimiera and nearly as alive.

From then on, they would often stroll through Błonia Park together. A resplendent spring surrounded them, though now and again a blustery cold wind would sweep in, with a reminder that all changes were relative, and that the past never definitively disappeared and could return when you least expected it. The Rudawa River overflowed its banks, and here and there the meadow turned into impassable swamps. The usual fogs scattered to the solemn bellowing of the livestock, driven out to graze for the first time after long months of wintering.

On their walks, Kazimiera's little face, angular as always, was adorned by dark blond locks that she painstakingly curled before retiring to sleep, and a tall white collar with fine lace accentuated her neck, long like the Kraków swans'. She wasn't particularly attractive, but to Lypynskyi she was the most beautiful woman in the world. What he wanted above all else was to embrace her, and to hold her in that embrace until his final breath. He wanted to take care of mundane affairs, go places, study, be sad, grow tired, meet with like-minded colleagues—and do all of it holding her in his embrace. Kazimiera occupied the depths of his soul. A delightful new sensation was filling him up, and without reservation, Lypynskyi took that feeling to be happiness.

IN MAY, HE WROTE to his parents that he had met a girl he hoped to marry. Klara Lipińska immediately arrived for an inspection of the bride, and Kazimiera proved not to her liking.

"She's too self-confident, she's a coquette," was his mother's verdict. "She's excited by novelty and scared off by humdrum. But that's what life is, son—humdrum!"

"I've already decided," Lypynskyi cut her short, though perhaps he suspected that there was a kernel of truth in his mother's words. Kazimiera had a passionate nature; she yearned for festivities, adventures, and heightened feelings. For the time being, Lypynskyi had been giving her that. The sparks between them hadn't died down yet, and when they argued about current political topics, the air around them became as hot as a blacksmith's workshop. He didn't budge for her, and she didn't budge for him. Their discussions could last for hours, and Lypynskyi would hold back only when he noticed tears on her pale cheeks. Then Kazimiera would joyously clap her hands like a child and, for the entirety of the ensuing day, celebrate her victory, repeating, "Come on, Wacław, admit that you were wrong." Sometimes he would admit it, but more often than not he would deny it, and the discussion would reignite with even more vigor.

No, for now there was no shortage of intense emotions between them. But could it go on like that forever? At night, Lypynskyi had mentally measured out their married life to the littlest detail, but Kazimiera was poorly suited for the role that had been prepared for her, that of loyal companion and docile assistant. He who had had the imprudence to fall in love with this Erinys was the one who needed to be loyal and docile.

FOR LYPYNSKYI'S MOTHER, however, one argument outweighed all of the bride's flaws and shortcomings: Kazimiera was Polish. So excited at the prospect of her son marrying a fellow Pole that she was nervous, Klara Lipińska awaited her son's marriage with fearful trepidation, lest it fall through. In the family of one of her acquaintances, a tragedy had recently occurred when a young man, in defiance of his parents' will, had unexpectedly decided to up and become Ukrainian, and then, on top of that, married the first best Ukrainian girl he met. She, of course, turned out to be some uncouth peasant girl from a remote village. To avoid communal condemnation, the family had no choice but to publicly declare their son disabled. Klara Lipińska had very much feared a similar scenario and immediately decided that even the worst Polish Kazimiera was better than some hillbilly Ukrainian named Paraska.

The day after meeting the bride, she was supposed to settle procedural matters with the older Szumińska, as was the custom, and ask for Kazimiera's hand in marriage on her son's behalf. The ladies secluded themselves in Mrs. Szumińska's office. The young couple, meanwhile, discussed women's suffrage on the couch in the living room, pretending to be oblivious.

"Denying a woman the opportunity to vote in elections on equal footing with men—that's some kind of Stone Age!" Kazimiera was ardently arguing. She followed this subject closely and had even sent a letter to the Viennese women's weekly *Die Arbeiterinnen-Zeitung*, in which she passionately described Polish women's expectations of receiving the right to a political voice. For some reason, that letter never did get printed.

"If the female residents of the Grand Duchy of Finland go to the polls—and that's how things look!—that'll be an abasement to all those who consider themselves vanguards of the European community, to all of us!" Kazimiera continued.

The mothers came out of the office. Klara Lipińska was flushed beet-red, her hands clenched in resolute fists.

"It's not all that simple," Lypynskyi began, but, looking at his mother, stopped short.

Mrs. Szumińska didn't waste time on niceties: "Kazimiera, I was honest and told our esteemed guest everything that I think of her son. I don't consider him a good match for you but will give permission for the marriage if you yourself want him. So, do you want him?"

Klara Lipińska was so enraged that she was shaking. Kazimiera lowered her gaze to the floor hesitatingly. Lypynskyi froze. In those few dozen seconds of uncertainty, he again reexperienced all the pain that this girl had managed to inflict on him. It seemed as though at any moment she would erupt with laughter and exclaim contemptuously, *Mother, who would marry this yokel? How could you think that of me? I was only waiting for a suitable opportunity to have my revenge.* Lypynskyi recalled their quarrel in the church, and a suspicion flashed through his mind that the recent rendez-vous in Błonia Park, the invitations home, the strolls, and the pleasant conversations were nothing more than a preparation for the most insidious and hence the most perfect plan of revenge that the female intellect had organized to date. Had this been the case, the plan would've been successful. Lypynskyi would have been completely destroyed.

"I want him," Kazimiera replied softly, and at first it seemed to Lypynskyi that this was his imagination whispering.

"What are you mumbling, Kazimiera? Can't you say what you want clearly?"

Kazimiera stood up and—like a soldier, her head held high—pronounced the same thing loudly and clearly: "I want him."

She wasn't looking at Lypynskyi—as though she had already achieved her goal and no longer needed him or anyone else. Maybe her plan of revenge was much more intricate and a million times more ruthless than anyone could have imagined.

"So, it's been decided," the hostess of the gathering concluded irritably. "You must forgive me, but I'm not feeling well and must go lie down promptly. Would you like any tea, Mrs. Lipińska? If so, I'll see to it that it's brought."

Klara Lipińska could no longer restrain herself.

"Thank you, but it's time for me to go." With these words, she flew out of the apartment like a tempest, never to return.

"What an intolerable family! To accept your proposal of marriage so begrudgingly?" Klara Lipińska would later complain to her son. "I can't imagine how you're planning on sharing a life with them. I've seen such arrogant behavior before, to be sure, but not from someone who's completely bankrupt."

The Szumiński's financial situation was no secret. Yet Lypynskyi was the last to be concerned with it.

When the betrotheds finally found themselves alone, Kazimiera was aloofly studying a bee that had just flown in through the window and now couldn't find its way back. An awkward silence expanded in the room, so much so that it was dizzying, but neither of them could compel themselves to say something to dispel it. The new status of their relationship was so unexpected that they were both immobile with fear. The bee was hysterically flailing against the windowpane, which had been washed painstakingly in preparation for the Green Week festivities preceding Pentecost. Kazimiera waited. At long last, Lypynskyi mumbled, "Women's suffrage would make sense if women received an education on par with that of men. Without education, the right to vote is a meaningless plaything. How are women going to know who to vote for if they don't know how to read or write? Their husbands will make the decision either way."

"Women know how to read and write!" Kazimiera objected heatedly.

"I'm not saying that all of them don't, but many . . ." Lypynskyi fell silent, while Kazimiera rushed to the window and threw it wide open to help the bee fly free. The bee hurtled between the pane and the frame and stopped buzzing. Lypynskyi walked over to help.

"I don't need any help!"

But she wanted him to help.

Lypynskyi set about trying to coax the insect out of its hideout with the curtain, though he did so, as was customary for him, very ineptly. The bee flew down his collar, and a sharp pain shot through his whole body. He grabbed his neck and howled as if he had contracted apian rabies from the sting. Kazimiera laid him down on the sofa, whispering, "What happened, Wacław? I'll send for a doctor, but tell me: What happened?"

"Yes, send for one," Lypynskyi replied, his tone softening to a premortem moan, "but it might be too late. I'm dying. There's not enough air for me to breathe, Kazimiera. I'm dying."

His pallid face was bathed in sweat, his hands froze over, his eyes grew bleary.

"Christ, can you tell me what's wrong with you?"

"The damned bee bit me here, in the neck." And he turned back the collar of his shirt to show her. Kazimiera exhaled. She wanted to laugh but didn't. Instead, she suddenly leaned down and kissed him on the lips.

The pain subsided, and the world ceased to exist. The kiss was barely palpable. It was more of a whiff than a kiss, a spurious touch, a fleeting, one-footed jaunt into quicksand—a poke of a toe, just to break the sand's stillness but not get sucked in whole. Lypynskyi had a right to this kiss, as they were now engaged. But he didn't have the courage to claim it. Kazimiera pulled her head back, and he didn't stop her.

Many years later, he would replay this scene in his mind over and over: the bee, his cries, her fright, her kiss. Though, no, it wasn't a kiss but a proffer of a kiss, a proffer of herself, as if to say, *From now on I'll be yours, take me, take my mind and my body.* But he didn't take her, he shoved her away. It didn't matter that he did so out of great fear; Kazimiera retreated back inside her shell, offended and shamed, and never showed herself to him again.

This would be the most terrible mistake of Lypynskyi's life. All of his subsequent mistakes would be but consequences of this first one.

"I don't think it's worth troubling a doctor," Kazimiera declared, standing up abruptly.

Sprawled out on the couch, Lypynskyi helplessly squeezed his throat with numbed fingers, as if willfully throttling himself.

"Have you never been stung by a bee, Wacław?"

"Never."

"It isn't deadly." Kazimiera's face sharpened like a dagger.

Lypynskyi remembered that he should still escort his mother to the courtyard. He rose from the couch.

"I'll stop by tomorrow as usual, at two o'clock."

Kazimiera nodded, and he quickly gathered his things and abashedly slipped out into the street.

THE WEDDING TOOK PLACE in that same church where the young couple had previously quarreled so spiritedly. Only the closest relatives attended the ceremony. Uncle Adam Rokicki, the owner of the large estate outside Uman, was too busy with the threshing to make it but invited the newlyweds to visit him at his homestead. Lypynskyi responded that they wouldn't manage to visit him that year, perhaps the following year, but before committing to doing so, he'd consult with Kazimiera, as they were now a family and decided everything together.

Together, they decided to move to Geneva to enroll in a sociology course at a university there. They both knew French quite well. They both wanted to get away. They sent their belongings in advance by mail, and some acquaintances in Geneva helped them find an apartment just opposite the university at the address Rue de Condol 4. Then the newlyweds headed off for their honeymoon in Venice. They spent two weeks in a luxury hotel on the island of Lido di Venezia.

At first, they held hands constantly. There was something new about this for both of them—that new type of unguarded intimacy, when there's no need to be on defense, when there's no need to mentally sift through relevant topics for conversation or analyze the words you've heard, searching for a hidden intimation or accusation in them. They could simply hold hands and not say anything. Her hand was always cold. His was as well. Kazimiera would spend the entire day splashing around in the water: she didn't know how to swim, naturally, just pretended. He sat on the shore in a folding chair, shirt buttoned up to the last button in the scorching sun.

Who knew what these boundless marine depths concealed? Big fish could bite off his feet.

This was the first and last time Lypynskyi saw the sea. Later, whenever salt hit his lips or skin, he would invariably think of his wife.

But now, here she was, smiling, happy, her hair poking out from under her hat. He was rushing toward her, but each step that he took separated them, didn't bring them closer but distanced them, took her away from him. The closer Lypynskyi wanted to be to Kazimiera, the less of her he had left, and whenever he'd come up right next to her, she'd disappear entirely. She'd dissipate, dissolving like a droplet of seawater in a river's floodplain. The aftertaste of salt in his mouth alone would serve as a reminder that she had ever existed at all.

In time, to be able to expel Kazimiera from his memory, Lypynskyi would give up consuming salt in any shape or form. The "sans diet," as he'd call it. A life sans salt and sans flavor. A life without Kazimiera.

VII.

SOOT

(Me)

THEY SAY THAT ONCE upon a time, the great Renaissance paintings looked quite different than they do now. The soot from the candles that settled on their surfaces for centuries—up until the invention of electricity—is now impossible to rub off; hence, not a single museum visitor will ever look upon the original again. One can only speculate at the gamut of colors hidden beneath the smoky overlay.

The past is nothing but a conjecture of the past. The soot that so densely coats lengthy intervals of time is a historical circumstance, while reality is that which, in defiance of everything, emerges through it nonetheless. What comprise our reality aren't necessarily the most important details of the entire painting; conversely, it's the secondary, often trifling minutiae that you probably wouldn't have noticed if you were actually seeing the principal thing.

That's how I've stored my personal past in my mind too. The trifling, secondary details play a more important role in that past—or more precisely, in my memory of it—than do the principal ones.

The principal ones are all coated in soot. I can't navigate the past of my own life. If someone were to quiz me on my knowledge of myself, I would most certainly fail. My neighbors would test higher. Yet I have a very good memory of involuntary glances, cast furtively when willpower failed me; of fears that never did get realized but hold me firmly in their grip until this day; of the unexpected smell of linden trees, and of asphalt drenched by summer rain, and how I ran over it at breakneck speed, spattering my raspberry-colored velvet pants with puddle mud. I remember very well the desire that made my head spin. I wanted everything. And I wanted to experience everything firsthand. Is this hunger not sometimes called youth?

This hunger often made me stay when it would have been wiser to run. I didn't leave, for instance, upon learning that my first golden-haired man was married. Actually, it would've been strange to expect a staid university lecturer two minutes shy of becoming professor to be living a bachelor's life. Wedlock is some sort of requisite initial phase certain types of men need to go through before daring to move up the social ladder. First they must get married, and only then can they do the rest: build a career, publish books, reflect on the meaning of existence, get drunk with colleagues after work—in short, live. Such men are born already married. Dolefully, I was coming to the conclusion that I was sinning, but I didn't know it for a fact. Perhaps because I didn't know that I loved him.

WE BEGAN TO meet regularly at a small, cozy pub not far from the university to talk. It was a game. We just talked. He told me right away, for instance, "My wife used to study the same thing that you're studying."

I asked what her name was, how old she was, and what she looked like: Valentyna, five years older than me, pretty.

"I don't doubt she's pretty," I assured him.

"Yes—yes, she's pretty."

Valentyna never came up in conversation again.

Our conversations at the pub could last for hours, late into the night, until the weary waiters would begin to make a show of flipping over the chairs of the neighboring tables. Then we would pour the wine we had ordered into disposable cups and slowly sip the last of it in some dark little courtyard nearby, sitting on the low iron railings that typically enclosed the flower beds in front of houses. No one would have taken us for a university student and her instructor. We more resembled a melancholic poet and a frivolous damsel with a weakness for sweet words. Those sweet words never did get uttered. Nor did I look like a frivolous damsel in the proper sense because I never wore short dresses with plunging necklines. Actually, I never wore dresses at all, so perhaps my only resemblance to a damsel was in name.

But there was nonetheless something in me that attracted him. My audacity? Our shared interest in literature? My wit? Was I witty? What is it, actually, that pulls certain people toward one another? There must exist some mechanism that drives us—or at least some criterion, some sign that we use to pick a focus for our tenderness from the vast sea of other living beings.

Sometimes we would sit and look into each other's eyes. He'd be stroking my hand, just barely, while I pretended not to notice. In those moments, he would look infinitely sadder than usual. His eyes would flare, the bridge of his nose would crease, and his brows would furrow as if he felt great regret for something he was losing. Or that he never had. That's it: it was sorrow for something unattainable. I'd quickly come up with a new topic for conversation because I couldn't bear these torturous silences. I'd burst into laughter and pull my hand away. Our game would continue.

During lectures, we behaved, as usual, antagonistically. He'd gently prod my impregnable fortress in the back rows, and I'd ungently brush him off, which he'd ignore, continuing on with the lecture. When finished, after saying goodbye to the class, he'd signal to me with an inconspicuous gesture that we could meet up that day. I'd go flying over to the pub, where he was already sitting, lost in thought over a folder of papers, with a few books under his arm and a glass of cognac under his nose. I'd enter, and he'd smile. But with what looked like bitterness. Increasingly, regret muddied his gaze. Increasingly, he drank. Increasingly, his comments grew harsh, and when I'd ask what he wanted from me, he'd respond in almost a shout, "I don't want anything from you! I don't know what I want!"

HE WAS MY FIRST READER. One time I brought him a printout of a novella that I had written on my brand-new computer, under the influence of our strange unrealized relationship. He took the manuscript home and promised to give it a look. I didn't take writing seriously; it was more like an exploration of my own self, a form of entertainment in the midst of unbearable longing, but the entire week, waiting to see what he would say, I didn't know what to do with myself. I very much wanted to live up to his expectations. To tether him to me with my talent. To have him see my full beauty, which likely wasn't noticeable from the outside.

When we met up again, he solemnly handed me the manuscript and said that he liked it. He had read it straight through, in one night, which had frustrated his family members. His lack of sleep made no impression on me at all; for me, it was a common side effect of our "unrelationship." But what did concern me was the term "family." Who was he referencing? His wife and a cat? A dog? Children? All of the above?

"Do you have any children?" I suddenly asked.

"Two."

He didn't look at me as he said this. I started to cry.

At that moment, some man approached our table: "Why are you bringing students to tears, Professor? Was she not prepared for class?"

I quickly wiped my face. Stiffly and unconvincingly, he tried to explain himself to the man, mumbling something like, *I didn't make her, she just teared up on her own, there's a situation with her family* . . . I snatched the manuscript off the table and ran out of the pub without saying goodbye. Our game had come to an end, that much was clear.

So too did his course on Ukrainian Baroque literature. My entire student cohort, breathing a sigh of relief, gladly delved into the considerably more comprehensible but exceedingly tragic and tearfully romantic Ukrainian literature of the nineteenth century. The lectures were given by an exceedingly boring instructor whose name I don't recall, remembering only her good-natured singsong voice and her readiness to shed tears to Taras Hryhorovych Shevchenko's ballad "The Drowned Maiden." This instructor seemed to have come out from under Shevchenko's pen herself. I skipped her lectures shamelessly and didn't make anything of it.

I also didn't show up for my Baroque literature exam. This sort of disobedience could've had serious consequences, including expulsion from the university, but the matter didn't get as far as expulsion because an A miraculously appeared in his handwriting in my transcript booklet. The prefect of the class, whose job it was to address such things, reacted with a telling silence. She probably figured that I had backstairs influence at the university.

When we'd cross paths by accident, we'd walk past one another, electing the most distant trajectories possible. In the narrow hallways of the Ukrainian studies department, this wasn't easy. He'd nod and so would I, then we'd both immediately turn away. In the spring, he wore a long gray overcoat that appeared silklike but definitely wasn't silk, which flapped open as he walked, making him look like an archangel who had descended to the sinful earth on a humanity-saving mission. His golden hair had grown longer and curled into gentle locks, while a few days' worth of stubble added a decade to his years. Nothing could be gleaned from his shadow.

I SANK INTO a leaden depression, barely eating at all and not sleeping. The uncertainty is the most irritating in such cases. What was going on with him—that other side of our nonexistent relationship? Was he tormented or, conversely, glad that everything had been managed without casualties? Was he rejoicing at my pain, or did he not even think about me? The inability to talk to him was driving me crazy. I began talking to myself and imagining what his response would be: undoubtedly, something rational and reassuring.

A friend of mine who was studying violin at the university invited me over to his apartment. After smoking our fill of marijuana, we ran a bath and climbed in clothed. We lay there, he on one side and I on the other. The water wasn't all that warm. I remember vividly this experience of climbing into a bath dressed, casting aside all prohibitions, freeing myself of them because who said this wasn't allowed? In a soaked sweater and pants, I felt as free and clean as if I had just been born and the world was mine to discover. I felt light, like his overcoat that appeared silklike but definitely wasn't silk.

"Don't furrow your brow," the violinist was instructing me from the opposite shore. "Imagine that your soul is on the bridge of your nose. Be gentle with it! Stop wrinkling your nose!"

For some reason, he considered the forehead and the space between the eyes the most important part of the body and would get very tormented when he saw creases there. My distress didn't move him in the least. The violinist's sister had spent eight years carrying on with a married man, then finally snapped herself out of it, broke things off with him, and found herself another guy, who later turned out to be married as well.

"My situation's completely different," I moaned.

"My sister always says that too. Christ, I just don't understand where in the world the two of you get this idea that you're the chosen one. What's so different about you?"

We put on roller skates (it turned out he had two pairs) and, still wet after our bath, skated back and forth between the living room and the kitchen until the neighbors below began to ring the doorbell incessantly.

I've never done anything more deranged before or since. For a brief while, it even seemed that I was starting to fancy the violinist. During a walk across the dam outside the city, I clumsily tried to kiss him, to which he said, "Why are you ruining everything? Can't a man and woman just be friends?"

"They can, I guess," I replied somewhat disenchanted, and at that our friendship ended.

MY ANGUISH CONGEALED so much that I could no longer find the air to breathe. Time passed mercilessly, one minute at a time, and with every new minute that passed, I became cognizant anew of myself as the most unfortunate creature on this planet. Time expanded and clogged my blood vessels, took away my hearing and my voice, blurred my vision. My body, wasted away, became disproportionately bony. I seemed to be swimming in circles in an aquarium, densely filled with anguish the consistency of gel, while people examined me through the glass like some rare animal. I survived the day only because I learned to divide it into short distances, talking myself into suffering through one, then sprinting over into the next, where things would get easier.

"A little longer, and it'll be twelve," I'd tell myself to the drone of the computer first thing in the morning, lying in my bedroom. (I hadn't attended university lectures in a long time by then.) At twelve, I was allowed to try to sleep through lunchtime. Enduring the anguish seemed easiest in my sleep.

"A little longer, and it'll be five," I'd tell myself when I couldn't manage to fall asleep at noon. At five, my parents came home from work. I'd settle in on the little divan in the kitchen, cover myself with an old green throw blanket, and watch my parents have dinner. I concocted adventures from the day of cut classes—I lied blatantly quite often back then—or simply listened with delight as they unaffectedly conversed. If I managed to forget about myself for even a minute, I was happy; that's why I found pleasure in the routine travails of post-Soviet Ukrainian life, like lack of money and corruption. I also found pleasure in hardships outside my immediate world, like problems of family friends and, in particular, acquaintances dying—because nothing distracts from personal suffering like someone else's death.

I often imagined that I myself was dying. My swollen body was being pushed up to the surface of the aquarium face up, while he, my handsome golden-haired man, beat his head against the glass and, choking on grief, lamented, "No! No!"

In the evening, I'd stuff myself with sedatives, readying myself for another difficult night, during the course of which I'd write my stories, cry, doze, muse, cry, and finally remind myself, "A little longer, and it'll begin to dawn." And when dawn was about to break, I'd crawl into bed, only to begin this whole cycle of torments over again in a few hours.

Maybe you just have to undergo a bout of proper suffering, at least once? To excruciate oneself in order to determine the size of one's soul—XS, S, M, or XL? Mine was somehow sizeless.

———————

A LOCAL PUBLISHER agreed to publish my novella as a stand-alone book, despite it really being just a long story. I should've been happy, but I couldn't feel anything. I just insisted that the book launch be held in the pub where we once used to meet.

Quite a lot of people showed up because, at that time in post-Soviet Ukraine, books weren't published all that often.

And here again, soot coats the principal details of my past, leaving me with only the secondary ones . . .

I remember only that I sat before a smiling audience, joking incessantly as I crumpled the nicely bound little book in my hands. It was bright yellow. The wooden chair under me creaked now and then. The audience kept bursting into benevolent laughter in the vein of, *Look at how lovely she is, she's joking, her youthful energy spouting like a fountain, she's writing something in such difficult times, her spirit unfailing, how lovely.* The faces of those present metastasized into one continuous blotch. I read excerpts of the novella, and no one understood anything.

"Why, you don't understand any of it," I said, and the blotch exploded with laughter. *She's self-aware and ironic too, this really is lovely!*

Among those present, one face pulsated—his. He had arrived late, so he had to stand by the entrance, cowering against the door-jamb. When the others laughed, he smiled, just barely, likely to not protrude too much from the general background. When the presentation ended, he was the first to disappear, leaving me unsure if I had merely hallucinated him.

I headed home late that night on the last trolley bus. At the stop outside my parents' house, I noticed a lone motionless figure that was sitting Buddha-like on a block of concrete and staring at the full moon. Its crimson disk dangled over the suburban tract on the other side of the road like the sword of Damocles.

"The launch was fun," the figure uttered, and I froze in trepidation.

"What are you doing here? How do you know where I live?"

"I looked it up in your student records. I wanted to congratulate you on the book."

He was slurring; it was clear that he was terribly drunk. I stepped closer. He wanted to stand up but almost toppled over. "You're drunk," I said as sternly as I could.

"Come here."

Like an obedient doll, I walked right up to him, the smell of cognac tickling my nose. The moon grew menacingly redder above our heads.

There wasn't another soul around, just a little group of drunks hanging out on the steps of a convenience store about fifteen meters away. He embraced me, looking doomed, and began to grope me. I didn't resist. He kissed me, and I too felt intoxicated.

"Be mine," he whispered, "marry me."

I instantly sobered up.

"How can I marry you if you're already married?"

"Married?" Again, he almost toppled off the block of concrete. "Oh right, I'm already married."

I couldn't tell if he had really forgotten about his marital status or if, driven to despair, he was playing the fool.

"And she's pretty," I continued.

"She's very pretty."

"But it's all the same to me."

He fell silent for a moment or so, contemplating my words, and then started kissing me even more desperately. Despite the desperation, we were both overcome with relief.

I remember the moon was so close and so low that I had the urge to push it aside with my hand, to screen it with a curtain so that I might luxuriate in the darkness, as I deserved. I saw every tiny detail in his face. His drunken whispers sounded like a revelation; his fair hair blazed like the Golden Fleece of ancient heroes.

But he wasn't a hero. And neither was I. In my first real love story, the leading characters were behaving more like antiheroes— paltry cowards and liars who were apt to use love to justify any cruelty whatsoever. His wife turned out to be the heroine: a woman who suddenly and involuntarily found herself the target of fire on my and his battlefield and didn't flee, even though her chances at victory were less than mine.

I saw her not long after, when she stopped by the university one day to see her husband. She was slightly stooped and excessively thin, with a large, humped nose protruding from her pale, gray face. Her hair was fair, just like his. Her head was lowered and meekly tilted to the side, like an infallible Madonna's. They said goodbye to each other on the stairs, and the Madonna set off down University Street toward the city's central square. For a while I traipsed indecisively behind her: everything inside me buzzed, my cheeks were burning, my legs giving out under me. Finally, I caught up with her and blocked her path.

"You're Valentyna, right?"

She nodded. "And who are you?"

I didn't respond, just breathed hard.

"I know who you are," she said finally. "I pictured you differently."

"What do you mean?"

"You're pretty."

She took my arm in hers, and together we walked, slowly. From the side, someone might have thought we were best friends. No one had ever told me that I was pretty.

OUR FIRST MEETING was followed by heart-to-hearts, and then heated quarrels, in which she nonsensically claimed, "I love anyone who loves my husband," to which I nonsensically claimed, "You can't break something that isn't broken"; all of this followed by jealousy, pain, bouts of despondency, and suicide attempts on both our parts, condemnation from our respective families and friends, hatred, and, at last, fatigue and the slow onset of indifference. The entire journey from the genesis of my feelings toward him to our complete estrangement lasted a few exhausting years. The golden-haired man never did become mine. He also didn't remain hers. I barely remember the details anymore, just little snippets of them: the crimson moon above, the dam outside the city where I liked taking walks, our secret getaways to a little house in the mountains—and then the train, my worried parents who'd come to see me off on the platform, me waving through the window for them to leave but them not leaving. The train heaved into motion. I was smoking in the train's vestibule, and the cigarette smoke was suffusing the space around me densely, like sheep's wool.

A stranger was smoking next to me.

"A difficult goodbye?"

"Nah," I replied. "I've had harder ones."

The stranger peered at me.

"You aren't the author of that book, are you? The one with the bright yellow cover?" And he named the title.

I nodded sheepishly.

I'm embarrassed to hear the titles of my books on other people's lips. They seem so infantile.

"I was at your book launch. I sat in the front row."

"I'm sorry, but I don't remem—"

"You read an excerpt about a young woman who couldn't sleep because her upstairs neighbors were making a racket, and when she finally went to complain, she found a squirrel family calmly sitting around, shelling walnuts, in an otherwise empty apartment. I laughed."

"You remember that level of detail?"

"Oh, I don't forget anything."

The train was carefully crossing the Dniester River. I put out my cigarette, then said, "It wasn't just the squirrels keeping the woman awake."

"I figured. I felt sorry for her. She was special."

"Everyone thinks they're special, but in reality, we're all ordinary."

"That's not true. You're special. I'm a fan."

And the stranger cast his eyes onto me with sincerity, blue as the sky on a frosty February day.

"Do you know what the Dniester flows into?"

I was at a loss. In that moment, I didn't know if I knew.

VIII.

ROKICKI'S LEGACY

(Him)

INHALE—EXHALE. IN THE SUMMER of 1907, Lypynskyi fell off a horse and didn't breathe for several minutes. He was taking part in festivities organized in his honor by his maternal uncle, Adam Rokicki, the wealthy Polish landowner from outside Uman in the Russian Empire. With this event, he was presenting Lypynskyi as his heir and introducing him to the community. Rokicki had no children of his own. All the local aristocrats of greater or lesser stature gathered for the festivities, eager for the horse races in particular. It was Kazimiera's first time in Ukraine. She sat on the spectator benches, occasionally exchanging a word or two with Rokicki's wife, Henrykha Henrykhivna, a quiet and delicate German who had been Polonized. When Lypynskyi fell, Kazimiera shut her eyes and squealed. Rokicki bellowed like a bull and rushed down from the stands to the racecourse, darting onto the track, even as the race continued, to pull his nephew's body out.

Lypynskyi told everyone that he could not remember those few minutes when he didn't breathe, saying he was unconscious, but in fact, he remembered everything quite well. Those few minutes lasted forever. His lungs stopped moving, as if they could no longer take the pain that had been filling them in recent months, as if any more pain simply wouldn't fit. In vain, his uncle shook him and pounded his chest with his fist, trying to squeeze out some sign of life. Kazimiera stepped up onto her bench and watched, frightened. Henrykha sobbed. The doctor was already running to the casualty with his medical bag. The sun shone so brightly that Lypynskyi involuntarily squinted, as if trying to make out individual rays in the unbroken stream of light, which pierced him like arrows. It grew so quiet that he could hear the slow current of the Hirskyi Tikych River and the characteristic chug of his uncle's nearby water mills. The apricot trees rustled, wild strawberries ripened in the humid shade of the untouched meadows, and Lypynskyi detected their subtle and exquisite scent. In the stables, the thoroughbred steeds, which his uncle had selected himself, were neighing, while in his two-story house, countless paintings and drawings of horses hung silently on the walls—his uncle's precious collection.

Rokicki had a thing for horses. His stallions could outstrip the latest trains, and, in fact, they could cover the distance from the estate to the Uman train station—a full sixty kilometers—in under an hour. "All this will be yours," Rokicki had said to Lypynskyi when he was just departing for Kraków to study. A Pole, he was as loyal to and respectful of Ukrainian culture as his nephew would one day be. Twice a week, he would make his servants change into Ukrainian Cossack dress—embroidered shirts and the bright-colored balloon pants called *sharovary* ("We must respect local traditions!")—then he himself, even in the hottest weather, would throw the traditional felt cloak of the Cossacks over his shoulders, harness a charabanc, and, with this ensemble and accoutrements, drive off to markets in towns sixty to seventy kilometers away.

"He isn't breathing," the doctor said with a shake of the head. "His sternum is badly injured."

Though Lypynskyi could hear these words just fine, he was fixated more on the words Kazimiera had uttered a few hours earlier, which now played in his mind on a loop. They had been riding through the lands surrounding the estate. Kazimiera sat in her saddle with uncertainty, struggling to share her husband's enthusiasm. "Don't be offended, but the grasses outside Kraków smell exactly the same," she had noted. Due to a flurry of aggressive horseflies, the outing had to be concluded prematurely. "I'm not offended," Lypynskyi had replied.

LYPYNSKYI WAS A GOOD RIDER. On horseback, his stoop would disappear, his long, lean body attaining a perfect silhouette, his still-young face becoming manly and focused, and his eyes squinting like those of a hawk in search of a tiny field vole. Horses obeyed Lypynskyi like dogs. The day before, his uncle had half-jokingly quipped that a victory in the races wasn't obligatory, of course, but he very much expected it. A victory for Lypynskyi would mean unhindered entry into the upper society of men—and having his own heir would be even better.

Lypynskyi had told Kazimiera about this as he donned his jockey silks. "Everyone around here is asking the same thing: When will our family grow?"

"And what do you answer?"

"Nothing, otherwise I'd have to resort to rudeness. I don't want to spoil my uncle's warm welcome."

Kazimiera was getting dressed as well. A light cream-colored dress set out by the maids lay on the bed. Kazimiera herself was still twisting and turning in front of the mirror in her white undergarments. Lypynskyi watched her out of the corner of his eye. Such moments would remind him of how much he loved her.

He embraced her timidly, and Kazimiera recoiled.

"Wacław, you're always stressing that you're in no rush to have children, but every action of yours attests to the opposite. I'm not ready to become a mother right now, but you're indifferent to my feelings!"

"That's not what I—I didn't, I wasn't trying to—"

"What did you want, then? You know where children come from, don't you?"

Lypynskyi turned away and buttoned his shirt. Kazimiera yanked the cream-colored dress on.

"Do you ever ask me what I want?" she asked, almost yelling.

"There's no need to. That's all you talk about."

"I want to go back to Kraków after this visit, that's what I want. I don't like it in Geneva anymore."

Lypynskyi, conversely, adored the city. It was only in Geneva that he could study sociology, which had turned out to be even more interesting than he had anticipated. It was through sociology that Lypynskyi had immersed himself in how people organized socially, economically, and politically with those like them—a great mystery that had intrigued him all his life and that he was finally close to understanding.

"I didn't register for classes this fall and will be returning to Kraków in October," his wife said in conclusion, more calmly now but no less ruthlessly.

"I thought we made those kinds of decisions together . . ."

"And what is it you think we're doing now?"

"Kazimiera, you do understand that either way we won't be able to live in Kraków forever, don't you? My inheritance is here in Ukraine, in this estate. Sooner or later, we're going to live here."

Kazimiera was dumbfounded. Disgust and fear washed over her face simultaneously.

"Never," she hissed through clenched teeth. "I'd sooner die than live here. Living here or dying—it's all the same to me."

What could he offer her? Only his love and his social status. But she pushed away his love and was disgusted by his status among Ukrainians. He needed to find something else to offer her, some third thing.

"HE ISN'T BREATHING," the doctor repeated.

"Do something, or I'll shred you to pieces," Rokicki said, his teeth gritted. This corpulent and coarse man, with his deep voice, volatile nature, and propensity for lewd jokes, wasn't regarded as being particularly tactful. But he was a man of consequence. His wife Henrykha came across as an ancient goddess in the paws of a rabid monster. Despite this, they suited one another like a sword and its scabbard. Even though Rokicki liked his amusements, he always returned to Henrykha, nestling against her graceful body, while she sat wordlessly, her fingers fiddling with the betrayer's wiry hair, signaling to him that this time too he had been granted forgiveness. Their life unfurled before Lypynskyi's eyes like a theatrical production, full of perils and delights, ups and downs. Everything about the uncle had the tincture of the affected, the theatrical—a bit from vaudeville and a bit from tragedy—and no one, not even his nephew or his own wife, was allowed behind the scenes, where his tender essence, disguised as a boor and rascal, was hiding.

Lying on his back and still not breathing, Lypynskyi saw a different uncle before him: a concerned and decisive one. Maybe it was due to Rokicki's volition that he finally stirred and wheezed, feebly gasping for air. Kazimiera came running. The doctor crossed himself. In Lypynskyi's chest, concurrent to the influx of fresh air, something was irrevocably shattering, breaking off, splitting, almost as if by returning to life, he was destining himself to dying from then on, only at a slower pace. Lypynskyi screamed once in excruciating pain and only then passed out.

He regained consciousness a few days later in a terrible fever. The doctor gave a diagnosis of pneumonia resulting from a severe contusion and displacement of the ribs. Kazimiera sat next to him the entire time, placing the palm of her hand on the patient's forehead every few minutes.

"I think your temperature has dropped," she would say optimistically.

"And I think quite the opposite—that it's risen," Lypynskyi would moan in response, and ask her to read to him. Kazimiera read newspapers, *Don Quixote*, then Thomas à Kempis, and when Lypynskyi felt completely horrible, she'd read *coś ukraińskiego*, "something Ukrainian."

"I don't understand Cyrillic well," Kazimiera would grumble unhappily before going to look for a suitable book in his uncle's library. All that was there in Ukrainian was Borys Hrinchenko's recently published four-volume *Dictionary of the Ukrainian Language*. It had been a gift from Lypynskyi to his uncle. Kazimiera would open the dictionary to a random page and bunglingly read off whatever Ukrainian words her eyes rested on, along with their short explanations. Lypynskyi would listen carefully and occasionally correct her pronunciation.

"*Loputsiok*. The young soft stalk of a plant, used for food." And she would burst out laughing. "*Loputsiok!*"

Lypynskyi would purposefully cough over her laughter.

Within two weeks, the patient had more or less recovered, and the couple headed back to Geneva. No further conversations about Kraków transpired. The evening before their departure, the mistress of the house planned an elaborate farewell meal, but Rokicki never did show up to it. Three of them sat at the table, enveloped in a gloomy atmosphere, as Henrykha ignored her husband's absence and tried to maintain small talk.

Lypynskyi saw that his uncle's wife had been crying, but couldn't make out why. He never meddled in her and Rokicki's private life, regardless of what was happening there. Henrykha was leaning in over her plate, feigning hunger, even though, since the very start of the evening, she had just been pecking at the fine porcelain dinnerware without placing a single morsel in her mouth. Her silhouette, which seemed almost carved out of white marble, cast a large, weighty shadow on the wooden floor.

Lypynskyi felt the weight of this shadow pressing on him that entire night. Kazimiera too slept restlessly. Dogs were howling in the yard and constantly waking her. Heaviness and tension hung in the air.

A few hours before dawn, when the night was no longer bearable, Lypynskyi heard Henrykha's cries. He sprang out of bed and ran to her room. The door was ajar. Henrykha was standing in the middle of the bedroom in a long white nightgown with a silver candlestick in her hands. She was flushed, her hair disheveled, her smooth face marked with deep creases of pain. There was no self-pity in her defensive posture, no weakness, only a desperate desire to finally put an end to her protracted agony. It was the look of an exhausted wild animal that had suddenly stopped running, to turn around and finally peer into the eyes of its predator.

Adam Rokicki stood facing her in his outerwear, his fists and teeth clenched. It was clear that he had just returned. But for the first time in the entire eternity of their marriage, he hadn't been forgiven.

"Son of a bitch!" Henrykha exclaimed. "I can't bear their smells anymore!"

"Quiet, you'll wake up my nephew," Rokicki hissed, only adding fuel to the fire burning in his wife.

"Boo-hoo, I'll wake up your nephew! Don't worry, he'll get over it. When he fell off that horse, you trembled over him like you never would've trembled over me. You fuss over him as if he's your own son!"

"Since I don't have a son of my own, I might as well treat someone else's child like my own."

An invisible bullet pierced Henrykha's throat. She screamed and wobbled, and then, using all the might she could muster, hurled the candleholder at her husband's head. Rokicki didn't manage to dodge the attack, and the candleholder slammed right into his wide forehead, bouncing away with a jangle.

"I'll kill you," he seethed, and moved in her direction. Henrykha wasn't scared, just crossed her arms over her meager breasts. Against the deathly silence, Lypynskyi could practically hear the tears trickling down her face.

Lypynskyi had to gather up all his paltry strength to hold back his uncle. He grabbed him by the arm and hung on it like a bratty little six-year-old boy.

"Uncle, stop!" he begged helplessly. "Stop! What are you doing?"

Henrykha let out an almost wild laugh. Rokicki freed his hand, spat, and walked out of the room.

Henrykha went limp and dropped feebly to the edge of the bed, as if scattering into tiny marble shards that no one would ever be able to put back together. Humiliated for being infertile, she was desperately wanting pity now, but no one could give it to her. Lypynskyi stood awkwardly by the wall for a moment before fleeing the battlefield, noiselessly shutting the door behind himself. The sun was just beginning to rise.

And in the morning, everyone was heading to the Uman train station together. From there, the Lypynski were supposed to travel west through the Russian Empire to the city of Zhmerynka, from Zhmerynka to Volochysk on the Austro-Hungarian border, from Volochysk to Pidvolochysk immediately across the border, and then on to Geneva, with stops in Lviv, Kraków, and Vienna. The move from one empire to another was felt first and foremost in the trains: Russian railcars were dirty but spacious, while Austrian ones were cramped but luxurious.

Rokicki was cracking crude jokes and guffawing at himself. Henrykha looked straight ahead pensively; not a single emotion could be discerned on her face; her eyes were dry and cold. Kazimiera was also silent. Everyone was pretending as if nothing had happened. Rokicki leaned over to his wife, timorously touching her shoulder. "Come on, isn't that so?" he asked. "Am I not telling the truth?"

Henrykha nodded that yes, he was telling the truth, and Rokicki, soothed, went on cracking jokes.

At the station, they said their goodbyes quickly, even though there was still plenty of time. "Everything that I have is yours," Lypynskyi's uncle repeated into his ear so that the women could not hear. Lypynskyi just nodded, not letting Kazimiera out of his sight through the corner of his eye.

"Thank you for your hospitality," Kazimiera said, approaching.

"You are always welcome guests here. Come whenever your heart desires."

"Of course," Kazimiera assured him, though she herself would never again return to these boondocks of Little Russia.

And on their way back home, Rokicki complained to his wife: "There's something inane about her. It's always Kraków and Kraków, as if there's nothing more to the world than Kraków. You're from Kraków too, and I've never heard you go on about it like that."

To which his wife responded, "Because you weren't listening."

———

IN GENEVA, LYPYNSKYI again began to feel ill. The doctors unanimously declared that with such weak lungs, he should live elsewhere. The local Bise winds had a very negative effect on tubercular consumptives.

"I have tuberculosis?"

"Not yet, but the esteemed gentleman inevitably will if he remains in Geneva."

Lypynskyi gathered up his library (it had already moved twice), sealed the wooden crates holding his notes and letters, withdrew from the university, and returned to Kraków, where his wife was already waiting for him. They didn't need to look for an apartment, since his mother-in-law, Mrs. Szumińska, had proposed that they stay with her, and Kazimiera had already agreed. Lypynskyi wasn't particularly resistant, though he nonetheless didn't start breathing easier. The air in the new apartment on Hugona Kołłątaja Street was more poisonous than any of the most dangerous Geneva Bise winds, and the stern faces of the two most prominent Polish kings—Kazimierz and Jagiełło—on the façade of Building No. 8 served as a reminder that sincere Polish patriots lived there. Lypynskyi wasn't one of them; on the contrary, he felt like a foreigner that had infiltrated a tribe of strangers and was now stuck for life.

Kazimiera once again became distant. It seemed she no longer wanted to do or learn anything, as if marriage were the death of the mind and the cessation of personal growth. Previously one of the best female students of Jagiellonian University—though they were, of course, very few in number—she was no longer interested in women's suffrage or the paths to liberalization of the Austro-Hungarian Empire. She spent entire days reading the tabloids or meeting up with girlfriends, feeding her indolence and irritation with nibbles of puffy Kraków pastries. In this regard, she was growing to resemble her mother more and more. Over dinner, she would relay information in brief spurts: "Excessive sweating can be cured with electric currents."

"I don't smell," Lypynskyi would answer. "My sweat secretion is fine."

Mrs. Szumińska's family doctor recommended mountain air for the lungs, and Lypynskyi gladly escaped to the town of Zakopane. There, in the Polish Tatra Mountains, he decided to freeze his pain into nonexistence, to finally squeeze it out of himself like an inflamed boil. He took up quarters at the Jeżewo Sanatorium. The owner of this sanatorium, Dr. Vilchynskyi, mostly took in Ukrainians, as he himself was of Ukrainian descent. There was a whole heap of them there. Tuberculosis was the favorite illness of the Ukrainian intelligentsia, and Zakopane was their very own Switzerland. Only the truly well-off could afford to splurge on Davos, the best resort town for lung health in Europe.

Lypynskyi lay in the Jeżewo yard, covered with a sheepskin, and counted the sharp tops of the spruces around him. Beyond the trees he could see jagged mountains. The patient's assignment was to just breathe, and he subjected himself to it completely. He breathed so diligently that hoarfrost would form on his well-groomed black mustache, making him resemble an old graying man who had been sent out to pasture. In the six months of his stay in the sanatorium, Kazimiera didn't visit once.

IX.

TUBERCULAR CONSUMPTIVES

(Him)

DURING ONE SUCH "AIR-TREATMENT" session, a slim smiling man in a buttonless overcoat walked up to Lypynskyi. It was rather cold—the tail end of November—and a biting wind was mercilessly flapping the edges of his garment, which the man was pressing to his body with his elbows.

"Mr. Lypynskyi, you haven't become my comrade in misfortune, have you? A fellow tubercular consumptive?"

Lypynskyi wiped the hoarfrost from his mustache.

"With all due respect, I just have pleurisy."

The man laughed. Only then did Lypynskyi recognize him. Vasyl Domanytskyi was the soul of the Ukrainian national movement. He was also a talented publicist, poet, historian, archaeologist, and ethnographer. Most importantly, he was the editor of the first complete edition of Taras Shevchenko's *Kobzar*. Shevchenko, less than fifty years after his death, was already considered a pivotal figure in Ukrainian literature, and *Kobzar*, his debut collection of poetry from 1840, had been republished by Domanytskyi in

1907 in a massive and unparalleled print run of six thousand copies, causing quite a stir among Ukrainians.

Everyone knew Domanytskyi. Female students fell in love with him at first sight, while men, especially professional colleagues, considered him their best friend after the first handshake. He was a sprightly man who was forever hurrying off somewhere, forever captivated by something, forever disheveled. If he disappeared for a week or two, it was because he had found and was now lost in some interesting old family archive. He didn't walk, he flew, which earned him the nickname The Wind. He was known for wearing a pince-nez and this old gray overcoat, buttonless from age. Domanytskyi had been vagabonding like this, without any buttons, for many seasons already. That's why he looked disheveled. And that's also why he, most likely, contracted tuberculosis. Alongside all this, he managed to produce an incredible amount of editorial work and writing, and was a regular contributor to the two most important Ukrainian newspapers: the Lviv-based *Dilo*, and the Kyiv-based *Rada*, which had launched in 1906.

Domanytskyi could have easily had a robust career in Russian publishing, yet he stubbornly worked on the development of Ukrainian literary projects for paltry pay instead; for this reason, many described him as a saint. There was talk that he didn't marry simply because he wouldn't be able to support a family. No one knew or wanted to know how Domanytskyi was financially getting by: he was flaunted like a diamond on a pile of simple river stones, and only when he began to crack—however impossible that may have seemed—did all of Kyiv's Ukrainian society chip in for treatment.

The publication of Shevchenko's *Kobzar* in St. Petersburg had brought Domanytskyi great fame but also a great deal of trouble. The tsar's censors had gathered their wits only after the appearance of the book and were now viciously taking vengeance on its compiler, sentencing him in absentia to three years in exile in

Vologda Governorate north of Moscow. With a counterfeit passport, the ill Domanytskyi had been forced to flee west. But the exile had nowhere to go. A month's stay in a "Zakopane hole in the wall," as the Jeżewo Sanatorium was described by Ukrainians, cost a good bit of money—two hundred fifty rubles, to be exact—and Domanytskyi's initial sojourn there was covered by a collection from Kyiv society (so that he spend time in the benefit of his health). Scrounging from the Kyiv sugar magnates, and not for the first time, *Rada's* publisher Yevhen Chykalenko ardently proclaimed, "Ukraine doesn't have the right to squander this man!"

Lypynskyi was rather flattered that Domanytskyi had approached him—someone six years his junior and still completely unknown.

"Vasyl Mykolaiovych! I'm genuinely surprised that you recognized me!"

They knew each other very superficially, owing to a series of illegal meetings of the Ukrainian intelligentsia that used to be held in the Kyiv apartment of the wealthy landowner Maria Trebynska. At the time, Lypynskyi had been in his final year at the First Kyiv Gymnasium, a prestigious preparatory school, while Domanytskyi served as the private teacher of Trebynska's children and the informal leader of the regular meetings in her home. During these *jours fixes*, the gymnasium students such as Lypynskyi were permitted to sit and listen, but didn't take part in the discussions. The young Lypynskyi, among other things, acted as the senior errand boy. Usually he was entrusted with obtaining literature banned in tsarist Russia, a rather innocent task, since the banned literature circulated around Kyiv almost unhindered. One time, however, he was caught red-handed with a copy of Mykhailo Drahomanov's *On How Our Land Became Not Ours*; only his notable lineage saved him from several months' imprisonment.

Domanytskyi pulled up a lounge chair closer to the reclining

Lypynskyi, lay down beside him, and likewise covered himself with a sheepskin. Then the two of them set to breathing together.

"Pleurisy, you say?"

"Yes, just pleurisy. Dr. Vilchynskyi said my odds at a full recovery are very good."

"He said the same thing about me. Projecting good odds is his job. And our job is to squander these odds."

Lypynskyi steered the conversation to a topic he found less irksome: "What's the news from Kyiv? Are they still doing searches?"

"The searches are much worse, my friend, much worse."

LYPYNSKYI AND DOMANYTSKYI quickly became inseparable in Zakopane. In the morning, they'd breakfast together in the sanatorium's dining hall with its huge windows overlooking the mountains, exchanging news from the newspapers they'd read and the letters they'd received. Next, it was time for respiratory procedures. They'd lie face up in the cold, discussing the pitiable situation of Ukrainian education and politics, and devising intricate plans to save them. It was through these exchanges that they founded the publishing house Peasant Booklet, with its series of accessibly written brochures on various behavioral-economic topics. The first brochure, "How Peasants in Other Lands Prosper," written by Domanytskyi, was published early the following year, in 1908, and cost twenty kopiykas. Lypynskyi borrowed the money for its publication—a total of four hundred rubles—from his father. Subsequent booklets were scheduled to be devoted to selling eggs abroad and silkworm breeding.

After lunch, Lypynskyi and Domanytskyi would stroll through the nearby hills and, on their way back, stop for dinner at one of the local restaurants. There they would be joined by other consumptives infected with the virus of Ukrainian community-building. The time passed swiftly and merrily. Lypynskyi spoke little, listening mostly. He addressed Domanytskyi by only his first name and patronymic, Vasyl Mykolaiovych, while Domanytskyi half-jokingly called Lypynskyi *"gente Polonus,"* Latin for "a Pole by pedigree." Lypynskyi would frown in offense but quickly get over it. He forgave his older friend's didactic tone because in him he saw a worthy guide into Ukrainian culture, someone dignified who would vouch for him in front of others. Domanytskyi lived up to this task brilliantly. He was first to recognize in Lypynskyi a historian who had long since passed the stage of archive-lover, someone who could even compete with the recognized luminaries of historical science. Truth be told, there weren't all that many of them. The master of Ukrainian historiography, Mykhailo Hrushevskyi, who lived in Lviv, was just then preparing the seventh volume of his magnum opus, a ten-volume *History of Ukraine-Rus'*. His figure cast such a titanic shadow that all the other historians seemed like tiny insects puttering around in the leftovers from the master's table. For a long time, Lypynskyi couldn't find the courage to become one of them. He had prepared a few articles but hadn't sent them off anywhere, as if awaiting the approval of someone he could trust, someone like Domanytskyi. Beyond offering mere approval, Domanytskyi considered Lypynskyi his equal and, by extension, the equal of every intellectual working with Ukrainian culture—a field that, due to its tiny parameters, was often cramped and reeking of intrigue and competitiveness.

By the 1908 New Year, Lypynskyi had sent his first two historical articles in Ukrainian to the editorial office of *Rada*. He declined any honorarium, of course, considering himself—a descendent of Polish colonizers—as a priori guilty before the Ukrainian people for the rest of his life. The formal induction into Ukrainian intellectual circles was a success: the articles were immediately printed, and the author was discussed with great interest.

"Now you can call yourself a Ukrainian historian without reservation," Domanytskyi said, which Lypynskyi diffidently eschewed because he had never formally studied history and would forever be just a well-versed dilettante.

Lypynskyi and Domanytskyi resembled each other physically, both having a stoop that likely resulted from the uncertainty of their chosen paths. One was nearing the end of this path, while the other was just embarking on it. In pulmonary weakness, too, Domanytskyi had advanced much further, having been spitting up blood for a long time already. People nonetheless found his company easy and comforting. Domanytskyi tried to approach everything with a sense of humor, and it seemed as though he didn't take his illness seriously—as if it weren't grabbing him by the throat but was merely a fleeting phase. Only the dark circles under his energetic eyes and his inflamed cheeks alluded to the impending end to his virtuoso performance.

"What are your plans for the spring?" Lypynskyi would inquire persistently, but he never heard an intelligible answer. Domanytskyi would've gladly stayed at the sanatorium, but his money was inexorably running out.

"Whenever I leave here, I'll likely die," he would joke dismissively.

At the time, with no earnings of his own, Lypynskyi was fully living off his parents. Nonetheless, he scraped up a sufficient sum of money from his allowance for Domanytskyi to remain in Zakopane for another three months.

"This isn't a gift," he told his friend when he began to resist. "Don't even think that. It's just a loan till better times. You'll give it back when the peasant books start to turn a profit."

BUT IN FEBRUARY, the always cheery Domanytskyi suddenly became taciturn and withdrawn: a certain individual whom he hadn't seen in over two years and with whom his last meeting had ended rather unpleasantly was coming to Kraków, just a little over a hundred kilometers away. This individual had informed him of her arrival in a letter, expressing a desire to meet again. Domanytskyi carried the letter in the inside pocket of his vest but didn't reply to it, just reread it a few times a day or simply fidgeted with it as if wanting to shake an ounce of her essence out of the piece of paper. Lypynskyi didn't ask any questions because he wasn't in the habit of meddling in other people's matters of the heart; just once, over dinner, did he carefully convey that he was ready to help if necessary. Domanytskyi sprang to life.

"Be my courier! Go to Kraków tomorrow, meet her at the train station, and pass along a message from me."

"If that's what you want, I'll go. I need to go to Kraków myself anyway to take care of a few private matters. What should I pass along?"

"That I'm very troubled, and that's why I can't meet with her."

HAVING OBTAINED PRECISE INSTRUCTIONS, Lypynskyi left early the following morning. Upon his arrival in Kraków, he still had enough time to stop at home and was wonderfully surprised by Kazimiera's heartfelt welcome. She spent an entire hour relaying the latest news about her sister's fiancé and then suddenly announced that she'd been taking swimming lessons for a month.

"Swimming? That's a strange pastime for a woman, but if you find enjoyment in it, then I have nothing against it."

"I want us to go to the sea again, Wacław. I want to be able to swim in the sea. We'll go again, won't we?"

Lypynskyi nodded without giving it much thought. He too had something to tell.

"There's something important that I want to share with you. I've established a publishing house with Vasyl Domanytskyi, the Ukrainian activist from Kyiv, who's staying in Zakopane with me. We're going to publish pamphlets for the Ukrainian peasants. The matter is very important, and I'll need to live in Kyiv to oversee the work, probably for about three years."

"Why doesn't Domanytskyi oversee it there?"

"He's forbidden from entering Russia."

"Is he a criminal?"

"Who in Russia isn't a criminal?"

Kazimiera turned away.

"Have you made up your mind to move to Kyiv for three years?"

"I don't know. For now, I want to explore if publishing is even for me. I was going to go and try it for at least a year."

"And me?"

This question didn't catch Lypynskyi by surprise, but he fell silent, hanging his head timidly. He had the urge to crush her in an embrace, to tell her that she was his wife and had to follow him—no, he couldn't force her, but if she loved him, then she had to go and not think twice. Without her by his side, wherever he may be seemed like exile. Without her, the entire world felt like a prison; he felt like his own prison.

"I walk through the interminable prison of myself," he muttered softly under his breath.

"What did you say?"

"Nothing. You should decide for yourself what it is you want. It would make me happy if you came with me, but I don't intend to force my wife into doing anything she doesn't want to do."

With that, Lypynskyi retrieved some things from his room, and they said goodbye.

"Come visit me at the sanatorium for a night or two," he added on his way out. "Dr. Vilchynskyi promised he wouldn't charge you for a short visit."

Kazimiera replied that she didn't know if she would manage to make it.

The train station was just a few minutes' walk from Hugona

Kołłątaja Street. The apartment's proximity to the train station had always seemed uncomfortable to Lypynskyi, as if the city weren't letting him in all the way, and the blare of the locomotive's horn was constantly reminding him that just as he had arrived, so he would leave, and it would be best to seek the refuge he'd so been dreaming of elsewhere. He walked out onto the platform just as a train from Lviv was pulling in. There were few passengers on it. Lypynskyi patiently waited for everyone to exit, then opened the door to the third compartment. A young woman gazed at him with surprise.

"Don't be scared, young lady," Lypynskyi said matter-of-factly. "I've been authorized by our mutual acquaintance to meet you and convey a verbal message."

"Domanytskyi isn't coming?" The young woman was Lesia, the daughter of the landowning Maria Trebynska, in whose home the *jours fixes* of the Ukrainian intelligentsia had regularly taken place. Domanytskyi had been her private tutor.

"Ms. Lesia, Vasyl Mykolaiovych is very troubled that he couldn't come today to Kraków. He asked that I apologize on his behalf and help you with your baggage should you need it."

"Coward!" Trebynska exclaimed. "He didn't have the guts to come himself, so he sent an errand boy."

"I'm no errand boy. I'm simply doing a friend a favor."

"Yes, I'm sorry. I didn't mean to offend you. Lypynskyi, no? I remember you."

The courier couldn't tell if the woman was crying or boiling with rage.

"Thank you for coming and letting me know. Otherwise, I would have waited in vain for this . . . buffoon."

"He truly feels terrible, but there was just no way for him to come."

Trebynska considered the situation agitatedly, then there was a shift in her tone: "Is he so ill that he wasn't able to come? Tell me the truth. I'll go to Zakopane!"

"Domanytskyi is ill, but not so ill that he can't travel short distances, dear lady. The sanatorium has undoubtedly benefited him."

"Buffoon," Trebynska repeated feebly.

Lypynskyi helped her carry her two suitcases off the train. On the platform, they exchanged a few more words; Lypynskyi inquired after the health of the elder Trebynska and politely passed along his sincerest greeting to Kyiv. Suddenly he seemed to spot Domanytskyi's stooped figure in the crowd, as if he had been watching them the entire time from a safe distance, but just as soon as Lypynskyi noticed the figure, it disappeared without a trace.

In Zakopane, he excitedly reported to his friend: "Just imagine, I was sure that I had seen you in the crowd on the platform! It was as if you were standing and watching me and Ms. Lesia."

"You're seeing things," Domanytskyi assured him. "Why would I do that?" He listened to the remainder of the report without particular interest.

"I brought you a little gift from Kraków." As he laid out a large soft parcel on the table, Lypynskyi almost beamed with pride. "This is my spare overcoat. Please take it because, by God, walking around in buttonless rags is unbecoming of you. I have no need at all for a spare coat. It's just lying around uselessly and getting destroyed by moths."

THERE'S ONE PICTURE in which the two of them are against a backdrop of mountains and in very similar overcoats—either standing or sitting, it's unclear. The overcoats have astrakhan collars and differ only in the cut of their lapels. On their heads, they're wearing astrakhan *kubanka* hats that Lypynskyi had bought a few days after gifting the overcoat; they wore them on a hike to Morskie

Oko, or the Eye of the Sea—the legendary mountain lake in Zako-pane, where the photograph was taken.

The hike took place in early April as the snows were begin-ning to melt. A rather large group convened. Professor Lepkyi and his wife had come from Kraków, as did two colleagues from the *Literary-Scientific Herald* in Lviv, with greetings from its editor-in-chief, Professor Mykhailo Hrushevskyi. Domanytskyi also invited his longtime acquaintance, the socialist Dmytro Dontsov, who had arrived in Zakopane to have his nerves treated after an eight-month internment at the Lukianivska Prison in Kyiv. He made a positive impression on Lypynskyi.

They walked for three hours. Everyone was bespattered with mud up to their waists because the thaw had turned the roads into slush, but no one complained once they finally reached the shore, and the lake unfurled before them in all its beautiful glory. It really did resemble a perfect eye, as if its waters had been delicately poured into an eye-shaped mold resting in a gorge of the Tatra Mountains. The ice that had lingered for all those winter months had broken up, and now it looked like a gigantic ocular prosthesis that had started cracking from old age.

They stopped for a break. Professor Lepkyi's wife handed out sandwiches. Meanwhile, Domanytskyi talked passionately about his new publishing project—a popular history of Ukraine that Mykola Arkas, the aging judge from Mykolaiv north of the Black Sea, had written with a lot of mistakes and that Domanytskyi had decided to edit (actually, rewrite) and fill with illustrations. He was enraptured by his work.

"This *History of Ukraine* is going to make a ruckus! It's so sim-ple and lively, almost like a fairy tale. This is exactly how we need to rouse the national consciousness of the general public—with accessible writing."

Lypynskyi promised to write a review after the book's publication. Dontsov, with his distinctive desire to be original, said that populism was a holdover from the last century and all efforts needed to be directed at the working class right now.

"I don't agree with you here, sir," Lypynskyi objected. "Our working class is decentralized and amorphous. It doesn't have its own political slogans and is unlikely to acquire any soon. Ukrainians are a grain-producing people. It's them, the grain farmers, that we need to be uniting and preparing for a future fight for the state. We can't force them into parties of gentlemen and serfs, as our socialists like to do."

"Are you speaking as a gentleman or as a serf right now?" Dontsov sniggered.

"My pedigree shouldn't be of your concern. But when it comes to a fight for independence, it's the people with wealth and proper education who will play the decisive role."

"Money is a temporary concept, Mr. Lypynskyi. One minute it's there, the next it isn't. But something else is surprising me. Are you being serious about a 'fight for independence'? In all honesty, I didn't anticipate hearing such naïve ideas from you."

Lypynskyi blanched. He had never been able to respond swiftly to direct insults.

"The Ukrainian state doesn't need to concern us," Dontsov continued. "According to Marx, social development will be the thing to make Ukraine."

Domanytskyi intervened in the conversation, or rather in its absence: "Lypynskyi and I are going to run over to that little hill," he said, and motioned at one of the mountains. "Do you still have some strength in your legs, Viacheslav? There's a surprise waiting for us up there."

Lypynskyi nodded and ambled off behind him.

"Dontsov has a reputation for being critical, don't pay attention to him," Domanytskyi said when the group was out of earshot. A steep path wound ahead of them.

"Those are exactly the types you need to pay attention to," Lypynskyi countered with a wheeze. "Every bit of lenience makes them stronger, and over time they commandeer the minds of those who don't know how to think independently. Once that happens, no one will be able to compete with them. But I'm rather weak with words. I don't know how to debate satisfactorily, especially when I'm being accused of naïveté."

"Let it go, my friend. Listen, instead, to how quiet it is."

They had indeed become surrounded by an incredible silence. The path had led them out onto a mostly flat area, not visible from below and covered in stones of a strange red shade. In the middle of this flatness sprawled another lake, completely different from Morskie Oko—murky and sinister-looking.

"So, did I surprise you? This is Czarny Staw, the Black Pond. I heard about it from the locals. I wanted to see if there was indeed a mountain pond above a mountain lake. And look, they weren't lying."

The men sat on a large rock and gazed in silence. The still, black water appeared dead. Everything around it portended if not death, then something contrary to life.

"Everyone's nursing their own black pond in their soul," the pensive Domanytskyi remarked somewhat dramatically. "My black pond is my love. It's just as unattainable. And just like this, I try my best to hide it from human eyes."

"Why didn't you want to meet Ms. Lesia? Why wouldn't you admit to her that you love her?"

Domanytskyi pounded his fist against his chest. "What for? What can I offer her? I'm no romantic, as many make me out to be. I know how much time I have left—one year, two, no more than that. I'll only ruin her life and force her to watch me die. I don't want that!"

The black water overflowed its banks and seemed to fill the entire expanse of land, making it equally black and muggy.

"And your black pond, *gente Polonus*? What's it like?"

Lypynskyi shrank into a slump. His unhappy marriage was no secret, but he himself never bemoaned it to anyone.

"With all due respect, Vasyl Mykolaiovych, I don't nurture black ponds. If I have something to say, I say it; if not, I keep silent. If there's a reason to, I'm happy, and when misfortune arises, I'm pained. I don't hide. God hasn't bestowed domestic happiness unto me and my wife. In the coming year, I'll probably get divorced so as not to torment either her or myself. It isn't a black pond in my soul, but a black abyss. I'll have to continue living with it somehow."

IN MAY, after an almost six-month stay, Lypynskyi finally made it out of Zakopane. As Dr. Vilchynskyi had promised, the pleurisy was fully cured, and the patient was eager to resume his crusade, this time in Kyiv. In addition to his lectures for the peasantry that made up the overwhelming majority of the Ukrainian population, Lypynskyi came up with the idea of publishing a Polish-language journal as a tool for converting rich local Poles to Ukrainian nationalism. He first headed to Kraków to begin packing his things and was startled to find his wife, surrounded by her packed belongings, waiting in the entryway of the Shumiński's apartment.

"I'm going to Kyiv with you," she announced resolutely, and for a long time, Lypynskyi wouldn't be able to believe his good fortune.

Domanytskyi also left Zakopane and spent the following summer in the village of Kryvorivnia with some friends. "I'm living a natural life," he wrote to Lypynskyi from the Ukrainian Carpathian Mountains. "I bathe in a stream, sleep on hay, drink milk from a cow, and spend my days lying in grass. It's beautiful."

"Take good care," Lypynskyi replied from Kyiv, "when you're on the riverbank. I'm not going to say don't drown, but be careful not to gulp down too much water." Then he added, "Fate has come to pity me a little. I feel the strength to work on our joint project. I'll tell you in confidence: My wife is expecting a child. She's unwell often, but we're very happy. We'll go to Kraków for the birth because my wife doesn't trust Kyiv doctors."

THE *HISTORY OF UKRAINE* that Domanytskyi was so proud of proved more successful than the author had hoped. Only one person didn't relish this success—Professor Mykhailo Hrushevskyi, the master of Ukrainian historiography, its tsar and god. He published a devastating critique in the *Literary-Scientific Herald*, and then, to make certain that Domanytskyi would read it, he brought a copy to a meeting with the author in Lviv and "forgot" it on the table. A series of public accusations and scandals commenced that only exacerbated Domanytskyi's physical condition. The prompt news of his death in 1910 in the French resort town of Arcachon wouldn't surprise anyone.

Again the Ukrainian community in Kyiv would raise funds, a total of nine hundred rubles, in order to have the body delivered from abroad. The police, fearing anti-government demonstrations, would forbid burying the celebrated exile in the city. The funeral would instead take place in late autumn in Domanytskyi's native village in the Zvenyhorod region. A modest delegation would arrive from Kyiv—seven individuals, bringing twenty funeral wreaths with them. One would be from Lypynskyi, who would be unable to attend because he was bedridden with illness.

A mix of snow and rain would be falling that day. The publisher of *Rada*, Yevhen Chykalenko, would give a heartfelt speech before a crowd of villagers, describing Domanytskyi as a pure and holy person (it's no wonder that he died at the same age as Christ) and his loss as exorbitant for the nation, "which has so many million bodies but so few actual people . . ."

"Tuberculosis and Russian autocracy are our greatest foes, and they feed off each other as they're able to," Chykalenko would note in conclusion.

At the time, Chykalenko would already be pondering the idea of acquiring a small villa on the southern shore of Crimea so that feeble Ukrainian writers, instead of dying in various foreign countries, could restore their health there. This would require mortgaging one of his own properties once again and yielding good harvests to be able to pay off the debts.

Lesia Trebynska wouldn't attend the funeral either. She will have just married and will be honeymooning with her young husband in southern Italy. As was Domanytskyi's wish, she wouldn't witness his death. His black pond would remain untouched and unseen by anyone—save for a cheerful little poem that could be found in the *Literary-Scientific Herald* of 1900, in the third issue, on page 232. The poem, full of optimism and a defiant faith in human progress, was dedicated to "Lesia T., a person of the twentieth century" and ended with the lines:

And that moonlit world
That still in our childish years
   Blinded our eyes through the window—
We'll give it to the poets,
While we ourselves fashion
   Electric lanterns for the night.

And the signature: *V. Dom.*

X.

THE QUEEN OF MOLD

(Me)

I HAD ALWAYS WANTED to be intelligent but squandered my chance, never actually utilizing my natural gifts for accumulating knowledge. Discovering had been my passion until another passion—the female one, the human one—triumphed. Instead of nurturing my mind, I trained at suffering. Instead of binge-reading, I washed down my agony with alcohol. I focused on love and neglected the high art of lucid thinking. The years that should have been devoted to painstaking daily self-education slipped by in a pursuit of personal happiness, which, in and of itself, is only an illusion of happiness, an illusion of a pursuit. I didn't become happier, and the lost time is now impossible to recover. I gained an intimate knowledge of my own feelings at the cost of wisdom.

As a child, I scoured all the local libraries just to gain a sense of the vastness of human knowledge. Whenever I recall my younger self with that gaping mouth and inquisitive gaze, I feel both pity and pride. Pride for my past and pity for my present.

———

MY LOCAL LIBRARIES weren't notable for any sort of unique holdings—they were more meager than adequate—but I delighted in their collections, and each time I visited one of them, I held my breath in the anticipation of making yet another book my own, of sucking it in like dry skin sucks in lotion. Anticipating a book was just as important as subsequently reading it, sometimes even more so.

I had cards for all the libraries, even the district ones, which had nothing to offer beyond daily newspapers, a few dozen grease-bespattered detective novels, and shelves of Soviet encyclopedias. I was convinced that treasures yet unknown could be hiding in these crannies, forgotten by civilization—some sort of long-lost thousand-year-old manuscripts from Kyivan Rus' or highly valuable incunabula from the Middle Ages. Perhaps I would've made a good archaeologist. For all my searching, I never did find anything, but I never lost hope.

The district libraries were staffed by kindhearted ladies in thick-framed glasses, dressed in gray or brown, sometimes with huge, impeccably plaited buns at the napes of their necks and puffy beauty marks on their chins. Their soothing presence generally lent the tiny libraries an almost familial atmosphere. I felt at home there, especially when the librarians—there were always two of them—would start watering the plants or unwrapping their lunch parcels. I'd sit right in front of them in the so-called "reading room," which consisted of two tables pushed together, and rummage through Soviet encyclopedias just as the librarians chomped on their lunches over easy chitchat with older regulars. The appetizing aroma of fried potatoes, always with a pickle, or pilaf, without meat but with tomato paste, would waft over, and my empty stomach would squirm.

I remember how one time I came to them with an assignment from my biology teacher to write a paper on the eye of a *khrushch*, or May beetle. The librarians exchanged confused glances—*The eye of a* khrushch?—and set about tearing through everything that they had about May beetles, all the way to Ukrainian folk songs, but didn't find anything about their actual eyes. They even forgot to have lunch. It turns out I had misheard the assignment and was in fact supposed to write a paper on the eye of a tick, a *klishch*, not a *khrushch*. The biology teacher was alluding to the fact that ticks were somewhat bizarre creatures: during puberty, they grow a fourth pair of legs, and their eyes are unique from other living beings—how exactly, I still haven't gotten around to figuring out. I'm still a little embarrassed about the whole ordeal.

THE PROCESS OF EXPANDING my personal universe by accumulating knowledge stopped sometime around age twenty-two. After that, I don't think I read a single book of substance or thought a single thought of substance. My body rotted through like a young tree whose crown has become overgrown with European mistletoe. This state could be described as "satiated satisfaction with whatever." I vaguely recall having even said something to this effect on a few occasions, but memory, so flimsy by its very nature, was evaporating even more with the toxic miasmas of my frequent hangovers.

After university, I moved to Kyiv. By day, I worked, and by night, I met up with friends whose universes had also stopped expanding. Holed up in our mix of fear and whimsy, and justifying our laziness to one another, we felt little, so we had to increase our inebriation regularly in order to intensify our feelings. We yearned for drama, bouts of crying, heated arguments, affronts, and permanent goodbyes—everything that, come morning, usually brings on discomfort and embarrassment. I liked to repeat that I knew everything about everyone, jabbing my finger into the chest of whichever friend I was talking to and yelling as I burst into tears, "I know everything about you! I see right through you!"

I had no idea where this teary know-it-all-ness stemmed from. My universe was molding from the inside, and in order to survive, I needed to constantly convince myself that my life was special, that I was busy with self-actualization and didn't need anything new or external. I was the queen of mold. And my friends were knights of the order of beer and whiskey bought with their last few hryvnias. When I vanished from their lives, they sighed with relief and became exemplary family men and women.

Looking back, I see how the queen of mold was relentlessly defeating the queen of libraries, one move after another, like in a chess game. I lost this tournament once and for all when I abandoned my long-standing habit of heading to the shore to at least catch a glimpse of the vast sea of knowledge and spend a few minutes mourning my inability to swim. For the queen of libraries, visiting that shore used to take the form of flitting from one library to the next.

For example, I used to regularly go to the local music and medical libraries even though I had no real interest in either field. Every Saturday, when I was in high school and then in university, I would also stop by the library of foreign languages—it was my favorite and was always empty—to simply meander through the stacks. It felt like I was walking around on a miniature globe or in a church, and all these French and Italian and German books were these gods' sacred writings. My ignorance didn't diminish their divine nature. I took English as my foreign language in school but never did manage to read in it. Despite this, I would check out my fill of English books from the library (a maximum of six were allowed)— for instance, *Jane Eyre*, *Alice in Wonderland*, *The Picture of Dorian Gray*, Milton's *Paradise Lost* with Doré's elaborate illustrations, an English translation of the Hindu Vedas, and some final one with a pretty cover—then haul this abundance of goods home. There, the books lay on my desk like on an altar the entire ensuing week, unread; I'd just stroke their bindings with reverence and look at the pictures if there were any. The following Saturday, I'd head off for a new batch.

"I'd like O. Henry's and Chesterton's short stories. And Mark Twain's too. And Golding's *Lord of the Flies*."

The young librarian, a graduate of the local university's foreign languages department, would note, trying to be helpful and not patronizing, that I had already borrowed *Lord of the Flies* at least three times.

"That's okay," I'd reply without batting an eye. "I like rereading books."

In addition to English, I tried to learn German, French, and Polish, and one time even bought *Spanish in 30 Days* to be able to read Borges in the original. I was looking for easy and quick methods— something that I could put under my pillow for the night, so that in the morning I'd be at least at the conversational level in some new language. As a result, I never really learned any of them and now chastise myself for putting in too little effort. I'll never master Latin now, or ancient Greek, or Sanskrit, or even Church Slavonic, for that matter. Ukrainian and Russian circumscribe my universe, like barbed wire around a prison. And the cognizance that I'll never break past the boundaries of this prison is sometimes too much to endure. My universe is minuscule, teeny, not even a universe at all but some sort of mini-verse; a boring, everyman's flatland on which nothing interesting happens other than moderate precipitation and mild seasonal changes.

I MARRIED THE MAN that I met by chance on the train. He was a historian but worked as a tour guide. He was good at his job, almost perfect at it. He was overall an out-and-out perfectionist, which is obviously what made me fall in love with him. This didn't happen right away; I only fell in love after I realized I had to be just as perfect to warrant being loved by a perfectionist. His love was inspiring. It wasn't even love, but adoration, almost worship. The fact that he hit me once doesn't contradict any of this. I fell on my back, holding my cheek, and he walked up and slapped me again, saying, "That's so that you can never forgive me." I forgave him, of course. We were both tipsy when it happened and barely remembered any of it in the morning. There was no mark on my face. I was, as usual, just craving intense emotions, or so I told myself. But later, I'd sometimes remember him leaning in before the second slap with that furious and cruel look, like a primitive man destroying the god of thunder's temple with full knowledge that he'll be struck by a thunderbolt someday. He wanted to punish himself with that slap, not me. He wanted to consume me, so that he might finally fall to the bottom of humanity and suffer like the damned. The quiet good fortune in which we lived together was suffocating him just as it was me, but we only let ourselves admit this in an altered state of consciousness.

Or, I understood everything incorrectly.

I often had the feeling back then that I didn't understand the true meaning of anything. It felt as though someone had blinded me and made me deaf, the way people used to do to jackrabbits, only to chase and shoot them, then nail them up by their hind legs on a barn wall. That way the blood would drain without damaging the fur. In an attempt to break free, to leap off the nail, I wrote from time to time, publishing a new slim book of stories every two years, but no one took any particular interest in my work because texts written by those confined to their own heads are dispensable and steeped in futility. My husband would reassure me, saying, "They just don't understand," but in reality, I was the one who didn't understand, not them. "They" always seemed to be doing fine.

———

I HAD THIS ANNOYING and cowardly cat, whom I nonetheless loved very much. He'd be asleep on the bed, curled up in a dough ball, whenever I returned home in the evenings; I'd shove my frozen hands into his soft gray-striped fur to warm up. The cat would half open his eyes in displeasure and immediately fall asleep again. He slept around the clock, save for a few hours in the dead of night when he'd succumb to cat antics. Then, he'd scuttle around the rented apartment like a maniac, cavorting all over me to his heart's content. He would jump on my stomach, my chest, my head, then claw lightly at my toes jutting out from under the comforter, and when I'd tuck my feet back in, the cat would poke his head under the comforter and ram his fangs into my calf or elbow. I'd yelp in pain, and he would leap triumphantly onto the window ledge, tipping over flowerpots as he flew. "I'll kill you!" I'd howl. By then it'd be three or four in the morning, and the cat would purr contentedly, knowing that I wouldn't do anything to him because I couldn't catch him.

When other people would visit our apartment, my cat would lose all pluck and morph into a paralyzed feline scarecrow with exposed claws and fur standing on end. Should someone be unwise enough to touch him in such a state, they might find themselves missing an eye.

But the worst hell was traveling with such a coward. Two hours would go to coaxing the cat out of hiding and finally stuffing him into a special wicker cage, which he'd pee all over before we had reached the train station. I'd have to abandon the taxi sooner than planned and clean the cage on the sidewalk with a roll of toilet paper that I'd prudently brought from home. As I did so, I'd have to pin the cat to the ground with my knee so that he wouldn't jump into traffic. Though it's unlikely he would've tried to run away because he was frozen from fright, his goggling eyes devouring the hostile surroundings. I'd be at once angry and amused. There's no bigger scaredy-cat, I'd say, in the whole wide world. My friends' cats could calmly travel long distances, but this one was never able to accept the simple fact that anything could possibly exist beyond his home. My cat's universe was just as limited and moldy as mine. At the time, I had no idea that I would soon outdo my four-legged ward—that I too would be lying flat against the sidewalk, submitting to those around me just as helplessly, afraid to move, speak, or even blink.

The cat always relaxed a little once in the night train. There, our surroundings were once again concretely delimited by a floor, walls, and a ceiling. The cat would sniff every inch of the compartment and fall asleep exhausted at the feet of some kind fellow passenger until morning. I would be demonstratively ignored after the tortures he had undergone.

THE LAST TIME I brought the cat to my parents' house, I did so with the intention of leaving him there for a while. But my parents didn't like the cat. He sharpened his claws on their favorite couch in the living room, freshly reupholstered in a gilded fabric. Golden threads flew around the apartment while my mother flew after the provocateur, menacingly waving a kitchen towel. A few times, she managed to thwack him on the tail.

"I'm going to leave him with you for a bit," I told my parents over dinner.

They suspected nothing.

"Are the two of you going on vacation?"

"I don't know yet, but I want to be ready when the time comes."

"Okay, just come get him soon. He's already destroying the sofa in the living room."

I changed the topic: "Do you remember how I used to haul books home from the library?"

"Yes," my father confirmed, "you read a lot when you were little. Though I never did understand why you brought home books about the injuries of World War I soldiers . . ."

"They had a lot of photographs."

"But," my mother butted in, "we were proud of the fact that you read in English."

"I didn't, I just pretended I could."

My parents looked dumbfounded. I regret having been too frank with them at times.

"In any case, you were a smart girl," my mother said at last.

"So, I'm not anymore?"

My parents again fell silent. They didn't think I was dumb; the direction of the conversation just struck them as unusual.

As I was packing my things to head home, the cat hid in the living room under the sofa, wary of ending up back in the wicker cage. I remember only the two little green flames burning right through me from the semidarkness under the sofa, begging to be left in peace amid the dust and golden tinsel strips. "My, what a scaredy-cat," was all I said to him in parting. After my departure, the cat probably didn't slither out for a few more hours.

THE FOLLOWING MORNING, I unlocked the apartment door with my key; my husband was still sleeping. It was half past six. I hadn't slept a wink the preceding night because the zealous conductor had cranked up the heat to over a hundred degrees. The passengers had to strip down to their undergarments, even though it was December and there was snow all over the ground. I felt as though I were liquefying, like a hunk of ore in a blast furnace, fearing that if I went back out into the cold, I'd congeal again, but deformed this time, so that no one would ever be able to recognize me again.

"Is that you?" the sleeping man whispered.

"I don't know," I replied, lying down next to him.

"I showed a group of Russians the tsars' Kyiv yesterday," the man said. He always shared news from work with me. I always listened with great interest.

At the time, I thought the man didn't suspect anything. Now I think that he was merely pretending to not suspect anything because how could he not have noticed my strange behavior in the preceding weeks? He was the only person who really saw through me, only he never admitted it, never jabbed a finger at my chest. I sighed, mustering up courage. The man woke up fully and drew me close to stave off the inevitable. *There's no need*, the frozen sky-blueness of his eyes was pleading, *don't do this*.

"I need to tell you something," I began.

"Maybe later?" He knew everything yet hoped that it would somehow pass. He wanted to skip the hard part.

"I don't love you anymore."

We lay in bed in silence, staring blindly at the ceiling. The man's embrace didn't slacken.

"That isn't true," he finally squeezed out, just as I was starting to wonder if I'd fallen asleep. "I know you, you're just missing novelty. You want to live many lives at the same time, but that's impossible."

"My life is too much for me. I keep feeling like I died a long time ago."

The man rose from the bed, his hands trembling.

"What do you mean, died?" He struck a match to light a cigarette, even though he had recently quit smoking. His hands were still trembling.

"I've grown moldy. I'm the queen of mold, do you understand?"

"I don't understand. You're a successful author, you have new books published regularly, you have a ton of friends who respect you, you have your own money—not a lot, but you're doing what you were meant to do. What mold? What kind of metaphor is that? Mild dissatisfaction is a natural thing. Do you think I enjoy eulogizing to a group of idiots about all the times that Tsar Nikolai II visited Kyiv? I get underwhelmed and frustrated too."

The man could come up with a rational explanation for everything. Therein lay his greatest strength and his greatest weakness.

"I don't love you anymore," I repeated, but louder and more confidently.

"Why? Give me a reason."

"There are no reasons."

"That doesn't happen."

"It does happen!" I was suddenly yelling and crying. He was breathing in smoke emphatically, his chest expanding.

"There's someone else, isn't there?"

An affirmative answer would have offered the rational explanation he was craving.

"Yes."

"How long?"

"It doesn't matter."

"There is no one else."

He feebly sank into the chair by the window. The building's groundskeeper was pulling garbage cans out onto the street. She always did so at that time of day, waking up the residents for work and school. People called her the trash rooster.

I opened the overnight bag that I had just brought in and began to toss more of my things in. The man watched silently, then suddenly asked, "Can I ask you for one thing?"

"Go ahead."

"I want to make love to you one last time."

"That's impossible."

I got dressed, took the bag—the contents of which would later turn out to be far from essential—and walked out of the apartment. The man remained motionless in the chair.

That's how I remember him. Still groggy from sleep and

destroyed by the unexpected news. Golden curls and sky-blue eyes. A sadness the size of the world, in which I was just a light breeze that had briefly disturbed the surface of some mountain lake.

AND THEN MY CAT suddenly died. My parents took him with them on a vacation and along the way, when the cat had predictably peed himself, forgot the safety regulations and didn't pin him to the ground with a knee as they were cleaning out the wicker cage at the side of the road. The cat broke free, filled with existential horror, out into the road—right under the wheels of a silver Daewoo Lanos.

For a long time, I blamed my parents for everything, perhaps to expel the unbearable feeling of guilt that sometimes bathed me in a cold sweat. In every cat I encounter, I see him. In absolute silence, I distinctly hear the soft spring of his paws from the window ledge down to the floor. The bites from his fangs still itch. The cat also appears in my dreams curled up into a dough ball; I shove my cold hands into his damp, warm fur, and he squints his eyes in displeasure until I finally leave him be. In the voice of the husband I abandoned, the cat says that he has forgiven me, that it's time to stop beating myself up. But I don't believe him.

XI.

ARAGATZ

(Him)

LYPYNSKYI'S VAGUE CALLING had finally obtained its geo-
graphic focus. He needed to seek out the soul of his envisioned
Ukrainian state where it had last been seen—in Kyiv. Lypynskyi
dove into the search with enthusiasm, so much so that he beamed
from head to toe. Even Kazimiera submitted to the monumental
beauty of this Little Russian capital, going out for walks often or
taking the tram down to Poshtova Square, not far from the university where she was taking Russian language classes.

It was June 1909. The thunderstorms were almost daily. Lightning pierced the Dnipro waters mercilessly, as if aiming at a criminal hiding there from God's wrath but striking innocent Kyiv
fishermen instead. After the storms, their bodies would be pulled
out of the river with dragnets.

The ruthless weather suited the city, with its bitter cranberry
kvass and the power-drunk, oppressive gazes of the omnipresent
Okhranka, the secret police that had long been an inescapable component of Kyiv life.

———

LYPYNSKYI FIRST TASTED *kliukvennyi kvas*, as it was called in Kyiv, with Ivan Franko, the eminent Ukrainian author and activist from Halychyna, who was also paying an unanticipated visit to Kyiv at the time. Together, they would ramble through the antique market in the Podil neighborhood on Sundays, where Lypynskyi would fish money out of his friend's pocket to pay for book after book. Franko couldn't do this himself: his gnarled hands were covered over with sores and blisters from creosote. He may have been the most renowned writer and civic leader in all of Halychyna, but he stank worse than Kyiv's homeless and also often made no sense. Lypynskyi watched him with pity and dread. For Lypynskyi, losing his mind would have been worse than death.

He had first met Franko in this very city, at the editorial offices of *Rada* on Velyka Pidvalna Street in April 1909, where he had stopped by to personally drop off his next article. Franko was sitting by the window in the company of a reporter named Yefremov and Metodii Pavlovskyi, the newspaper's editor-in-chief. Franko's gray hair grazed his shoulders, and his crazed eyes were glued anxiously to the little square outside around Kyiv's Golden Gate, as if awaiting a stealthy attack. No one knew how the ill Franko had made it all the way from Lviv in Austria-Hungary to Kyiv, nor where he had obtained the money that he was throwing around left and right. It was also unclear whether he had a visa, or even a passport, and when he was heading back, if he was heading back at all. Franko had taken up residence with the newspaper's publisher Yevhen Chykalenko. For Chykalenko, the honor of receiving Franko was accompanied by huge troubles with his care. Franko could neither dress himself, nor shave, nor even go to the bathroom on his own. He was also prone to going on about how he had had to flee Lviv because, as he put it, "that scoundrel Drahomanov wasn't letting me live in peace."

Mykhailo Drahomanov, an authoritative Ukrainian thinker and Franko's formidable rival, had been following him everywhere— out in the streets, in his own home, peering in his windows, giggling when his back was turned. He even watched him from the roofs of tall Lviv houses, his legs swinging, hallooing from up there, "Hey, Ivanko! Iva-a-anko!" Everyone knew, of course, that Drahomanov had died in exile fourteen years earlier, in 1895.

"He gave me no peace on the train to Kyiv either," Franko had grumbled to the newspaper staff, who struggled to choke back laughter. "He climbed up on top of the train car and would waggle his beard at me now and again through the window. His beard has gotten terribly long! He doesn't even look like a man anymore."

Then Franko had pulled a little bottle of creosote out of his bag, a remarkably potent and highly poisonous substance used to waterproof wooden railroad ties. Slathering his arms up to his elbows with the dark brown liquid, he had waved them every which way, dancing around as he did so as if warding off an evil spirit. "This is the only way to drive him away. Nothing else works."

Every day someone would assume responsibility for Franko and escort him to places that he might find interesting. As it turned out, there weren't that many in Kyiv: aside from the *Rada* offices, there was the Ukrainian club on Volodymyrska Street and the Ukrainian bookstore next to the train station on Bezakivska Street. The rest of the capital was, for all intents and purposes, a center of Russian nationalism: people spoke Russian, read the conservative monarchist newspaper *Kievlyanin* (with its credo, "This is Russian, Russian, Russian land!"), and otherwise existed in a state of privileged repose under the vigilant surveillance of the tsar's chancellery and members of the staunchly pro-Russian and pro-Romanov Black Hundred movement.

Franko was so moved the time he visited the Ukrainian bookstore that he burst into tears when Stepanenko, the manager, addressed him in Ukrainian, asking if he could be of any assistance. The bookseller didn't immediately catch on who was standing before him and, upon recognizing him, was overjoyed, then spent multiple hours ceremoniously hosting the distinguished guest.

Franko's mind wasn't always muddled. When the conversation would turn to Franko's favorite topics, he would come alive and communicate thoughtfully and clearly. Then it was possible to again recognize in the paranoid madman the most powerful Ukrainian intellectual who, over the past three decades, had distinguished himself in almost every field of human knowledge, starting with orientology and ending with the newly fashionable Western European psychotherapy.

ONE FRIDAY NIGHT, activists, despite how much Chykalenko tried to dissuade them, organized a literary evening in the Ukrainian club in Franko's honor. The club, which rarely drew a full house, was packed. Franko sat modestly on a wooden chair that had with foresight been placed a safe distance away from the front rows, so as to protect the more delicate ladies from passing out from the acrid stench of creosote. Lypynskyi brought Kazimiera, who was far enough along in her pregnancy that she had to leave in the middle of the event due to the smell.

Franko sat with confidence, oblivious. He hadn't experienced this kind of public attention in a long time, and it was evident that he was enjoying the affair to whatever extent that he could. He eased in by criticizing his Halychyna compatriots for their provincialism and the "Greater Ukrainians" for their passivity and lack of national consciousness, and then, right before the very end, he suddenly announced that he had translated Apuleius's *The Golden Ass*. Astonishment swept through the hall: few believed that it was possible to translate from a language as difficult as Latin in such a state of mental demise, while others didn't know who Apuleius was, to which Franko, somewhat offended, declared that the translation had been quite a success. "Apuleius himself came over and praised my translation. He said so himself: *'Das ist fantastisch!'* "

The hall burst into laughter, and Lypynskyi closed his eyes out of pity. Franko really had translated one of the tales of *The Golden Ass.* "The Tale of Cupid and Psyche" can be found in his fifty-volume collected works.

MADNESS FELT AT HOME in Kyiv. That was how Chykalenko put it.

"The hopeless struggle makes them lose their minds, dear friend," he said to Lypynskyi not long after the literary evening. He and Lypynskyi were sitting in the little garden of the Chykalenko home on Mariinsko-Blahovishchenska Street, as they often did late into the evening. The watchman was dozing peacefully on the bench against the fence. Lights glimmered in the windows. The publisher's large family included five adult children and an almost-elderly wife.

"Look at my editorial staff," Chykalenko said. "Half of them have ailing lungs or stomachs, and the other half are mad. The oldest Shemet brother, Volodymyr, for example, served time for revolutionary activity in Lubny and for his Ukrainian newspaper, and now flinches at the sight of his own shadow. He walks around Kyiv on tenterhooks and tells everyone that people are following him and want to kill him. His brain's out of sorts—a persecution complex—and there's no knowing if he'll come out of it. My editor-in-chief, Metodii Pavlovskyi, has been imprisoned twice already for articles in *Rada*, the first time for a month, the second for two months. So has my chief correspondent, Yefremov. It's a band of jailbirds. Even I catch myself getting used to the constant night searches, the interrogations; I mechanically hide important correspondence with friends, don't note last names in my diaries so as not to expose

anyone to danger; and when in the middle of the night I hear—for
some reason, the vermin come at night—that someone's banging
on the door, my first thought is to not forget the teakettle and the
baggie of Aragatz. I'll tell you this: any proper Kyivan must have
a teakettle and anti-bedbug powder on hand. I have both, and I'm
calm. Is that normal? It's normal. We've all gone mad. In his madness, the unfortunate Franko is somehow less insane than we are."

The police stations where the Ukrainian intelligentsia were routinely locked up—often as a preventative measure—were teeming
with bedbugs and lice. When Chykalenko's older son was tossed
into prison that summer of 1909, immediately upon returning from
studying abroad, the publisher appealed to all his contacts among
Kyiv's senior administration in order to smuggle him the life-saving
powder. Whenever the police let the boy out for short rendezvous,
his boots crunched with parasites. The arrest was timed to coincide
with the bicentenary of the Russian Empire's victory in the Battle
of Poltava in July 1709. Tsar Nikolai II himself came to Kyiv, and
the Okhranka picked up everyone with possible connections to the
anti-tsarist revolutionaries. The first to be rounded up were those
who had spent time abroad. Chykalenko felt responsible for what
transpired; if not for a family scandal, his son wouldn't have come
home from Switzerland at such an infelicitous time, and wouldn't
have had to sit out the festivities in the company of Kyiv's thieves
and prostitutes.

LYPYNSKYI WAS ONE of the last to find out about the
Chykalenko scandal, being, as a rule, oblivious to rumors and gossip. Moreover, he was very busy with his "missionary" work in Kyiv,
publishing a weekly bulletin and working on a historical almanac
that was supposed to accommodate the entire centuries-long evolu-
tion of the Ukrainian question in its two hundred pages. The almanac was being written in Polish for strategic purposes—so that it

might help sway Ukraine's Polish-speaking *szlachta*. Due to a lack of like-minded colleagues, Lypynskyi had undertaken most of the work himself: he wrote short overviews on particular topics and periods that later expanded into whole monographs, sought out suitable texts by Ukrainian authors and translated them into Polish, rummaged through archives, and copied old portraits for use as illustrations. Two hundred pages obviously weren't enough. Lypynskyi would abridge, cross out, then again add more material—hence the constant postponement of the publication.

Concurrently, he was traveling routinely to the cities of central Ukraine, to give public lectures for the Poles who were fairly numerous there, illustrating for them through historic examples their need for self-determination and to become "citizens" of Ukraine. In his travels, Lypynskyi was emphatically supported by his uncle, the Polish Ukrainophile from outside Uman. He personally sent invitations to Polish aristocrats he knew, and they would often attend the lectures out of respect to Rokicki, listening with clenched teeth.

"Poles don't have to stop being Polish to be Ukrainian," Lypynskyi would passionately reassure them from behind an improvised podium. That's how, in an attempt to resolve his own personal conflict between his lineage and his calling, he slowly arrived at "territorialism," which would become his best political idea. This idea ruled out any potential class or national enmity because it designated the "building component" of the future state to be common land, in contrast to the common blood of the nationalists or the membership in a common social class of the socialists. In Lypynskyi's vision, all of the inhabitants of this common land would unite in the land's interests, irrespective of their ancestry, language, faith, or occupation. Oddly enough, this simple and clear-cut plan for surmounting enmity in the multi-ethnic and socially stratified Ukrainian territories engendered even greater enmity.

When Lypynskyi collected his lectures into a book, its publication caused a great hubbub among Poles in both Ukrainian and Polish lands. They bought up all the copies and destroyed them, accusing its author of being either a fool, or a degenerate and an agent of the German Empire seeking to subvert the Polish cause. Two Warsaw newspapers, *Kurjer Warszawski* (*Warsaw Courier*) and *Goniec* (*Messenger*), printed an avowal by an alleged spy, who claimed that the members of the Ukrainian national liberation movement—and a certain Wacław Lipski in particular (his surname was deliberately changed, but everyone understood who was being referenced)—were not to be trusted because they were working off bribes paid in German marks. The journalists' turpitude stunned Lypynskyi. He responded to these "knights of lying," as he referred to them, with an irate statement in *Rada*, in which he promised to take both newspapers to court for libel.

"Will you help me?" he asked Chykalenko one day. "I'm not familiar with press law. I don't know a single lawyer."

"Leave it alone," Chykalenko replied. "It'll just cost you an unnecessary amount of money and nerves. How many such lies have been printed about me? Who haven't I allegedly spied for?"

But Lypynskyi didn't view backing down as an option.

"Accusations of bribery shouldn't be left unaddressed. This is an indelible stain on my reputation, which you wouldn't understand."

Chykalenko did understand. He helped Lypynskyi find a lawyer and, on multiple occasions, sent correspondents to Warsaw at his own newspaper's expense to cover the development of the legal proceedings. Nonetheless, he didn't meddle in the matter much himself.

"FOR THOSE OF US unhappy in our private lives," Chykalenko had said to Lypynskyi that spring, "public opinion doesn't matter anymore."

This once-energetic and feisty man with his hallmark fashionable goatee had now wasted away and weakened, grown taciturn, aged. His full fifty years emanated from his face as a heavy black shadow.

"If I can offer you any advice about anything, Yevhen Kharlampiovych—"

"No one can offer me advice. But I'll admit honestly, my dear Viacheslav, that in the last few years I've been at the very brink of suicide three times."

Lypynskyi was alarmed by that conversation. Pretty much anything could be expected from the publisher of *Rada*—an explosive verbal tirade, a scandal, a whirlwind romance—but certainly not attempts to cut short his life. Suffering in silence simply didn't suit Chykalenko. Normally he wanted the whole world to know of his misfortune and suffer along with him. And this time, it actually would before long.

Within a month or so of their conversation—right before the tsar's visit, actually—Kyiv was masticating with relish the details of new gossip: Yevhen Chykalenko, Ukraine's godfather, was in the middle of a conjugal tragedy. As it turned out, Chykalenko had been in love with a girl twenty-five years his junior for a long time but had kept his feelings private until it was clear that she wasn't indifferent to him. Then he became unleashed. Like an enraged bull, Chykalenko plunged headfirst into the maelstrom of new feelings, but his familial ties to the girl made the situation infinitely worse: she was his wife's niece. There was no hoping for an amicable separation. The affronted wife dragged Chykalenko through every possible circle of societal condemnation. The first thing she did upon learning about the betrayal was summon their oldest son from Switzerland and orchestrate a humiliating family mock trial. All five young Chykalenky took their mother's side. His closest friends weren't thrilled with what had happened either and subjected him to didactic discussions in hopes of talking sense into the rebellious husband and father. Needless to say, these attempts were futile. Chykalenko kept repeating that he considered his marriage to have ended long ago, since he hadn't physically lived with his wife in many years already, and he wasn't intending to sacrifice his personal happiness for the sake of antiquated moral principles.

The scandal ended with an even greater scandal: leaving the house to his family, Chykalenko moved into a new apartment with his beloved. From that point on, every outing of the couple would end in tragedy. One time, in a theater, one of Chykalenko's daughters pointedly refused to offer her hand to his young lover, turning away instead. In response, Yulia Mykolaivna (that was the name of the chosen one), who had a family history of tuberculosis, began to spit up blood. It would be a year before the couple would have any peace.

LYPYNSKYI'S "KYIVAN YEAR" was also reaching its conclusion.

Kazimiera was insisting on going to Kraków to give birth, which Lypynskyi wasn't necessarily opposed to. Since arriving in Kyiv, his enthusiasm had waned. He too now walked Kyiv's ample boulevards anxiously glancing over his shoulder, hid important letters from friends, and tried to not mention any last names in the little notebook in his breast pocket. Fear and madness were slowly taking hold of his once-lucid and rational mind, and physically escaping Kyiv seemed to be the only path to salvation.

Before their departure, Lypynskyi stopped by the *Rada* editorial offices to say goodbye. Chykalenko was just then plotting where to find an additional ten thousand rubles so that the unprofitable newspaper could be published the following year.

"Whenever *Rada* dies," Chykalenko was threatening, "then I

too will vanish from the Ukrainian horizons! I'll change one letter in my last name and will become a Romanian named Chykalesko, because it's embarrassing to be a part of such a rotten nation. I'll move away and leave this Asian kingdom of Russians!"

Previously, the newspaper had always been saved from complete bankruptcy by pure providence or someone's unexpected generosity. Chykalenko himself had already spent close to one hundred thousand of his own rubles on the national revival. He liked to repeat that it wasn't enough to be a patriot from the depths of one's soul; you needed to be a patriot from the depths of your pockets too. Admittedly, he rarely found allies in this matter, as Lypynskyi didn't in his own. His colleagues would suggest to their boss that he smear the newspaper with glue in the summer months: his mercantilistic fellow countrymen would buy it more readily, to use as fly traps.

A dispute had just arisen in the editorial offices over *Rada's* political policy. Lypynskyi voiced his dissatisfaction with the absence of a clear-cut and open pro-independence stance, which, in his opinion, was the only correct one in the conditions of the current political struggle.

"Ukrainians can only obtain what they want through their own state. Cultural autonomy isn't enough," he said, apparently a little carelessly, to which Chykalenko exploded.

"Come back down to earth, my good man! What state are you talking about, if the only Ukrainian newspaper in the Russian Empire has a few hundred subscribers out of all the millions of people? The villages are uneducated, and the cities are Russified. There's no one to read newspapers, and you're talking about a state! Who are we going to build it with? The Rusyns of the western regions and the Malorossiians of the surrounding regions haven't become Ukrainians yet. They haven't matured as a people."

"Haven't matured as a people, you say? What about you? What about me? Aren't we mature people?"

"Polish wolves like you, Wacław"—Chykalenko deliberately chose the Polish form of his name to jab him deeper—"will without fail howl in Polish when push comes to shove."

"That's a brazen lie!" Lypynskyi shot back as if scalded. "I don't think anything in my life till now has given cause for that sort of prognosis."

FOR A LONG TIME, Lypynskyi couldn't forget Chykalenko's words, which stung like a knife in the back and always surfaced in his memory whenever he felt weak. On top of things, financial hardships had definitively spoiled his relationship with his father, who didn't want to pay for his numerous publishing projects. Klara and Kazimierz Lipiński placed their only hope on the birth of a child: Such a momentous event usually brings even the most obstinate fools back to their senses. In becoming parents, even fools abandon their unrealistic dreams and find something sensible to invest their energy in, something that will provide for their offspring.

Kazimiera gave birth in a Kraków maternity clinic. She considered home-birthing to be an evil holdover from the past and firmly insisted on a doctor's support. Her modern convictions ultimately saved her life; the delivery proved to be unexpectedly complicated, and the doctors had to hastily perform an operation in the middle of the night. Lypynskyi spent the entire time sitting in a dark corridor, praying. He was handed the blood-smeared infant first; Kazimiera spent almost the entire following day in bed, unconscious.

The little girl lay in Lypynskyi's arms quietly, like a baby bird that, in consideration of its own safety, had to weigh everything carefully before chirping. Her wary eyes, large and black like her father's, were just barely open, as if waiting to see how Lypynskyi would behave—like an enemy or like a provider of sustenance and protection. Lypynskyi clumsily nestled his cheek against the baby bird, and only then did she begin wailing with all her might.

A day before the verdict in Lypynskyi's libel suit was to be announced, the Warsaw newspapers agreed to a settlement and apologized to the plaintiff. In a sizable retraction, *Kurjer Warszawski* assured its readers that all their accusations that he worked for Prussian marks were unsubstantiated, and Mr. Lypynskyi's energetic community work was based solely on ideological grounds.

They named their daughter Ewa.

XII.

A SPRING SO IMPOSSIBLE

(Him)

"YOU DON'T HOLD HER CORRECTLY. Be careful with her head."

"I'm being careful."

"She always cries whenever you're around. You frighten her."

"Babies cry."

"Your mustache—that's what she's afraid of."

"I'll shave it off."

"That isn't necessary. You look like a baby bird without one."

"Then I won't shave it off."

"What's new in the world? I feel so dumb, just up to my ears in diapers. I'm not keeping up on anything."

"Relax. You haven't missed anything, the world's still spinning. You just had a baby."

"Don't tell me to relax. I hate when you say that."

"I won't say it anymore. Give Ewa back to me."

"You don't hold her head correctly. She's afraid of you."

———

THE CHILD CRIED incessantly because Kazimiera wasn't producing enough breast milk. At three months, her supply had dried up completely. There was no choice but to travel to a faraway Polish village to stay with a first cousin whose wife had just given birth. She had agreed to help nurse, as she was producing enough milk for two infants.

When Kazimiera left, Lypynskyi stayed behind in Kraków. He felt abandoned and excluded. He was angry with himself, with Kazimiera, with everyone. To curb this frustration, he again dove headlong into work. Sometimes his mother-in-law, Mrs. Szumińska, would pop into the office to give an update on her daughter and granddaughter. Kazimiera wrote to her mother but never to Lypynskyi himself. This upset him even more. His letters to Kazimiera conveyed his growing exasperation:

"Are you planning on returning, and if so, when?"

"I too have a right to take part in Ewa's rearing."

"I'd like all of us to go visit my parents in Zaturtsi for Christmas together. What do you think, will that be possible?"

"We didn't visit my parents for Christmas, so maybe for Easter? I'd like Ewa to start getting to know her other homeland."

"Can't she be fed with regular cow's milk yet? What's keeping you there, Kazimiera?"

IN EARLY 1912, Lypynskyi's almanac *From Ukraine's History* (*Z dziejów Ukrainy*), which he had worked tirelessly on for three years, was finally published in Polish. It was a massive tome that not merely covered Ukrainian history but specifically explored Ukraine as a historically political entity. Poles had never before looked at their eastern neighbors from such a viewpoint. And they didn't look this time either. To Lypynskyi's great disappointment, the almanac went completely unnoticed. It was neither lauded nor censured by friend or foe. The print run sat in Polish bookstores unsold. Lypynskyi hoped that, in light of the scarcity of scholarly historical literature, someone from Ukraine would at least undertake a translation of some part of it, but even that didn't happen. The Ukrainian public was occupied with dreams of war. It was talked about more and more often as the only possibility for national liberation (or for the passage of Ukraine's lands from Russia—viewed by many Ukrainians as inherently Asian—to European Austria). In Eastern Halychyna, the military society Sich was formed, made up of only Ukrainians, which could serve as the foundation of a national army in the future.

"The newspapers smell of war," Chykalenko wrote to Lypynskyi from Kyiv. "This is our chance."

But Lypynskyi didn't share in the general enthusiasm. He was in agreement that war could work to the advantage of the oppressed, but the sacrifices it would bring would far outweigh the benefits. The best would die, he'd say, and when it came to building the state, there'd be no one to do it because the citizenry weren't properly prepared. There'd be no choice but to be dependent on external circumstances, namely, the moods of the masses and the resolve of individual people. The Ukrainian idea hadn't ripened yet; it didn't have a sufficient number of adherents yet. It needed another fifteen years or so.

EACH SUCCESSIVE DAY in Kraków became insufferable. Lypynskyi would hole up in his office and spend hours poring over articles, lacking the strength to write even a few sentences. There was droning in his ears, his vision was blurred, his mind refused to comply, and his thoughts would wander off to some other dimension. The aggravated Lypynskyi would set out for himself the volume of work he was supposed to complete before going to bed, but such quantities were impossible to accomplish, and he'd pace around his office feverishly until morning, when his exhausted body fell feebly from its feet.

"You have neurasthenia, esteemed sir," the doctors would say, prescribing Lypynskyi absolute calm and a complete rest from work.

"But I'm not doing anything!"

"Then rest. Don't think."

"I always need to be thinking."

"It's not helping, dear sir. It's not helping."

He thus went to visit his parents in Volyn, where he let his mother look after him for two weeks. Klara Lipińska tackled the task with great zeal. She nursed her son with herbal teas and complained liberally about her bad daughter-in-law.

"Kazimiera's behavior doesn't surprise me," she'd say. "This was to be expected. To be honest, I doubt whether she's all right in the head. They say that that can happen to women after childbirth—that they don't let their husbands near them anymore. You need to consult a lawyer. Lawyers can solve everything these days."

Before heading back to Kraków, the recovered Lypynskyi stopped by Kyiv for a day or two, made the rounds of his old acquaintances, and with sadness came to the conclusion that he had less and less to talk about with them. Even in Kyiv, Lypynskyi felt shoved out, thrown out of the process of life, as if he had gotten off at some stopover station and the train had driven on with a rumble.

He shut down all his publishing projects, citing a lack of funding and poor health. "I have neurasthenia," he lamented to everyone, at times boastfully. In reality, Lypynskyi had lost faith in the appropriateness and practicality of his chosen path. He yearned for quiet and calm, longed for his family, and often repeated that he now just wanted the simple things: to own his own home, work the land now and then, and watch his children grow up.

Chykalenko proposed that he become the editor-in-chief of *Rada*, but Lypynskyi categorically declined. A Catholic editor would undermine the newspaper's credibility. Besides: "Literary work is very nerve-wracking, and my health is poor. I was even deemed unfit for the Imperial Russian Army. Through my parents' residence in Zaturtsi, I was summoned to nearby Kovel for military exercises as a reserve warrant officer but was released after a few days without my even trying. That means I really am sick . . . There comes a moment in every man's life when he has the desire to settle down . . . The spring is so impossible this year."

Thoughts of his uncle's farmstead had finally captured his imagination. From Kraków, Lypynskyi wrote to Kazimiera, who was still in the village, that he was going to visit Rokicki to help with the sowing, to which she, as usual, replied with silence. But Rokicki welcomed him with wide-open arms.

"I think I'm finally ready to put down roots in my own soil," Lypynskyi said without unnecessary ceremony. His uncle, as it turned out, had been preparing for this conversation for a long time and immediately put forth a plan.

"I'm giving you ownership of my estate, Rusalivski Chahary. Take it, build a house for your family here, work the land, and my people and I will help."

Lypynskyi accepted the offer.

THEY SCHEDULED THE START of construction for the fall of 1913 so that Lypynskyi would have time to settle all of his affairs by then. Lypynskyi wanted to personally oversee the erection of the house, and the autumn months sufficed for this. The family was supposed to move into the new residence by the new year. Heartened, Lypynskyi set off for Kraków, readying himself for a difficult conversation with his wife. She had just returned from the village, having gained some weight and tanned. Ewa didn't cry anymore, just glanced distrustfully at the unfamiliar father with large black eyes.

"See? She doesn't even recognize me," Lypynskyi complained. "She takes after me, no? My eyes, my gaze ... I need to talk to you, Kazimiera. My parents can't support us any longer ... I have an inheritance, you know. Rokicki and I spoke. He gave me a portion of his land ... Why are you not saying anything?"

Lypynskyi outlined the construction plan for his wife and showed her the prepared sketches: "The windows of the house will face southwest, and you should see the views there! The library will need to be moved. The Ukrainian steppes are the prettiest in May."

Kazimiera listened attentively, examined the sketches, but didn't say anything.

With resignation, Lypynskyi packed his personal belongings with the intention of never again returning to Kraków. "I'll write how the work is progressing, but you two prepare to move after Christmas, okay?"

Kazimiera didn't respond. Later, it would become clear that during all these conversations, she no longer took her husband seriously. For her, he had long since lost touch with reality. The mad can talk very convincingly, but she wouldn't be duped.

Kazimiera walked Lypynskyi to the train station and stood on the platform as the train prepared to depart. Through the window-pane, she looked her husband straight in the eyes. He looked away, flustered, then spread out the books he intended to read during the long journey before him and stared at their covers instead. His mind was occupied with dreams of a happy new life on his own land, but Kazimiera's gaze—scalding him, straight through to his insides—foretold that there would be no happy life, no land of his own, only loneliness that would envelop and consume him. Kazimiera's gaze was hard as a rock. It was a rebuke of Lypynskyi, his definitive sentence. *You betrayed your family*, it said. *You sacrificed it for the sake of unrealized dreams. You prioritized your political convictions over your love for your wife and daughter. Have you ever actually loved anything other than that ghastly product of your imagination—a country that doesn't exist? Go move to your wild steppes, you wretch. Build your house in the wide-open Ukrainian grasslands. Your child's laughter will never ring through it.*

In despair, Lypynskyi pulled a watch out of the inner pocket of his jacket, but he failed to compute how much longer these tortures would last. Kazimiera's lonesome figure pulsated on the platform. Finally, the train heaved from its spot. The lonesome figure began to drift away, along with the world that, like a blanket, she had pulled over and onto herself. One large hot tear rolled down Lypynskyi's pale cheek then, forever soaking up the remnants of this unendurable moment into itself—her gaze, her rebuke, her unspoken last words. Lypynskyi brushed away the tear, and it splintered into millions of sunbeam reflections. He glanced out the window, hopeful to catch her image one last time—he wanted to remember it for all the coming lonely years, to hide it in the deepest cellar of his most secret memories, so that he might reminisce over this precious treasure on holidays—but the lonesome figure had already been replaced by Kraków's snaking streets, which jumped rapidly into his line of sight, one after another, as if showing off and trying to entice him to come to his senses and stay. Kraków had taken Kazimiera from him. Or maybe Lypynskyi had given her away voluntarily? Kraków was the altar of his sacrifice, the cemetery of his love.

When the city was firmly behind him, Lypynskyi breathed a sigh of sad relief.

But in Rusalivski Chahary, everything went wrong. The fall seemed intent on being rainy, and the construction of the house advanced more slowly than Lypynskyi had planned. The workers were lazy and dishonest, and Lypynskyi grew irritated, deciding at last to take all the work under his own control. In October, he was forced to move into the finished part of the building because leaving the building unattended overnight was becoming dangerous. Bands of robbers were roaming the area. One such band burned down his uncle's largest mill on the Feast of the Intercession. In another village, a group of well-to-do louts tortured and killed an old peasant woman. By day, Lypynskyi worked; by night, he trembled with fear.

"Burglaries, arsons, murders—and all of it seemingly for sport," he'd write to friends in Kyiv. "It's sad to look at our denationalized villages, increasingly out of touch with their Ukrainian culture with each passing day . . . My circumstances are such right now that any possible literary work is out of the question. I have no choice but to establish a household in the steppe . . . I feel forgotten and ostracized, completely out of society. I have no dealings with the world whatsoever. Even *Rada* has stopped arriving in the mail, even though I've requested it. Maybe they're worried that I won't pay, though I've paid as punctually as possible till now . . . My library has arrived, so I'll be able to write a little at a time. Don't think that I'm boasting, but it's the largest library in Ukraine on matters of history and sociology."

EVENTUALLY, LYPYNSKYI'S MANOR was burglarized. It was the dead of night. A sensitive sleeper by then, he heard whispering outside the window. But he couldn't stir. He was paralyzed. He knew that he would in no way be able to defend himself. The whispering died down; then he heard the front door creaking, as if someone were pressing against it with all their might. Lypynskyi considered running to the kitchen to find a knife but abandoned that idea because he would have been incapable of stabbing anyone. A cold sweat enveloped his entire body. He lay in bed without moving. *This is what your love for the Ukrainian land will end with,* he was thinking. *They'll slaughter you in bed like a piglet, and you won't even be able to defend yourself.* Then it grew quiet by the entry-way, as if whoever had been trying to break in had stopped. A brief wordless scuffle could be heard, and then a hoarse male voice said, "What is it you've forgotten here, lads?"

The "lads," of course, did not have an answer. They just mumbled something indistinct, something entreating. Lypynskyi rose from bed, threw on a dressing gown, and quietly crept to the door, grabbing a knife from the kitchen on his way just the same. The voice began speaking again: "Tell your people that this gentleman has around-the-clock protection. One more intrusion by someone, and that person will be left without a head. Do you understand me, lads?"

"We understand," came the reply, and the pardoned "lads" scampered off at full speed. Lypynskyi could hear their steps receding. Only once they were out of earshot did he find the courage to open the door.

On his doorstep stood an old gray-haired man with a thick curling beard. The old man was grinning broadly at Lypynskyi, clutching an old bayonet in his hands.

"Did the scoundrels trouble you, sir? Please forgive us for being such unwelcoming neighbors. There's been an increase in riffraff in these parts. The rich aren't very liked around here these days."

The old man's beard grew not downward, but stuck out every which way, making his head appear disproportionately large on his small body. He looked like a white-maned lion.

"People call me Zanuda. The name's Levko. If you like, I can help you with guarding the estate. You won't get anywhere these days without protection. And a kitchen knife won't help."

Lypynskyi recovered his wits and shoved the knife he was wielding into the pocket of his dressing gown. His voice was slowly coming back to him.

"Thank you, Mr... *Zanuda*," Lypynskyi uttered, unsure if Killjoy was the man's nickname or a real surname.

The old man laughed.

"I'm no mister. I come from generations of peasants. I work the land, and when I die, I'll go into the land."

"Me too."

"That makes both of us agriculturists."

IT TURNED OUT that the old man was a widower, and his children were grown. Lypynskyi proposed that the old man move in with him, and he agreed. He settled in the kitchen. During the day, he oversaw the workers, and at night, he guarded his master's slumber with a bayonet in his hands.

"God himself sent you to me," Lypynskyi would say with delight.

"Well, maybe not God himself, maybe just your uncle, but certainly not without God's will. When will the lady of the house and your daughter arrive?"

"We agreed on sometime after Christmas."

"Then we need to hurry, so that everything's ready by their arrival."

The illiterate Levko Zanuda loved most of all to sit in Lypynskyi's library and blow the dust off the old tomes. When the master of the house was working, he'd instruct the workers to conduct themselves more quietly, so as not to disturb the course of his thoughts.

"This is an erudite man," he'd say. "Such people need to be valued. He's writing an article about the Ukrainian people's six-hundred-year struggle for liberty right now!"

Lypynskyi's longtime friend Andrii Zhuk had commissioned the article. Together, they had planned to publish the periodical *Vilna Ukraina* (*Free Ukraine*) in Lviv, but in the end couldn't reach an agreement on an ideological strategy: Zhuk was a socialist, Lypynskyi was a convinced independentist, and the rest of the project's participants were partial to Poland and not as focused on Ukraine's independence. The article thus expanded into a fundamental political history of Ukraine.

Lypynskyi spent the long autumn evenings sharing with his guard his ruminations and doubts, and reading aloud what he had written that day. Zanuda listened attentively and even voiced observations. He carried letters for Lypynskyi from the post office; not one of them was from Kazimiera. The Catholic Christmas passed, Saint Sylvester's Day passed, the Feast of the Epiphany passed, and news from his wife kept failing to arrive.

"THE LADY IS LINGERING in Kraków," the old man remarked when spring arrived. Lypynskyi's health had again deteriorated. "The house has been built, and the lady hasn't come."

"She won't come," Lypynskyi replied, at that moment himself realizing this possibly for the first time. Heartbroken, he lay in bed with a fever, and once a day, Rokicki's wife Henrykha would appear to feed him.

"She isn't going to come," Lypynskyi would say to her. "Kazimiera won't allow her daughter to grow up in Ukraine. She wants to raise her to be as die-hard a Krakowian as she herself is. Kazimiera never understood me. Our marriage was a mistake. She won't be coming."

"Maybe things will still work out," Henrykha would try to console him.

"There's nothing to work out. My life is over. I built a manor for myself alone. Not a manor, but a huge coffin. For now, I'm still lying around, but soon I'll die. There won't even be anyone to nail the lid shut."

"There is no untimely death," Levko Zanuda would reassure Lypynskyi, who would usually turn away to the wall in silence. The first wheat sowing of his own, for which he had so prepared, he handed over completely to his uncle, only once venturing out into the fields on horseback just as the steppe was blossoming.

A heavy grief engulfed Lypynskyi, swallowing him with everything he had that was dearest to him. Work wholly lost meaning, the future ceased to exist, only the never-ending day, echoing with loneliness, which crept slowly like a slug over a dead body, droned before him. As he groped his way through the white fog that had enswathed him anew, unable to see even a step ahead, he was sure that where he was going, it wasn't worth expecting anything good. A scorched heart, scorched land. A helpless inhale–exhale, inhale–exhale.

THE FIRST WORLD WAR finally broke out in July, overfilling the chalice of Lypynskyi's personal catastrophe. This time, a new medical commission, of the Kyiv Military District, recognized the reserve warrant officer as fit to serve and dispatched him to the Fourth Dragoon Regiment of General Samsonov's Second Army, which was quartered in Bilostok right on the Prussian border. Lypynskyi was confident that he would die in the first battle. En route to his duty station, he wrote farewell letters to all of his close acquaintances, in which he asked forgiveness for having been so categorical in the past, and passed along his most sincere greetings to everyone to whom he didn't have the time to write.

"I feel like a droplet in a large stream," he wrote in a letter to Yefremov, the former correspondent of the now-discontinued *Rada*. "I'm going along with millions of our nation's sons and believe that our blood won't be lost in vain. From this blood will grow a better destiny for Ukraine; if it doesn't, it wouldn't be within Ukrainians' power to survive the terrible nightmare that's transpiring now."

During its campaign in East Prussia, the Second Russian Army suffered a crushing defeat, its commander General Samsonov committed suicide, and hundreds of thousands of soldiers were killed or taken captive. The remnant soldiers drowned while trying to wade across the Masurian Lakeland. The wounded Lypynskyi, upon finding himself in cold waters, grasped the mane of someone's horse and thus managed to make it to the opposite shore. The horse, however, did not.

When he was admitted to a military hospital, Lypynskyi barely spoke or opened his eyes, just coughed occasionally, then wiped away from his chin the blood he had spit up. In addition to severe hypothermia, doctors diagnosed a nervous breakdown and sent him off to complete his treatment far away from the front, in Poltava. There, Lypynskyi grew truly guarded around people because what he saw when he looked at them horrified him.

From then on, every person he encountered appeared to him to have only one eye—right in the middle, at the bridge of the nose. That's how it looked to Lypynskyi. Everywhere, he saw one-eyed men and women, even children. The human world had become a world of Cyclopes. *I've gone mad*, Lypynskyi thought. *I won't survive this war. And thank God.*

XIII.

SONIA THE STRONGWOMAN

(Me)

MY THIRD AND FINAL golden-haired man went out one day to invite a friend to be a witness at our wedding. I stayed behind in the apartment alone and prepared a pail of hot water.

I learned how to wash floors from my Grandma Sonia, the one whose own father left her on the steps of a children's home—and then himself died of starvation in the gatehouse of a factory complex. Grandma Sonia used to say that the important thing about washing floors was to not leave dirty streaks. "When I see," she would say, "how some housewives think they're washing a floor but are really only swishing mud all over it, I lose it." You have to wash a floor twice. If you wash it only once, assume that you've spent yourself in vain; the floor will be just as dirty. The first time, wash without wringing out the mop too much, even leave it dripping a little when you pull it out of the bucket, and the second time wash it clean, with the mop wrung out well. Then you need to leave the front door open to create a draft—and it's better to open a window as well—so that the floor dries quickly. And no walking on the recently washed floor. If you really must, take off your shoes.

Grandma had polished and perfected her process over decades of working as a cleaning woman in a music school—the one that was attached to the Polish church and had once been a Catholic monastery. Grandma would head off to work as twilight was already falling. Solfeggio scales were still being practiced in the more far-off cells, somewhere someone would be clacking at a piano clumsily or squeezing a few final tears out of a violin, and Grandma would exit the service room, toting with vigor a giant pail of water and an enormous mop with a three-meter handle—a mop that looked more like a cross awaiting a crucifixion. Dragging the cross on her shoulders, Grandma Sonia traversed from one building of the music school to the next. She scrubbed until midnight, and then would open the windows and wait until the floors had dried.

I too opened a window. It was the cold middle of March. My life was falling into place: I had published my first novel, which had proven more popular than my stories and novellas, then moved from Kyiv back to my hometown, news of which my parents accepted relatively calmly, with only Mom saying in a moment of irritation, "You know, I never did understand you."

Grandma Sonia was her mom. The two of them differed only in their stature and the quantity of their facial wrinkles. Mom was tall and slender, while Grandma Sonia bowed closer and closer to the ground with each passing year, as if trying to pick up something she had dropped and couldn't find. Her ability to bend in half had amazed me since I was little. When, for example, the time arrived to dig up the onions in the small garden outside of town—Mom had been issued the plot in the final year of the Soviet Union's existence and lost it in the first year of Ukrainian independence—Grandma Sonia would volunteer to tend to it and would take me with her so that I would be "predisposed to work from a young age." That little garden was also home to cucumbers, zucchini, and one large pumpkin that someone later stole. Grandma Sonia would sit me down next to her and deftly lean over the onions with a small hoe in hand, not bending her knees in the process, only planting her feet a little past the width of her shoulders. The corresponding pose in yoga is called Prasarita Pada Uttanasana. For years to come, whenever I needed to bend down, I would always envision my grandma, an onion in her large rough palms. Sometimes the image would blur in my mind, and I would no longer be sure if it was Grandma Sonia or Mom. As third in line, I'm just as tall and slender as the second and as the first had once been.

For much of my life, this resemblance troubled me. I was hardly pleased by it. When I baked my first *pampushky* with plum butter and brought them to my parents to try, Grandma Sonia, who was living with them by then, swallowed one in silence, while Mom twiddled another in her hands, poked it with a finger to check its fluffiness, and placed it back on the plate with the pronouncement that she would taste one later because she wasn't hungry at the moment. She never would have admitted that my fritters, though I had never specifically been taught to fry them, had turned out precisely the same as hers or Grandma Sonia's. We all had a common *pampushky* gene.

We also had a common forefather, who had left his daughter on the steps of a children's home during Stalin's man-made famine, the Holodomor.

THIS STORY, WHICH I HAD HEARD OFTEN, probably wasn't worth believing in its entirety because Grandma Sonia, per my calculations, had been three or four years old when it took place. I remember almost nothing from when I was three.

In any case, little Sonia was dropped off on the steps of an orphanage by her father, who then ran off to fetch some plum-butter *pampushky*. Sonia waited a few hours, without budging. She sat quiet as a mouse, so the grim housemothers of the establishment didn't notice her right away. "Come inside," one of them called out finally, but Grandma Sonia shook her head, saying, "I'm waiting for my dad, they've gone to fetch some jam-filled *pampushky*." It was growing dark, and the housemothers lost their patience and set to dragging her into the orphanage, but she resisted and screeched with all her might: "Let me go! My dad will be back any minute with *pampushky*!"

Every time I listened to Grandma's story as a child, I would burst into tears at this point. In telling her tale, she never forgot to mention the *pampushky*, as if they were the main protagonists of the whole story and not the little girl in her first hours of orphan-hood. It was then that this little girl—and, by an automatic process, all of her progeny—developed this protective *pampushky* gene. The gene lets itself be known at those moments in life when something so horrific is transpiring that you could die from a surplus of emo-tion. That's how it was for my grandma; that's how it is for me.

Grandma Sonia always said the exact same sentence about her mother, never supplementing it: "They had a magnificent voice and died when I was eight months old." That's all. Not a single word more. What's strange is that my grandma spoke in a western Ukrainian dialect and referred to her parents in the third person plural, though she herself had only moved to western Ukraine after World War II as an adult. Her homeland was the most central part of Ukraine, the dialect of which became the literary language for the rest of the terri-tory. On occasion, this Ukrainian of central Ukraine broke through in her speech, and then I would fish out those unknown words and expressions with my bare hands like golden minnows out of a pond. I would try to remember them; some I would even write down.

In her retellings, the *dietdom* alone, which is what she called the children's home, invariably remained the *dietdom*. The rest of the details would change. The time spent sitting on the stairs changed from a few hours to an entire day. The seasons changed. Sometimes it was warm, while other times it was snowing and the little girl was numb with cold. The housemothers addressed her differently— sometimes with sympathy, other times with indifference because the orphanage was bursting with abandoned kids whose parents had also run off to fetch some *pampushky* and would "be back any minute." The Holodomor wasn't in full swing until 1933, so what I know for sure is this: it was still only 1932, because it wasn't until after my grandma's escape from the children's home that people were truly swelling from hunger and lying unconscious against fences. She and one other little boy (in some versions of the story he was her brother) decided to run away when the orphans started receiving a bowl of water with three beans for the entire day. Their survival instinct whispered that out there, among the people, their chances of surviving were greater.

They fled by night through a window. There was no subsequent search for the children to speak of. At the local bazaar, those who still had some money or something to sell would give Grandma Sonia and her friend morsels of bread. People were selling anything they had that wasn't fit for dinner, but that could prove useful to someone else who was also close to starving. Kerchiefs, worn undergarments, sheepskin coats, boots. Whoever brought out books to sell went home hungry. There were days when no one handed Grandma anything. Then she and her friend (or perhaps it was her brother?) would gather plum pits off the ground, crush them with a large rock, and eat the little seeds.

I PUSHED MY HEAD out the window and watched the pigeons perched on the building across the street. They were weaving nests for themselves on the neglected open balconies and laying eggs. Once in a while the building's owners would toss the eggs off the balconies onto the asphalt below. The pigeons would then sit on the roof and dispassionately observe the destruction of their offspring.

In the building facing mine, on the floor level with my apartment, a little elderly couple had a little shaggy white dog. The couple generally spent the entire day boozing in front of the TV. The husband, thin as a rake, would shuffle from the living room to the kitchen for his next serving of alcohol in long johns, shirtless. A few times, I had even seen him without the long johns, completely naked. The woman moved rarely. She lived on the couch and was incredibly fat. I made note of the fact that alcohol sucked some people dry and inflated others. The woman I had also seen naked a few times. The couple had no curtains on their windows. I didn't have any either, but neighbors took no interest at all in my life. The light of day seemed to concern only their light-haired shaggy dog, who hung out on the windowsill, his nose shoved up against the pane. He stared outside apathetically but immutably, so that nothing escaped his attention. He couldn't miss something. On occasion, our gazes would meet.

This time, the doggie wasn't in his customary spot. A spring wind gusted into the room, but I wasn't cold in my short-sleeved T-shirt, as if my sensory organs had been shut off by someone. Mechanically, I set to washing the floor. Water dripped from the mop onto the parquet. I added essential oil to the water but caught no whiff of its lemon scent. The world had contracted to the dimensions of my body; beyond it, nothing more existed. All the bodily orifices and sluices through which contact between my inner self and my surroundings should have been transpiring had shut tightly. I felt like a scarecrow that could nonetheless move as if it were alive. Shut off, confined, restricted by my own body. *I walk through the interminable prison of myself.* I began washing from the far-right corner of the room.

"Why are you washing as if you haven't eaten in three days?" I could hear how Grandma Sonia used to exclaim while keeping an eye on how I, as a child, was executing her detailed directives. Then she'd snatch the mop out of my hands to once again, for the hundredth time, show me how to do it right. With each freshly rinsed mop, you needed to catch the last third of the area you had just washed. If you didn't, dirty streaks from the preceding swoosh of the mop would remain. "Don't be scared of the mop! Give it more muscle!"

GRANDMA SONIA HERSELF was very strong. At age sixty, she could carry a hundred-kilo sack of grain on her shoulders thirty meters. I don't know how she managed it. I wouldn't have been able to even budge that sack. My parents either. It was only this incredible, innate strength of hers that saved Grandma Sonia from a premature death.

She should have died, for instance, back when she was husking plum pits. Or when, after fleeing the *dietdom*, she was utterly lost and somehow found her way home by rote. She and her friend had gotten separated by then.

"The chances of him still being alive are practically nil," she said one day at age eighty. "He was older than me." Until then, Grandma Sonia had always imagined her friend living somewhere safe and sound—that he had successfully made it through the famine of 1933–34, that he had grown up, gotten married, had children, and not died in World War II. His name was Roman.

"Or was Viktor his name?"

"No, Viktor was the son of the milkman that you worked for as a hired hand."

Grandma Sonia weighed my words. "Ah, yes," she replied with uncertainty.

―――――

SHE HAD FOUND her way home, back to the house she had grown up in, by accident. One day, some man at the bazaar recognized the little beggar girl and led her as far as the fork in the road beyond which the gardens of Sonia's father began. Before dying of starvation in the factory gatehouse, my great-grandfather had owned a large farmstead, a pond of fish, and two very long barns of hay. Grandma Sonia bathed in the pond, as she had done in the past. Now it was completely overgrown with rushes, and the little girl almost drowned, entangled in the roots. The barns stood empty. Yet their house was freshly whitewashed, its door wide open. Grandma Sonia joyously ran inside but encountered no one she knew there. Someone had outfitted the bright room with shelves and stocked them with groceries and household items for members of the Communist Party. This was now a general store for the elect. An elderly man in a coverall was puttering behind the counter. Grandma Sonia pressed her back against the wall and kept quiet as a mouse.

At this point in the story, I too would always burst into tears.

The expression on the salesclerk's face was warm and sympathetic. He walked up to Grandma Sonia, and she squeezed against the wall even more, as if wanting to grow into it, embed herself in it forever. Sometimes, as the story was told, the store would be empty; other times, a few neighbors—newly minted Communists—would be waiting in line, clenching lifesaving coupons for bread in their fists.

Someone noted calmly, "This girl lived here once."

It's possible that the name of Grandma's father was uttered then too, because it would have been logical if, upon recognizing the girl, someone had voiced the surname of the whole family. For instance, "This is the daughter of So-and-So. They used to live here." But Grandma Sonia was never able to recall more than I'm describing. Her father forevermore remained nameless. She herself always remained nameless too—merely "that girl," "the girl from there," Sonia the Strongwoman. A dove egg tossed out of a nest that by some miracle didn't break.

The man in the coverall cut off half a loaf of white bread for her and led her outside. I think he even stroked her head. He seemed to genuinely feel bad for her. The little strongwoman bit off a hunk and hid the rest of the treasure in her bosom.

Then she was heading somewhere—she didn't know where—and found herself at the cemetery where her mother was buried. The one who sang very well and died when Grandma Sonia was eight months old. According to some tellings of the story, a ledger stone covered the grave; according to others, it was just a mound of bare earth with an iron cross. Nearby, members of the Sanitarian Service were digging a large pit into which they were piling locally gathered corpses of the starved.

Grandma Sonia lay face down on the ledger stone (or on the bare earth) and, if I recall correctly, began screaming very loudly. Anyone who still had the strength to scream was of no interest to the sanitarians. Abandoned and ignored, Grandma Sonia screamed so hard that she forever strained her voice, which must have been just as pretty as her mother's. From then on, she spoke softly, almost inaudibly, her voice more like the rasp of an old wooden door. As a child, I was scared of her voice.

"If I hadn't screamed so hard back then, I could've sung like her," Grandma liked to repeat, turning the radio that was playing the songs of her idols Anna German, Anatoliy Solovianenko, or Nina Matviienko up all the way.

NOW, AS I mopped, Anna German's ballad "The Echo of Love" began to rise from the depths of my body, trying to break free. To distract myself, I scrubbed the parquet adamantly, after each dunk of the mop not forgetting to catch the last third of the area I had just washed. "We're a lo-ong echo of one ano-o-other," Anna German sang to me, and my heart clattered in time with her polished voice, harder and harder.

ACTUALLY, GRANDMA SONIA once let slip that it was possible she wasn't screaming then as she lay on the grave, but singing. She knew a few songs from somewhere and had wanted to sing herself to death with them, in order to finally unite with the mother she had never known. In the evening, a pack of hungry dogs appeared and tore open Grandma Sonia's bread-filled shirt. The white loaf instantly vanished in the jaws of the main she-dog. Why hadn't she torn apart the little girl after the bread? Is it possible she pitied her?

An entire day passed. Then a second. Then a third. The sun rose and set behind the poplars, but Grandma didn't move from the grave because there was nowhere to go. That's how she would always say it, trying to rationally explain the behavior of a child only a few years old: "There was nowhere to go." When I would ask if it had been cold and scary at night, my grandma would reply that she didn't know.

"I remember that I was screaming really hard," she would recall time and again. "And that the sun would set behind the poplars. And so it went on for many days. I ate nothing. I just slept and screamed."

And then a little girl she'd never met appeared from somewhere and took her away from that cemetery. This new friend was still a child herself, just twelve years old. Hand in hand, they walked away, and Grandma Sonia, time after time, glanced back as if regretting to leave such a cozy spot.

———

IN TEN YEARS' TIME, during World War II, all of those places—Grandma Sonia's house, the very long barns, the orphanage, the bazaar, the graveyard—all this the Germans would burn down. Absolutely nothing remained of the village, the name of which I don't even know, save for the incongruous recollections of one orphan. And now that orphan was lying in a room that had once belonged to me, in my parents' apartment, in a state of delirium. Thoroughly wasted away, Sonia the Strongwoman was clinging to life with desperation because that was what she knew best: surviving had been the point of all her near-ninety years. Having enough to eat. Having a roof over her head. Doing everything in her power so as not to be tossed into a pit and buried along with everyone else. Trying to wash yourself clean from tragedy your whole life was pointless: Washing floors taught you that. No matter how much you scrubbed, dirty streaks would emerge regardless.

"JUST IMAGINE, SHE can't remember anything anymore," Mom had said to me recently in amazement, because it was genuinely difficult to imagine Grandma Sonia without her reminiscences. "She calls your dad Roman one time, Viktor the next. Me she doesn't seem to see at all. But she eats a ton, and her strength hasn't left her yet. When we left Sonia on her own for a few hours the other day, she poked out a hole in the front door with her cane. We need to pull her diapers on for her."

That's when I asked my mom, "How did what happened to her affect you?"

She looked at me guardedly. "What do you mean?"

"The *pampushky* and the *dietdom*."

Mom shrugged. "What was there to be affected by? That's how

things were, and that's all there is to it. She wasn't the only one. That's what those times were like—horrifying. But she survived."

"But she was crippled."

"Why in the world crippled? How can you talk like that?" Mom's face even flushed.

"She was broken. I bet she never told you that she loved you."

"She did." Mom turned away. "It's just, who thought about love then?"

"You've never told me that you love me."

Mom's face reddened even more. She exclaimed something indiscernible and, infuriated, rushed out of the apartment. She had come to size up my new place. I didn't run after her; I prepared a pail of water, opened the windows, and began washing the floor. Water (to wash, to wash oneself, to wash away) was always the thing I needed most, my greatest compulsion.

AND SOMEWHERE IN THE MIDDLE of the floor, between the sofa and the bookshelves, it finally happened. My heart suddenly relocated into my throat and began pulsating with unfathomable strength. My chest clenched so tight that I was no longer able to fill my lungs with air. A fear stronger than I had ever felt gripped and paralyzed me, and my mop fell to the floor with a clunk. I went down in its wake. I saw nothing, heard nothing, felt nothing—only my heart pulsating in my throat. Time had stopped. The end had arrived and begun to stretch into eternity. I couldn't breathe; I couldn't scream. Grandma Sonia had screamed everything out before me. Her tragedy hung on to the living and refused to reach its end. It refused to let us, its prisoners, go.

May death come already, flashed through my head, but I didn't understand whose death it was I was wishing for. Hers or my own. And whether this death would bring some sort of relief.

———

MY THIRD GOLDEN-HAIRED MAN returned from his friend's house and joyously announced from the doorway that everything was ready for the wedding. We'd have a modest civil ceremony in the company of our closest friends. Just us and two witnesses, as we had planned.

Upon finding me sprawled in a puddle of dirty water, he said, "We need to go to the hospital."

I got up as if nothing had happened. Only the incredible weakness pervading my body corroborated that the attack hadn't been a fabrication of my imagination.

"Everything's okay now."

"No, it isn't. We're going to the hospital." The man took some money out of our hiding place in a book, in anticipation of having to bribe the doctors. "Throw on a sweater or something."

I stared, unperturbed, out the window. The little shaggy white dog from the apartment across the street didn't appear. Where was he? Why wasn't he here when he was so needed?

"I'm waiting." The man was losing his patience. "We need to get you to a specialist."

He grabbed me by the arm and pulled me—not forcefully, but insistently—toward the door. I resisted, wanting to shout, *They'll be back any minute with* pampushky! The man wouldn't have understood: I had never told him my grandma's story. As we neared the door, my heart once again began to creep up to my throat.

"What's the matter? Don't you care about your health at all?"

I wrenched my arm free and returned to the living room, to the pail and mop. I wanted to fill the pail with clean water and wash the floor anew. To add in more essential oils, to pour in the whole bottle. For a few minutes, the man watched everything, offended. Finally, he asked, "Can you tell me what happened?"

In the window across from mine, the apathetic little muzzle of the little shaggy white dog appeared—my comrade in misfortune. Now we were both prisoners of our respective large architectural cages. Going forward, both he and I would only see the world through the dirty windows of our own residences.

"What happened is that I'll never go outside again," I said.

The man stood stock-still. He couldn't tell if I was joking.

But I wasn't joking. I was finally at peace. The mop moved forward and backward, to the right and to the left.

XIV.

THE INTERNAL WILD STEPPE

(Us)

A WORLD OF CYCLOPES: What would it have seemed like? How would it have felt? What did Lypynskyi think when he encountered his first one-eyed creature? Did he realize immediately that it was an illusion, an illness of the mind; that the one-eyed people were actually fine, that it was the person seeing them that wasn't? Was he fathoming just how the ongoing world war was forever changing the world, forever changing mankind, forever changing him? Did he, a person of the glorious old epoch of empires, grasp that a new era was setting in—one in which there would be no more victorious marching of the strong and healthy to the jaunty clang of shiny weaponry, just the disparate and lonely glances of madmen like him, cast about fearfully in the utter silence?

When you looked, it would no longer be possible to anticipate what it is you'd see. Human consciousness had revealed its dark sides—the previously unknown ones—and the demons that had been skulking there from the moment of their creation had finally broken out. Through the unbridled madness of modern war, the world had ceased to be a place where one could be sure of oneself, and the terror unleashed by this new reality gripped Lypynskyi in the same way that it gripped me a hundred years later.

Lypynskyi had an existentialist nature and, simultaneously, a corporeal one, because he would hole himself up in his chest, in some center invisible to X-rays, and direct his body and mind from in there like a rag doll. Terror became a full-fledged organ of his body but remained invisible, so that it couldn't be excised with a scalpel. I stopped going outside when I realized that I too possessed this same terror.

I BEGAN TO STAND on my head.

One doctor told me that sometimes it was beneficial to see things from a different angle, in particular upside down.

When I'd stand on my head, the entire weight of my body would shift to my shoulders, neck, and skull; I would be exerting myself to such an extent that I wouldn't have a chance to examine anything around me. Standing on my head, I comprehended that an upside-down world was different—completely different—but I didn't really have time to notice how so. The blood coursing through my body, after some resistance, would first slow down, then—reluctantly, almost with a screech—come to a stop, and finally, under the influence of earth's gravity, turn around and flow in the opposite direction. All the while, my head would throb deliriously, particularly my eyes, and there'd be a din in my ears. I would last like that for a few dozen seconds, then softly drop onto the cushions of my big toes and, for another minute, lay face down, my knees tucked under me. I would be scared to return to my customary vertical position again. Maybe a customary position had never existed at all. There was no being sure of anything anymore.

"World War I has broken out in my chest," I would joke to my third golden-haired man, who understood nothing and took my reclusion as an alarming sign. He would try to persuade me in every way imaginable to go out for a walk and breathe some fresh air, to which I would reply that I could breathe perfectly well out the window too. In reality, any attempts at breathing well were unsuccessful because breathing itself had transformed into penal hard labor.

"Breathe deep, inhale–exhale," the man would bid me, to ease my suffering. For some reason he believed that deep rhythmic lung work was relaxing and overall healthful. That isn't true. As soon as I would try to control my breathing process, especially how deeply I inhaled, the terror of not being able to take in the next portion of air would become tremendous—quite simply, all-consuming. It would seem as though I had forgotten how to breathe, had unlearned it, had lost that ability, and, by exhaling, was dooming myself to a slow convulsive death from oxygen deficiency.

IT WAS THEN that a certain doctor visited us, a friend of one of the man's friends, since I was refusing to go to the hospital. She heard out my complaints listlessly and measured my blood pressure. She wanted to draw some blood for analysis but, despite protracted efforts, never did manage to get the needle into a vein. Finally, she informed me rather flatly, "I'm not really seeing any physical abnormalities."

I gave a little smile, because after everything I had been through, that sort of diagnosis sounded like mockery.

"There are obvious problems with my heart," I objected, and the man nodded spiritedly that yes, with my heart, he could attest to that.

"I've had pangs on the left side of my heart for a long time now," I continued, and showed her where exactly the pangs occurred, below my left breast.

"That's from nerves. That's not where the heart hurts."

The doctor took my hand, which was still holding on to my left side, and moved it to the center of my chest, a little below my throat. "That's where the heart hurts."

I was at a loss, even disappointed. My heart had never hurt there, but I had been certain that my attacks were cardiac in nature.

"It's worth doing an echocardiogram, but I think that you're perfectly healthy. Change your lifestyle, spend more time in the fresh air"—here the man again nodded spiritedly—"quit smoking if you smoke, and don't drink coffee or alcohol. Your attacks are from nerves."

I had the urge to spit in the doctor's face. I turned away.

"But she doesn't go outside," the man jumped in. "She hasn't gone out in a month, no matter how much I've asked. She can't even get close to the door."

The doctor didn't say anything in response, just motioned quickly with her hand—a gesture I only half glimpsed—and went to the hallway for her coat. Maybe she made a cuckoo sign. People like me just pretend to be sick, so we drive people like her crazy. We think that the whole world owes us something; we can't pull ourselves together; we're lazy weak beings—hypochondriacs and malingerers. Hmph. The man paid the doctor a hundred hryvnias, and she left. From the doorway, she added, "Standing on your head helps with panic attacks. It's overall beneficial to sometimes look at a problem from a different angle."

The next attack occurred that very evening, a hundred times stronger than the last. The man slowly led me by the hand around the apartment, the way one leads the elderly, and tried to calm me down, ordering me to breathe deeper.

"If it doesn't get better, we'll call an ambulance."

"I know that it won't get better. Call one now," I was whispering, but the man never did call an ambulance. By then, he too had evidently stopped believing in any physical causes to my illness.

———

I LAUNCHED INTO READING old newspapers. All I did for entire days was just wash the floors and read. First I studied everything I could find on the internet; then I got in touch with the librarian at the regional library, who remembered me from when I was a university student. Claiming illness—not quite a deadly disease, but almost—I persuaded the good, kind woman to let me take old bound newspaper books home for the weekend. My third golden-haired man would stop by the library on Fridays, five minutes before closing, to pick up the newspapers, and would then return them for me Monday morning. The librarian could have been fired for such antics. I reassured her that I was researching an extremely important topic and that the book I was currently writing would be my last. Perhaps I even believed it.

"What do you need this old junk for?" the man would sometimes ask, to which I would respond, "I want to understand what time is." He would shrug. Soon he began to distance himself from me, slowly but undeniably. That's how this new terror that consumed me came first between me and him, and eventually between me and everyone who had ever been important to me.

The only things I ever felt anymore were fear and, on occasion, a driving curiosity. The desire to discover the root cause, to discern the meaning of something that had no meaning at first glance, was the only thing that, apart from the panic attacks, could still occupy me at times. I no longer felt love, gratitude, tenderness, hatred, or guilt. There was no joy; there was no despair. Nothing disturbed my one-dimensional coordinate system, save for curiosity. I couldn't satisfy this curiosity with the present, so, in desperation, I turned to the past, so be it that it belonged to someone else. Old newspapers, random stories, and forgotten unimportant facts served as my lifebuoy.

"The Government Department for Alcohol Sale reports that in 1905 in Tsarist Russia, with a population of 132,240,000, a total of 75,037,174 pails of vodka were sold."

"Last year, Mars was located in a position that allowed astronomers to examine it closely. Through the help of telescopic observations, the Italian astronomer Giovanni Schiaparelli asserted that there were very straight, artificial-looking canals on Mars, both wide and long ones, that could be the work of intelligent beings."

"*Ukraina Stelo*, the first Ukrainian periodical in the Esperanto language, has commenced publication in Kolomyia."

I needed to organize the past for an important experiment. That's the only way I'd be able to deduce some common law out of the boundless quantity of individual details, to construct a history of history, to understand—or at least approach understanding of—the mystery that was still keeping me from definitively drowning in the gloom of the subconscious. Time? What is time? Maybe it's a sagging crag, and human life is just a frail sapling trying to clasp on to it with its roots? A glimmering flame that pierces the endless darkness? A singular cry in an apathetic voicelessness?

Why do I even exist?

Questions without answers bounced back to where they had come from—back into the utter nothingness of my existence.

I imagined how Lypynskyi—until recently, a promising historian and publicist, an upstanding community activist, a husband and father—abandoned and forgotten by everyone during the most intense years of the war, roamed the environs of Poltava aimlessly. There, east of the Dnipro River, Reserve Officer Viacheslav Lypynskyi looked after the backup horses. The white fogs that he had seemingly subdued long before enveloped him fully again, head and all. On Protopopivskyi Boulevard, his gaze stumbled hundreds of times on the bust of Ivan Kotliarevskyi, the one that had caused such a commotion among the Ukrainian citizenry in 1903. Now the bust seemed like any ordinary mute hunk of metal erected someplace, by someone, for some reason.

Why did he, Lypynskyi, even exist?

LYPYNSKYI'S BODY TEMPERATURE remained elevated for months as the illness began to desiccate him from the inside. "I run around for a day, then I'm in bed for three," he wrote in his trusty breast-pocket notepad, the pages of which remained empty more and more often. In order to conclusively normalize his personal life, Lypynskyi sent a letter from Poltava to his wife in Kraków, in which he released her from any and all marital obligations to him and offered—once the war was over, if he survived that long—to divorce officially. In the letter, he stressed that he was by no means renouncing his daughter and promised to do everything befitting a father, so that Ewa would not want for anything. Kazimiera, as usual, didn't reply. Perhaps her response simply got lost in the whirlwind of military events. One such letter sought its addressee for over a year and arrived when it was already too late.

"Where are you, son?" Klara Lipińska was asking, simultaneously informing Lypynskyi that she and his father had had to evacuate from the family estate in Zaturtsi eastward, to Zhytomyr, and that the day following their escape, the house lay destroyed beneath its fabulous columns. Kazimierz Lipiński, a nobleman bearing the Brodzic coat of arms, couldn't endure this and, as the letter informed, had died at age seventy-one from sudden cardiac arrest.

As soon as he received the letter, Lypynskyi requested leave. He found Klara in a tiny Zhytomyr apartment, wasted away like a gray-haired ghost. She cried for a long time; she hadn't expected to see her son alive.

"I don't know if I'm happy that I survived," Lypynskyi admitted honestly over a modest lunch. "I can't shake the feeling that my life is over already too."

"You have no right to say such a thing!" Klara exclaimed. "Wishing for your own death is an unforgivable sin."

Lypynskyi didn't respond.

"You have a daughter, after all. Think about her."

"Maybe I do, maybe I don't. I don't take part in raising her, I never see her, I don't even remember what she looks like"—and here Lypynskyi was exaggerating, because he never would have been able to forget his baby bird's face that once nestled in his arms.

"And what about your Ukrainian state? American President Wilson is promising the right to self-determination for unfree peoples. The prospects may be good before long."

"Since when does Ukraine and its statehood interest you?"

Klara served her son his favorite linden tea and noted that the ruddiness in his cheeks was very unhealthy. Consumptives were often that ruddy.

"I got nipped by frost while crossing the Lakeland," Lypynskyi replied. "I can't seem to recuperate."

Klara relayed that his younger brother Stanisław was making plans to rebuild the destroyed family manor, in order to engage in the agricultural selection of potatoes and wheat in Zaturtsi after the war's end. "That's good, he should rebuild it. I already have my estate."

What's true was that Lypynskyi hadn't been at Rusalivski Chahary since July 1914 and only occasionally received short notes from the unlettered Levko Zanuda that had evidently been dictated to someone else. The guard would laconically send word that the fields had been sown, then that the wheat was flowering, then that the crop had been harvested. His notes reassured Lypynskyi that the Uman region was calm and the little house was awaiting its owner. But the owner was in no hurry to travel there.

"Your father and I were always proud of you," Klara Lipińska said to her son in parting.

"You called me a fool."

"Fools also evoke pride, sometimes even more so."

That was the last time they saw each other.

LYPYNSKYI RETURNED TO his duty station in an over-crowded train wagon. Soldiers, mostly deserters who were quitting the front, sat in the aisles with weapons in hand. When the train accelerated too much or made a sharp turn, those sitting on the roof lost their balance and quietly fell onto the tracks, their deaths unsurprising.

"Have you heard?" the passengers who had managed to squeeze into the train at the station in Myrhorod, not far from Poltava already, were crying excitedly. "There's a revolution in St. Petersburg! The tsar's abdicated!"

A clamor arose. Some soldiers couldn't hold back their tears.

"The end of the war!"

"Freedom!"

"Freedom!"

It was February 1917. Euphoria was spreading through the air like some toxic, vexatious bacillus. There was bedlam in Kyiv too. Through the efforts of predominantly leftist autonomist circles, the Tsentralna Rada—the Central Council—was formed there, becoming a first Ukrainian parliament of sorts. On March 17, the history professor Mykhailo Hrushevskyi, who had been arrested at the start of the war, was elected its chairman. Now Hrushevskyi was hurrying to Kyiv from exile to commence fulfilling his duties.

The time to act had arrived, Lypynskyi had no doubt. Serhii Shemet, a cloth factory owner and likable patriot from the noble Ukrainian family of Shemet-Kezhhailo, bearers of the Lebid coat of arms, was waiting for Lypynskyi at the train station in Poltava.

"We need to organize into a political movement!" Serhii Shemet declared. Serhii's younger brother Mykola had studied with Lypynskyi in Kraków and later, in 1905, had been the founder of the first Ukrainian newspaper in the Russian Empire, *Khliborob*. Tsarist reactionaries had imprisoned a Shemet brother for this newspaper, just not Mykola, but Volodymyr Shemet, the oldest of the three, who then developed a severe delusional disorder that he was forever being followed and persecuted. Now Volodymyr was being treated in a clinic for the mentally ill. To everyone's surprise, Mykola became an officer and fought on the side of the Tsar's army, while Serhii Shemet, the likable patriot, engineer, and factory owner, energetically engaged in political activity.

Serhii was a man of tall stature, with unusually straight posture, as if he had been fitted with an oak plank instead of a spine and, hapless, couldn't bend down even if he had wanted to. He barely moved his neck, didn't turn his head, and never lowered it; in order to check if a phaeton driving past had spattered the hem of his topcoat, Shemet would fold at the waist to almost ninety degrees just to keep his neck, wrapped in an elegant white collar, straight. His eyes were little, his teeth were large—overall, he looked a bit like a rodent—and later, because of his gnawing character, it would be said that appearances are never deceiving.

Now Serhii Shemet was persuading Lypynskyi to become a member of the newly formed Democratic Agrarian Party.

"To the best of my knowledge, Viacheslav Kazymyrovych," he said, "our views regarding the unconditional independence of Ukraine are fully aligned."

"Yes," Lypynskyi answered, "but the paths to take to this independence matter. Democrats, as you call yourselves, have never built a state out of nothing anywhere in the world. Only strong Ukrainian monarchical rule will be able to keep our land from chaos right now."

"And where will you enjoin us to look for a Ukrainian monarch? Perhaps we should borrow one from the Germans or the Austrians?" Lypynskyi didn't yet have an answer to this question. He ruminated over Shemet's proposal for some time and finally decided to write the party statute, in the margins of which he scratched four words: "Honor, discipline, idealism, nobleness." No one understood the purpose of those words.

"BEFORE ENGAGING IN community work, the spirit of one's internal ruins must be overcome," Lypynskyi would say, more to himself than to his fellow party members. "One's internal wild steppe must be tamed."

Unexpectedly, an incredible calm enveloped Lypynskyi. His body temperature normalized, and the world of Cyclopes turned back into a world of normal people who yearned for change. The time for action had arrived, he decided: it was now or never. His long-standing dream of being witness to the emergence of a Ukrainian state was on the verge of being realized. Lypynskyi couldn't and had no right to stand on the sidelines.

The tragedy of his personal life retreated to the very edge of his soul, into the Tartarus abyss where, according to Greek mythology, the rebelling Titans had been cast. Lypynskyi peeped in there less and less often, and to the frequent queries about his wife he replied succinctly, "God gives familial happiness to some, and not to others. I wasn't given any."

In June 1917, the first congress of the Democratic Agrarian Party took place not far away in Lubny, attended by over a thousand delegates.

In Poltava, Lypynskyi would wake up at five o'clock in the morning and work on his writing projects. At ten, he'd meet with like-minded acquaintances or those he wanted to sway to his side. After lunch, Lypynskyi would carefully study the press and the arguments of his political opponents, particularly the Socialist Revolutionaries and the Social Democrats who were now in power in Kyiv and—wooing with their revolutionary slogans of "Down with the masters!" and "Land to the peasants without buybacks!"—were fostering hopes of autonomy for Ukraine in the framework of a democratic Russia. Lypynskyi didn't believe that Russia—even if a democratic one—would be loyal to Ukraine. In the evening, he'd write letters, sometimes twenty at a time, in which he polished his political views. The Bolshevik coup that autumn put an end to autonomist Ukrainian politics, which had envisioned Ukraine's future within a democratic Russia, and in January 1918 the Central Council proclaimed the full independence of the Ukrainian People's Republic, with Hrushevskyi as its president. Four days later, the Red Army occupied Kyiv.

Putting his officer rank to use, Lypynskyi actively Ukrainianized tsarist military units by appealing to individual soldiers' national identity, though, as one of his contemporaries noted, "the Bolsheviks had better slogans than the Ukrainians." The poorer peasants, who had nothing before then, rallied into gangs and created mini-revolutions wherever they happened to live, burning down the estates of landowners and wealthier, property-owning peasants everywhere. The powerlessness of the Central Council of the Ukrainian People's Republic only invigorated the general chaos, and it was proposed that President Mykhailo Hrushevskyi be strung up on the building where the council met, in lieu of a coat of arms.

IN APRIL 1918, a local Bolshevik gang neared Lypynskyi's manor, and the watchman Levko Zanuda came out to meet them with a bayonet.

"Move over, old man, this estate is subject to nationalization. It now belongs to the people."

"In order to socialize it," said the old man with the beard that resembled a lion's mane, "you'll have to step over my corpse first."

"If that's what you want, then here you go," said Hryhorii Velbivets, one of the attackers who happened to be from Zanuda's home village, before cutting off the old man's head with a saber. The head flew several meters through the air. At that same moment, the manor that Lypynskyi had built with such love for his family burst into flames. His hopes had long since burned away; now it was his library and archive burning, his unfinished fundamental political history of Ukraine, his letters, and the photographs of him and Kazimiera, which, unsurprisingly, he would regret losing the most.

He would dedicate his next book to his "loyal friend and good neighbor" Levko Zanuda, who, as he would describe it, had been killed by "evil and dark people." Lypynskyi would often imagine the hairy head flying through the air; sometimes the head would appear in his dreams, winking with its bulging eyes as if to say, *Don't be afraid of anything, I'll take vengeance on the miscreants, they'll pay for everything yet.* The miscreants, however, would remain unpunished, and the villager Velbivets, later an active Communist, would take pride in his deed till the end of his life, exaggerating how far his victim's head flew more and more with each passing year.

IN THE SPRING OF 1918, German forces liberated Kyiv, and on April 29, at an agrarian congress held in the theater building of the Kyiv Circus, a Ukrainian State headed by Hetman Pavlo Skoropadskyi was proclaimed. This former tsarist general was an indirect descendant of the final Cossack hetman from the eighteenth century, Ivan Skoropadskyi. Thus, a Ukrainian monarch had turned up on his own. He offered Viacheslav Lypynskyi a ministerial post, which he declined due to his poor health, saying that heading a Ukrainian embassy was the most he would be capable of. His ambassadorial candidacy was quickly approved, and

Viacheslav Lypynskyi became the envoy of the Ukrainian State to the Austro-Hungarian Empire. The once-mighty empire had only months left.

He embarked for Vienna alone. There was no one on the Kyiv platform on the other side of the window of his compartment; no one was seeing him off. His mother had just died in her sleep, and his brother was rebuilding the family's country estate. Out of habit, Lypynskyi laid out before himself the books he intended to read on the journey, then started when a stranger poked his head into the compartment and immediately closed the door and left. Kyiv's hills slowly receded into the distance and, with them, the country whose birth Lypynskyi had so eagerly awaited.

It was so cold in the train car at night that Lypynskyi had to request an additional blanket. He was coughing. They passed the Russian–Austro-Hungarian border quickly. In Lviv, the train stopped for an hour, and Lypynskyi got off to stretch his legs. In Kraków, when the train stopped for half an hour, he didn't exit the car; he didn't even glance out the window. He arrived in Vienna early in the morning. He walked out into the Northwest Train Station and, to escape the begging cripples, immediately hired a carriage to Hotel Bristol.

"WHO IS THIS LYPYNSKYI?" my third golden-haired man asked me. I remember that day very well. It was a Friday afternoon. I was lying in bed, surrounded by books and newspapers on all sides, and my head was muddled with all the information that I was swallowing like sea plankton, by millions of tons at a time, unable to satiate myself.

"Why are you studying his life in such detail?"

"There are just certain things about him that I find very interesting," I replied.

"You haven't gone out in three months. This isn't normal."

Only then did I notice that the man had put on his coat and was waiting to tell me something important.

"Are you meeting up with someone?"

"No, I'm just leaving. I can't do this anymore. You need professional help."

Our gazes met a few times. The man's sky-blue eyes were murky and filled with pain, even despondency.

"Don't do this," I pleaded. "Don't leave me. I love you. I want to marry you."

"When I leave, you'll be forced to reach out for help. You need help, don't you understand that? You're sick."

He leaned down to hug me, but I didn't move. I heard the door to the apartment open and close, and listened as the footsteps on the stairs grew more distant. My chest was pounding wildly. Unable to bear it, I jumped out of bed and went after him barefoot. I opened the door and ran down to the first floor. I darted outside. I shouted his name; I was screaming, I think. My eyes went dark; the world became plasticky like a toy; then everything turned upside down as if I were standing on my head. Under my feet, the blue sky dangled.

I exhaled and frantically tried to inhale but couldn't. I leaned against the wall and helplessly sank to my knees. The man was nowhere in sight; maybe he had gotten into a cab.

"Are you okay?" I heard a voice above me. It was the very fat woman from the building opposite mine. Her shaggy little white dog came running up and licked my face.

"Help me back into my apartment, please," I whispered.

The woman reached under my arms and helped me stand up.

"Maybe I should call an ambulance?" she asked with what even seemed like worry.

"Yes, call an ambulance. I don't feel well at all. I'm very sick."

XV.

VIENNA

(Him)

HE WAS PAINFUL to look at. This city of relentless wind had
now transformed into a city of endless frost. By 1920, it seemed as
though the war had sucked all the life out of him, all the warmth,
leaving only a chitinous shell over him, like from a long-dead
insect. The magnificent Viennese palaces stuck out amid the poverty and misery like the idols of yore—mute witnesses to a past
lavishness. From a distance, the green chariots jutting from the
roofs of the government structures that lined the Ringstraße
looked like moss-covered crosses in littered, neglected cemeteries.
Which dignitaries and functionaries were lying in these cemeteries and why had long been forgotten. The uniforms, blue as the
sky, had disappeared; the elegantly dressed, carefree crowds milling in the streets had disappeared; pedestrians swiftly passed by
in threadbare clothing and with troubled countenances. Everyone
in the city was cold and hungry, even the animals in the imperial
zoo. Wine and water were the only sustenance available to everyone. Coal and bread were now the most sought-after commodi-

ties, worth their weight in gold. The society women of Vienna were ready to sell their bodies and souls for them. Their husbands had either died or been maimed in battle for the sake of the now-dead Austro-Hungarian Empire and, short an arm or a leg, were begging outside the churches. Any healthy man spotted walking down the street was likely either a *Hochstapler*—a swindler and a fraud—or some emigrant. There were more of the latter in Vienna now than there was sewage in the Danube.

Just a few years earlier, in the local cafés, writers and philosophers, artists and architects, psychologists and composers—the entire bloom of that majestic imperial epoch that World War I had definitively brought to an end—had been writing, drinking, conversing, and lazily awaiting the onset of a new era. Georg Trakl and Oskar Kokoschka, Gustav Klimt and Otto Wagner, Joseph Roth and Hugo von Hofmannsthal—all of them sat here. Sigmund Freud smoked his twenty daily cigars in Café Central. Leo Trotsky played chess. They lived and created here, listing the cafés as their return postal addresses. But when the era that everyone had so been waiting for finally arrived, those that had been most eager for its arrival would prove the least likely to witness it, some dying and others simply leaving.

The poet and addict Georg Trakl, unable to forget the inhuman carnage near the Ukrainian town of Horodok outside Lviv, ingested a lethal dose of cocaine in November 1914. The artist Oskar Kokoschka took a bullet in the head near Lutsk, and survived, but never returned to Vienna. In 1918, the artists Gustav Klimt and Egon Schiele died a few months apart—the latter from the devastating Spanish flu epidemic, at just twenty-eight years old.

Viennese cafés abruptly emptied. Vacant tables appeared, and newcomers, mostly foreigners, unceremoniously grabbed the seats. These were the previously unnoticed people who the mighty wave of war had scraped from the bottom of the great empire and pushed

out onto the surface of its ruins. Ukrainians, for example. Had anyone even heard of them just a few years earlier?

THE CHIEF OF VIENNA'S POLICE, Johann Schober, had con-
scientiously reported to Count Burián, the imperial foreign minister of Austria-Hungary, the arrival of the Ukrainian diplomatic
mission and that it had taken up residence at Hotel Bristol. Count
Burián didn't believe in Ukraine, but at noon on July 5, 1918, he
had met with the envoy of the newly created Ukrainian State, Viacheslav Lypynskyi, and personally accepted his credentials.

"How's the situation on the eastern front?" he had asked his
cachectic guest, though he knew perfectly well the latest news from
his ambassador in Kyiv, Count János Forgách. The war was ending, and each state, as it ratified peace treaties, was trying to hag-
gle whatever it could from whoever it was negotiating with. At the
negotiations in Brest-Litovsk early that year, the Ukrainian mission
had insisted on the partition of Halychyna and the integration of
its eastern part, with its predominantly Ukrainian population, into
Ukraine. An appropriate pact between Austria-Hungary and the
UPR had been signed. But Count Burián was in no rush to put it
into effect because he had already promised Eastern Halychyna to
the Poles. (Within months, the original copy of the pact would be
secretly burned in Berlin, and Envoy Lypynskyi would find himself
sending official letters of protest wherever he could in vain.)

"We're waiting, Your Excellency Mr. Minister, for the ratifi-
cation of the peace accord," Lypynskyi began firmly. "Regarding
the matter of the division of Halychyna, we're taking a principled
stand. Its eastern part ought to go to Ukraine."

Such directness piqued Count Burián. "And we're waiting for
Ukrainian grain!"

"It's growing, noble sir. The harvesting will be soon. There'll be
enough Ukrainian wheat for everyone, I assure you of that."

When the guest had taken his leave, Count Burián summoned Schober. "Keep an eye on him," he advised his chief of police. "Especially who he's meeting with and what he's discussing. To whatever extent possible, check his mail, particularly encrypted telegrams. And spell out for me in a separate report who in the world these Ukrainians are. I've never even heard of them, yet suddenly here they are out of nowhere!"

"Count Lypynskyi is a Pole, Mr. Minister," Schober remarked courteously. "I reported on him to you last week."

"A count? A Pole? Why is he so fixated on Halychyna being part of Ukraine?"

"I'll try to find out."

"Please, do find out. But write more briefly, Schober. I don't have the time to read your novels."

Schober and Count Burián were externally similar, like two drops of water. They differed in that one of them, a haughty and pompous aristocrat, was nearing the end of his career without suspecting it yet (in a few months' time, Austria-Hungary would fall, and he'd sink along with it into the ignominious past), while the other, the product of a modest family with many children, was just beginning his career. An ordinary policeman, Schober would twice hold the post of federal chancellor of the young Republic of Austria, subsequently serving as vice chancellor as well.

ON BEHALF OF AUSTRIA'S FOREIGN MINISTRY, Schober tended to the "matter of the Ukrainians" personally from the very beginning. Outside of Ukraine, Schober was likely the only person who had a consummate understanding of Ukrainian politics and attached at least some significance to it. Between the lines of Schober's dry, meticulous reports to the ministry, a faint fondness toward the object of his surveillance was discernible, possibly for the simple reason that a hopeless pursuit always looks beautiful. At first glance, the formation of a Ukrainian state did indeed look beautiful; it was just a pity that few were able to fully appreciate its subtle aesthetics.

In his reports to the leadership of the new Austrian republic, Schober wrote that the withdrawal of German forces from Kyiv had left Hetman Skoropadskyi alone with and at the mercy of revolutionary forces. A few days after the fall of Austria-Hungary, in early winter of 1918, the troops of Otaman Symon Petliura (a journalist, no military education, a neutral-to-negative personal reputation) had captured Kyiv and proclaimed the restoration of the Ukrainian People's Republic. The government of the UPR was named the Directorate, and Volodymyr Vynnychenko (a writer with radical views, no military education, loyal to Bolshevism, a hysteric) was appointed its first head. The Ukrainian monarchy had fallen, not lasting even a year, and Ukrainian anarchy had taken its place.

Surveilling Envoy Lypynskyi, Schober saw how he was increasingly cowering and bending before the foreign powers, like a tree whose trunk was softening from excessive heat. The news of the change of power in Ukraine caused a boil to form on Lypynskyi's neck, which began to fester, and during a minor operation, the doctors discovered gangrene. They had to cut all the way to the throat. The patient spent a month after that sitting bandaged up in his hotel; after recovering, he resumed his diplomatic work even though the state whose diplomat he was—the Ukrainian State, or the Second Hetmanate—no longer existed.

Lypynskyi received guests and looked for funds, passports, and visas for various delegations, missions, and political refugees, more and more of whom were arriving in Vienna with each day. In Lviv, after a quick overthrow, the West Ukrainian People's Republic had been formed, also in November 1918, but the advance of Polish troops soon forced its government to cede city after city. By the autumn of 1919, the government of this state—together with its new dictator, appointed a few months prior to head an emergency government—finally ended up in exile in Vienna as well. The embassy of the WUPR rented rooms in the Zita-Hof Building on Mariahilferstraße, and the WUPR's dictator Yevhen Petrushevych (private address: Laudongasse 28/8, 8th District) would for a number of years still cherish naïve dreams and hold talks with the rulers of neighboring countries in hopes of securing assistance in the fight against the Poles. The army of Halychyna, which had previously fought side by side with the UPR, made an unexpected alliance with Anton Denikin's supporters, the anti-Bolshevik White Russians, whereupon the Directorate of the UPR—possibly out of revenge—tried to gain the support of the Poles at the price of Halychyna. In sacrificing Ukraine's western territories, Petliura, now the president of the UPR, hoped to save at least some lands for Ukraine. A terrible conflict erupted between the elites of Halychyna and Greater Ukraine, which put an end to efforts to unite Ukraine's central and eastern lands with its western ones.

LATE ONE EVENING, an exhausted Lypynskyi returned to his hotel suite, and the porter obligingly helped him with his outer garments, whispering in his ear that some strangers were waiting for him in his private rooms, probably with requests for favors or help.

"Be careful, Mr. Envoy, these people didn't give their names. Maybe they're Bolsheviks, come here to kill you. They have these funny hats, like the Tatars from Mongolia."

"Have you ever even seen Tatars from Mongolia, my friend?" Lypynskyi asked half-jokingly.

"I haven't, but that's about how I always imagined them."

The guests were laughing boisterously. They were wearing two mink coats apiece; decorative silver tableware and cutlery grabbed hurriedly as they fled Ukraine jingled in their bags; and a few gold chains each with huge gold crosses lay heavily on the women's necks and ample breasts. The "great migration of peoples"—the mass "exodus" of Ukrainian democracy—was in full swing.

IN STARVING VIENNA, these newcomers from Ukraine behaved like grand seigneurs, throwing around state funds in hotels and restaurants and having such fun that Ukrainians began to be viewed as some rich nation—about as rich as Americans but markedly less cultured. Their ill repute became so firmly fixed that for a while Viennese hoteliers refused to admit people with Ukrainian passports at all.

The new revolutionary government in Ukraine considered Lypynskyi a cursed landowner and a Polish scoundrel but didn't bother him, either acknowledging his professional qualities or simply not having the time to be picky, occupied as it was up to its ears with continual wars with the Bolsheviks, Denikin supporters, Poles, and intra-Ukrainian otamans. Kyiv, like a loose woman, changed hands over ten times during this tumultuous period, and each new seizure ended in bloody purges of the predecessors. There were days when the Kyivans didn't know who was in charge of the city—the Ukrainians, the anti-Bolshevik Russian Whites, or the Bolshevik Russian Reds. And inevitably, Kyivans who welcomed the coming of the first, the second, or the third could always be found.

Finally, in January 1919, the government of the UPR was forced to evacuate Kyiv in its entirety and never return again. The last train with the remnants of the Ukrainian intelligentsia, all involved in one way or another in the struggle for independence, left the capital a little over a year later, in June 1920. This train traveled slowly, traversing every kilometer with incredible difficulty, waiting out shelling at destroyed stations and, now and then, rebuilding with the hands of its own passengers the destroyed railbed. Some train cars were missing flooring, to say nothing of windows or bedding. At the forced stops, secretaries, publishers, and writers, accompanied by wives and children, suffering from hunger and thirst, fetched water in little bowls from neighboring villages and solicited hunks of bread from the dubious populace. The villagers, exhausted by the endless combat, didn't trust anyone anymore. What's more, the word "Petliurites,"—as these members of Symon Petrliura's UPR Directorate were called—no longer aroused sincerely patriotic feelings in them, as it had previously. Now that word elicited fear and condemnation because the Petliurites always retreated, and the power void they left would always get filled by the Bolsheviks, who always shot and killed.

IN VIENNA, ANOTHER ENVOY with the word "Ukrainian" in his title appeared in 1920—Yurko Kotsiubynskyi, the envoy of the Ukrainian Soviet Socialist Republic and the son of the now-deceased eminent Ukrainian writer Mykhailo Kotsiubynskyi. He scoured the Austrian capital in a commissar's leather coat and persuaded the floundering Ukrainian emigrants to return home to help build the Ukrainian Soviet Republic, which had been proclaimed in Kharkiv the preceding year—for the time being, as he would say, the only legitimate republic in Ukraine. To many Ukrainians, national communism really was starting to seem like a not-so-horrible political alternative, all the more so because the former Ukrainian leaders had long since fled to Austria and lived either in Vienna, like Mykhailo Hrushevskyi, the chairman of the Central Council (private address: Klostergasse 10, 6th District) or in Semmering, a former imperial health resort, like the author Vynnychenko. They considered Russian Bolshevism their closest ally, even when this "ally" had entered Kyiv in tanks with "Death to Ukrainians!" signs and ousted them into exile. Now Ukrainian leaders were puffing cigars in Viennese cafés, continuing to develop socialist ideas in front of a group of unpracticed students, "babies," as the local journalists quipped.

About Vynnychenko, the journalists wrote that "it won't be a pity if the Bolsheviks hang him as a politician because he did Ukraine a lot of harm as a politician; but as a writer, it will be a pity, as there are so few writers in Ukraine." "It is more practical," the press would rejoin about Mykhailo Hrushevskyi, the former master of Ukrainian historiography, "for the esteemed professor to enlighten bourgeois Europe with the light of socialism from the Herrenhof than have to endure it firsthand."

The Herrenhof was a café on Herrengasse in Vienna. The left wing of the Ukrainian emigrants would gather there at noon. Their opponents—the independent democrats or individuals without a distinct ideological position—would take their seats an hour later in Café Central across the street. In one of the alcoves of the Tsentralka, as the latter was called by the Ukrainians, Viktor Pisniachevskyi (a physician, bacteriologist, and journalist; poor vision; a charismatic and hot-tempered rabble-rouser; private address: Majolikahaus, Linke Wienzeile 40/38, 6th District) was assembling an editorial staff for his newly founded weekly *Volia* (*Freedom*). At this time of day on Herrengasse, the Ukrainian language completely drowned out German. Pisniachevskyi ruled in the Tsentralka like some governing premier. Everyone who wanted an audience with him, while waiting their turn, sipped dreadful-tasting coffee with wet red sugar at the nearby tables.

In the first issue of the weekly, Pisniachevskyi—tall, skinny, with thin whiskers and a pince-nez, sharp of tongue and chin—wrote to his readers, emigrants just like him: "Far away in this foreign land, in days of 'grief and tribulation,' in 'days of scatteredness,' we begin our difficult work. Much of the Ukrainian intelligentsia have dispersed throughout the cultured world. They live here and there, some of their own free will and others involuntarily, plodding at their jobs and, like bees from flowers, collecting real-world experience into their own hives. But the time of liberation will come. The bees will rise into the air and fly off in great swarms to their native apiary."

Over a dozen such periodicals arose in Vienna at that time. They could be purchased, along with freshly published Ukrainian books, at the Goldschmidt Bookstore at Wollzeile 12 in the 1st District. Every political force and every embassy, using the funds they had taken with them while fleeing Ukraine, produced some newspaper in which it fervently waged war against its political opponents. The pages of these newspapers witnessed the birth, development, and death of ideas that would never come to fruition and often weren't even useful. The bees themselves would never see their native apiary again.

IN THE SPRING OF 1919, Lypynskyi ventured on a short trip to Halychyna, which would be his final one to the region. He wanted to speak with the senior leadership of the UPR—those who hadn't fled yet—and see with his own eyes what was actually going on. Stanislaviv, in the foothills of the Carpathian Mountains, remained virtually the only city under Ukrainian rule. There, in Hotel Union, Lypynskyi met with Colonel Petro Bolbochan, whom Otaman Petliura had been keeping under house arrest for many months now on suspicion of preparing a revolt against him. Lypynskyi, on the other hand, considered Bolbochan one of the best and most professional Ukrainian military men, of which there were few in the Ukrainian army.

As a sign of protest, the detained Bolbochan wrote an open letter addressing the leadership of the UPR: "We're fighting Bolshevism, the entire cultured world is rising to fight it, and yet the newly established Ukrainian government is going out to greet it! Here you are pushing yourselves into the top ranks of global politics as ministers, otamans, and leaders of a large state when you don't even understand the simplest things in life."

In early June, an impromptu military court sentenced Bolbo-chan to death, and with Otaman Petliura's approval, the sentence was carried out with two shots to the head from a revolver. Lypyn-skyi had already returned to Vienna by that time. He received news of the colonel's murder via telegram in the lobby of Hotel Bristol. It was crowded—some large delegation was checking in—so few noticed how Lypynskyi, losing his balance for a moment, sank down onto a sofa upholstered in red satin by the window and began to weep bitterly. A stranger walked up to him and silently handed him a handkerchief. Lypynskyi wiped his tears and blew his nose.

"Thank you, dear sir, my nerves are completely shot. Leave your address, and my maid will send you the handkerchief washed and ironed."

"There's no need," the stranger replied. "Keep it."

Glancing at his Good Samaritan, Lypynskyi exclaimed in sur-prise, "You bear an incredible resemblance to Count Burián, the minister of foreign affairs of Austria-Hungary!"

"I don't even know who that is," Schober mumbled, and disap-peared into the crowd.

At that moment, Schober was fulfilling his task of gathering information about the well-known Ukrainian figures who had found refuge in Vienna, so his superiors could know their plans. Schober compiled a table, listing each figure's name and, alongside it, their address, the position they had held in Ukraine and which party they belonged to, their personal characteristics, contacts, and whether they were a possible threat to Austria. The list was six pages long. For greater clarity, Schober Germanized the Ukrainian names, though not always uniformly: Andrii became Andrei one time, Andreas another, Mykhailo—Michael, Hryhorii—Gregor, Mykola—Nikolaus, Ivan—Johann, Osyp—Josef. Only Lypynskyi for some reason was left with his hard-earned Viacheslav. The col-umns next to his name noted: former envoy, resigned due to disagreement with the political direction of the UPR, ill, doesn't pose a risk, place of residence still unknown. Lypynskyi was immediately removed from surveillance.

LYPYNSKYI REALLY HAD grown very sick. With the last of his funds, he left for Baden for treatment at Gutenbrunn Sanatorium, where he would consider what to do next. He couldn't return to Ukraine because he would have been immediately shot for his work in Hetman Skoropadskyi's government. He couldn't afford to remain abroad. His wife had reached out from Kraków and asked for money; she and his daughter were almost starving. Lypynskyi promised to think of something.

In the meantime, a reception of the Ukrainian press was held in the Kursalon music hall in the Stadtpark, Vienna's large central park, in honor of the UPR's new envoy to the Austrian government, who expressed "hope for the imminent victory of the Ukrainian cause."

"All people, without exception, seem crazy to me," Lypynskyi wrote to Yevhen Chykalenko, who had just lost all his money and property and would soon move to Vienna as well. "But maybe I'm mistaken, and I'm the one that's crazy? What else is there to hope for? Ukraine no longer exists. . . .

"Nonstate pigs can't be refashioned into state eagles," Lypynskyi wrote to his friend. "It's a nation of churls, wreckers, and 'fourleggers,' no better than animals."

Lypynskyi had thought up the word "fourleggers" himself, just as he had the word "selfstatelessness." He flaunted his neologisms in conversations with his new maid Fin Yulí.

A feeling of absolute defeat coated everything around him: the streets, the people Lypynskyi met, even himself. The defeat tasted like fine sand. Lypynskyi would take in a mouthful of it and grind his teeth at night, trying to spit it out, instead biting the insides of his cheeks until they bled. At times attacks of uncontrollable sobbing would overwhelm him, and in such moments Lypynskyi felt like a good-for-nothing worm, a failure who had lost everything that had ever been his. His dream had been right there in his hand—not paradise on earth, just his own independent state—but it had been snatched away from him and trampled by people who never understood its value.

Lypynskyi's university friend Mykola Shemet, an officer in the UPR's army, upon receiving an order to shoot at his rebelling compatriots near Lubny, shot himself instead.

Though he had an aversion to weapons (as well as to umbrellas), Lypynskyi regretted that he hadn't kept some sort of pistol at his disposal. A bullet in the temple would have helped him too, finally quelling this unbearable internal pain that returned every morning as soon as he opened his eyes and held him in a tight embrace until he once more sank into a heavy, stone-like sleep.

"I wanted to become a stone, but I'll become sand instead," he'd say to himself. "I'll scatter ingloriously, I'll vanish in the tiniest crevices of time, and no one will remember me because failures are the first to be forgotten. No one will tell the story of how vigorously I strove for victory and what I sacrificed for it, but there will undoubtedly be those who will write how loudly I cried and will relish how briefly I'll be mourned."

"Mr. Envoy!" an unfamiliar voice called out to Lypynskyi just as he was departing to the sanatorium for treatment. "Mr. Lypynskyi!"

A short, stooped man with almost no hair on his head but with a thick ruddy mustache was standing next to the exit. The furious porter was trying in vain to get rid of him.

"I've already told you that there's nothing worth waiting for here, that the gentleman is no longer an envoy!"

"Who are you?" Lypynskyi asked, addressing the ruddy-mustached man.

"Mykhailo Petrovych Savur-Tsyprianovych," the man introduced himself desperately. "I'm a secretary. I worked in the office of the Ministry of Education under the Directorate government. We were evacuated in full from Kyiv."

"What languages do you know?"

"I know German, French, and Russian."

"Do you know Ukrainian?"

"It's my native tongue."

"Come visit me at the Gutenbrunn Sanatorium in Baden, just south of Vienna, in a month. I lost in politics, so maybe I'll write something worthwhile. If we reach an agreement, you can be my secretary. I'm looking for one right now. I can't pay much, but it'll be better than nothing."

Tsyprianovych thanked him. His eyes welled with dog tears of devotion, but he brushed them away with the sleeve of his frayed frock coat. The hotel door swung open from a strong gust of wind, and Lypynskyi exited, covering his face with his hands. A carriage was waiting for him. Vienna's Central Train Station receded in the distance. Ahead of Lypynskyi, a desolate scorched wasteland was already opening up.

MANY YEARS LATER, in July 1927, another chance encounter would take place in this same hotel at Ringstraße 1. En route from Berlin to Styria, Lypynskyi would make a stopover in the familiar walls to recover a bit. He'd be in the process of carrying in his belongings when heavily armed police units would come marching down the street toward the Parliament Building. A staid man would watch the procession through the lobby window.

"There's unrest, a lot of unrest," the worried porter would say to Lypynskyi. "Who knows what will happen?"

A bit later, panicked screams and loud gunfire would be heard from outside. Dense black smoke would come rolling in from the direction of Maria-Theresien-Platz. The staid man, who would look horribly familiar to Lypynskyi, would continue to soak up the events outside the window with expressionless eyes.

"The Palace of Justice is on fire!" people would be shouting from that direction. "There's shooting! Many dead!"

Some nimble courier would come running into the hotel and hand the staid man a note. The man would read it quickly and hide it in the pocket of his well-tailored, expensive suit jacket. He'd stand there for another minute, as if paralyzed. And then he'd feebly sink onto the sofa upholstered in red satin and begin to weep bitterly. Lypynskyi would hand him his handkerchief.

"Thank you," the man would say. "My nerves are failing me."

An indelible bloodstain would creep across the impeccable career of the two-time chancellor and longtime chief of the Vienna police. Despite numerous reservations, Schober would give permission for the use of weaponry during a mass demonstration against an unjust court verdict. Eighty-nine innocent people would be killed.

"Are you in Vienna for long, Mr. Lypynskyi?" Schober would suddenly inquire, after blowing his nose and wiping away his tears.

Lypynskyi would shake his head energetically: "By no means, dear sir. I'm just passing through for one night. Living in Vienna, with my lungs, is pure suicide. There are always winds blowing here . . ." He'd start coughing. "Where do you know me from, sir?"

But Schober would be gone. That same evening, after dinner, Lypynskyi would find the laundered and ironed handkerchief with his initials on it in his hotel room.

XVI.

BOMCHYK LAUGHS AND EATS

(Me)

THE DOOR SHUT BEHIND ME and a complete silence enveloped the room. My mind raced: *Who am I, and what am I doing in this world? Is my world delimited by my body? By how far I can see? By the apartment I live in? Does it even exist at all, this world of mine? Will it go on existing if I close my eyes, if I pass out, if I die?*

I lay in that total silence, consumed by my fear of disappearing. I could hear it—this fear—thudding fiercely inside me, trying to break its way out. I clenched my teeth firmly and pressed my hands against the plateau of my chest to keep it from splitting open. I needed my fear to stay contained; it had no right to break loose. It had no right to become physical.

I was an inconsequential being who had suddenly become deathly afraid of life. The world had suddenly become too vast around me, just as there had suddenly become too much of me in the world, too much of my body. I dreamed of diminishing my body to the size of a pearl and hiding in a shell on the ocean floor. I dreamed of closing myself up. Of shutting off the light. Of shutting off the unbearable silence.

Without my noticing, my body had slowly prevailed over my intellect. Now, years later as I write this, I understand that this should have been foreseeable: I had neglected my body for too long. Driven to despair, it had switched into autonomous mode and taken full control over me. It was saving both of us, however it could. Whenever I tried to push myself out of my shell, it whispered with dizziness, pain in my temples, and nausea: it was dangerous there, outside my apartment. Venturing out into the world wasn't worth the risk, it cautioned; everything I needed was here, inside.

BUT, AS IT SOON TURNED OUT, I didn't have everything I needed in my hideout. In a week of solitary living, I ate up my whole stock and was beginning to go hungry. I was overcome with a constant and incredible desire to eat. I'd stuff everything I saw into my mouth until my stomach swelled up like a basketball and I felt exhausted and sleepy. Fear protected me from the dangerous world; food, in turn, protected me from my fear. With a full stomach, I was less afraid. And now I was out of food.

On Sunday, my parents came to visit and brought two liter-sized jars filled with potato dumplings that were still warm and cabbage rolls from the day before, also stuffed with potato and drizzled with pork cracklings—my favorite. Barely chewing, I devoured the gifts while my parents watched me wordlessly, as if they had come to have a look at a sideshow at a zoo.

"It's our opinion," my mom finally began, "that you need to stop being a drama queen and pull yourself together."

"Pulling myself together is impossible," I replied with my mouth full, unconcerned and not attaching any particular importance to what had been said. But for my mom, that was a signal to launch an attack.

"We know about everything. We know that you two aren't together anymore and you're living alone now. But you've become an invalid! You don't leave the house! Tell us"—here her voice became tender—"what happened? We'll help, just talk to us."

My father couldn't take it anymore and walked out to the living room. He avoided high vibrations of emotions whenever possible.

"I don't know what's going on with me," I said to my mom, but she waved her hand dismissively, as if to say, *Yeah, yeah, you're just being dramatic.* "I've started having these attacks, as if my heart will explode any minute or I'll just suffocate . . . I don't know how else to explain it."

"Then go to the doctor."

"A doctor was here and said I was healthy."

"That means you're fine!"

"I'm not fine."

My mom exhaled loudly, her powerlessness palpable. "Are you insinuating that you're having problems with your head?" She was ashamed. I could see it.

"I don't know. Maybe."

"If you want, I'll talk to Nina." Nina was Mom's neighbor, who worked as a nurse at the regional psychiatric hospital. "Maybe she can recommend some good pills. These days everyone's taking pills."

"That isn't necessary."

"If you're going to keep financially relying on us, then we're going to make this decision for you."

I went back to my dumplings and cabbage rolls. My father came back into the kitchen. "Look, don't eat so much or you'll end up like Grandpa Bomchyk," was all he said.

GRANDPA BOMCHYK, my father's father, weighed a hundred and fifty kilos when he died. That was a lot, for Grandpa Bomchyk. In his youth, he had been slim. I had seen photographs in which my grandpa, thin as a rake, is embracing a mottled cow, his favorite. He used to take care of that cow as if she were a princess: he talked to her, milked her, combed her tail and, with a special brush, her belly and neck, cleaned the dried dung off her calves, let her lick salt out of a large bowl (what for, I don't know), and even played the harmonica for her when no one was watching. The cow died before I was born, accidentally having eaten her fill of wet clover. Bomchyk tried to puncture her bloated stomach with an awl to release the gases, but it was too late. And Bomchyk missed her stomach in the process, so a butcher had to be called to finish up the matter. The bovine princess was twisted into sausage links, and my father ate them for the next half a year without any qualms at all.

After that, Bomchyk owned many other cows but never once took a photograph with any of them.

He also began to rapidly gain weight.

This process was in no way related to the cows; it's just that I remembered him as that thin man in that one and only photograph with the legendary Mottle. In it, Grandpa is dressed in a tarpaulin shepherd's coat with a hood because it's raining. It's late autumn—that blessed moment before a long winter when each ensuing day in the pasture may turn out to be the last if snow falls overnight. Cows graze the most assiduously then, in anticipation of the inevitable snow.

I remember how one time the snow started dusting first thing in the morning, when Grandpa Bomchyk and I and the cows were in the field. The cows were slowly being covered in a white gauze, like ridges of distant mountains. In the gorges between the cows' spine ridges, more snow was gathering, but the animals calmly went on grazing. Their calm unfurled in every direction around us. Bomchyk and I were sitting on folding chairs nearby, under a shared daisy-patterned oilcloth, which had covered the table in the summer kitchen until recently. We delighted in the idyll.

———

"SO WHY DID Grandpa Bomchyk get so fat?" my mom suddenly asked. She never liked Bomchyk all that much because she considered him unserious. Grandpa was indeed prone to poking fun often and at everyone, including at her, saying that a "bride is a thorn in the side." My mom never did forgive her father-in-law that phrase.

"Because he began to eat a lot," my father said.

But that was only a half-truth.

Before he began eating, Bomchyk used to laugh a lot.

He used to laugh so loudly that sometimes even the windowpanes in his little house would jingle. He had built the home with his own bare hands, back in the 1950s, the same year that a collective farm was established in his village. When Bomchyk laughed outside, all the neighborhood dogs would howl in accompaniment and the chickens would cluck louder than usual. Whether inside or outside, he wasn't embarrassed to open his toothless mouth wide when laughing; his plastic teeth spent most of their time warming in a mug on the windowsill of his summer kitchen. The kitchen was a stand-alone structure, with a clay floor, which he had also built himself. On the light blue windowsill, a strange red clock tick-tocked next to the teeth. It showed what I as a child understood to be the strange local time: depending on the season, time in Grandpa Bomchyk's village differed from conventional time. In the winter, I knew that half past eleven really meant half past one. In the summer, at four p.m.—which was five p.m. to the rest of Ukraine—Grandpa Bomchyk, laughing, would drive out the cattle (sometimes he also had goats, and even had a sheep once), leaving a few hryvnias on the windowsill for me to go buy myself an ice cream and a pack of Vatra cigarettes for him.

We spent one summer and one winter living together, just the two of us, and those were the happiest times of my life. I laughed along with Bomchyk. The locals called me Bomchykova, as if I "belonged to Bomchyk."

My grandfather naturally earned his nickname Bomchyk, "the Jingler," because of his endless jokes and tall tales. He tossed them around whenever he had the chance, casually, effortlessly, lightly, as if jingling a small bell that was always in his pocket. He was always kidding: to me, as a child, it felt like he never spoke the truth. But maybe there was no truth; maybe truth didn't even exist. I inherited my distrust toward everything that others deem to be true from him.

"WE'LL STOP BY in a week," my parents said, concluding their visit. They packed up the empty jars unceremoniously and walked out into the corridor arm in arm. I always made a mental note whenever they touched each other. For me, these touches signified tenderness and a contented trust. In my mind, they also denoted security, maybe because I regarded their mutual love as proof of their love for me. There were years, however, when my parents didn't touch at all and even avoided looking at each other. Maybe those were the years that I felt most lost.

Once on the stairs, my mom called out matter-of-factly, "I'll go ahead and call Nina."

The door closed, and the apartment once more sank into silence. I was alone with myself again.

To entertain myself, I remembered that once upon a time I had wanted to learn the Chinese martial art of kung fu. So I looked for lessons online. I placed my laptop on a table and clumsily repeated the simplest exercises in the middle of the room at the instruction of the teacher.

Actually, I wasn't the one who had wanted to learn kung fu; my father had wanted me to. He considered himself to be a kung fu master, even though he was one of those self-taught people who, in the late eighties, subscribed to Soviet magazines like *Technique of the Young* or *Martial Arts of the Planet* and met up to spar with friends in the district gyms that reeked thoroughly of men's sweat. I say "men's sweat" because, to the best of my knowledge, I was the only female to ever set foot in there.

My mom worked the night shift when I was little, so my father would drag me with him. We walked, two "kung fuists"—a kung fu master and the daughter of a kung fu master—with hands clasped, down evening streets, one tall and the other little, the tall one moving fast and the little one having to trot along. These are unusually fond memories for me now. We've never walked with such intimacy since.

The gym consisted of many rooms. The largest was completely lined with mats, and another one had exercise machines and thick ropes hanging from the ceiling. This second room smelled not only of sweat but also of rubber and iron. In the third room, which would be opened especially for me so that I wouldn't get in the way, there lived a piano (possibly for rhythmic gymnastics classes for the nonexistent females). I plunked on it while the men beat each other up. My father accidentally broke an opponent's leg one time, an arm another time. He himself had his nose broken once and toes broken twice. He was always bandaged up, or bruised, or limping with dislocated joints and sprained tendons.

Bomchyk would laugh at him.

"Look, by the time you get the hang of this kung fu stuff, you'll be in no shape to fight anymore. You look like minced meat."

My father was thin. Bomchyk was fat by then. Bomchyk never bothered with his body. His generation just didn't find it necessary. He worked hard, and when he wasn't working, he was sitting under the walnut tree and smoking, and when he wasn't sitting, he was lying in his tiny bedroom, listening to the radio. He called his tiny bedroom a hut, while the other two rooms in that house of his that he had built with his own hands were known as the big room and the new room. Grandpa Bomchyk's unexercised body served as a receptacle for the accumulation of unutilized laughter, which is why, over the years, as the reasons for laughter grew fewer and fewer, his body began to increase in size. It simply swelled from a surplus of giggles that had yet to come out.

IN A SIDEBOARD in the new room, Grandpa Bomchyk kept a small decorative box with what he considered his "valuable papers"—his passport, his military ID booklet, his pension certificate, his cow record books (which noted when each cow had been with a bull, when it was supposed to calve, when it calved), and two Orders of Lenin. The Orders of Lenin had been awarded by the government of the USSR for outstanding service in building socialism—namely, for meritorious work at the Lenin Collective Farm, the one established in his village the same year he was building his house with his bare hands. This decorative box always allured me, even though as a child I already understood that something was off about it. Now I know what exactly it was: valuable papers for normal people would've been, at the very least, documents for land, for a house, for some sort of property. But Grandpa Bomchyk didn't have those kinds of papers because he never had anything of his own. The fields on which he had spent his whole life toiling weren't his; the clover that he mowed every morning wasn't either. Even the house that he had built with his bare hands didn't belong to him. In the nineties, when private ownership returned to Ukraine, Bomchyk could have privatized his house and lands—it would've cost him almost nothing, and he would have finally had proper "valuable papers"—but such a prospect no longer tempted him. A military ID booklet and Orders of Lenin in a decorative box somehow sufficed.

The strangest thing was that Bomchyk was never actually in

the army. During World War II, when Halychyna was occupied by German forces in 1941, he was still considered too young. His older brother joined the SS; he'd send photographs from the barracks where they were being drilled but didn't sign them because he was illiterate. Grandpa Bomchyk also kept one of those photographs in his decorative box. On it, some sub-unit of the division is lined up against the backdrop of a nicely decorated New Year tree, all the soldiers smiling, though the overcoats and helmets issued to some are clearly too big and they were drowning in their uniforms. The new year of 1944, which the young men from Halychyna were so joyously welcoming in the photograph, wasn't a fortunate one for them. In six months, all of them, together with my grandpa's older brother, would be killed by the Soviet Army near Brody, just east of Lviv.

When Soviet rule arrived to stay later that year, Bomchyk had just turned eighteen. While meeting with the commission that was supposed to determine his physical readiness and send him to the army, he played the part of the village idiot: he shook his hand under the doctors' noses, saying, "Oh my goodness, I have a hand! Can you see, it's a hand! I have a hand! Look!" The hoax worked, and the dummy was rejected by the army and instead sent off to Chelyabinsk in west-central Russia for six years to work in a foundry. There, Bomchyk melted down church bells collected and transported from across the Soviet Union into weapons. Meanwhile, his old friends back home in Halychyna ran off to join the Ukrainian insurgents and roved about the surrounding forests until the last of them were found and shot. A collective farm was established in his home village; people had their land and livestock confiscated, then were forced to work for free and routinely hand over meat, eggs, and milk from their personal households to the state. Life quieted down.

"In Chelyabinsk," Bomchyk would tell the drivers of the collective farm's trucks and machinery once he had returned back home, "I bathed three times a day in a tub of gold."

"And here, it's once a day in a tub of manure!" The drivers would laugh, and Bomchyk would laugh too. He cleaned the collective farm's stables before getting upgraded to a driver.

WHAT I LOVED most when living with him was waking up— one of those desires that you grow out of with age. I would be woken by the pleasantly noisy and unceremonious tumult of the living world. Before even opening my eyes, I'd discern the buzzing of flies under the hanging light. Wasps and bees that had accidentally flown into the room buzzed differently, menacingly; that kind of buzzing made sleep restless. Hens, in anticipation of a laid egg, would settle in on the concrete right under the window and purr lazily, while those that had just laid an egg clucked like mad. Bumblebees hummed in the thicket of grapes against the neighbor's fence, and turtledoves cooed in a frenzy from the tops of utility poles. I'd also listen to the wooden winch creak and the aluminum bucket hit the cool water with a jangle when Grandpa Bomchyk drew water from the well. A gusty wind from beyond the village would strike against the old gate, cobbled together out of planks and greened from age, which led to the garden and the outhouse.

When my parents would come to visit, I'd wake up to the clanking of dishes in the summer kitchen and the knocking of five-liter bottles that my mom had already washed with baking soda and nettles, getting ready to fill the bottoms with horseradish, garlic, dill, and currant and cherry leaves, then stuff with cucumbers for pickling. The cucumbers would just then be soaking in a large wash tub to release their bitterness. My father, meanwhile, would have already gone walking barefoot in the morning dew and, by then, would be doing tai chi in the yard or twirling a huge "fighting stick" in his hands, tapping on my window with it so that the "kung fu master's daughter" would finally get up.

"You'll sleep through the whole day," he'd holler, and Grandpa Bomchyk, who'd filled up on sour milk pastries by then and was sitting under the walnut tree smoking, would chuckle. "Jeez, stop waving that stick around. You're making my head spin! Enough!"

My father had an insatiable need to know how to defend himself. Grandpa Bomchyk had no such need, even though he was the one who had had the opportunity to take up arms. But his real battle in life he lost for the simple reason that he never engaged in it.

WHEN BOMCHYK RETURNED from Chelyabinsk, in the grove where we would later graze cows together, a few of his insurgent friends were still hiding in an improvised bunker. The collective farm was already operating. One by one, the people had their land and livestock taken away, even their wooden threshing barns. (I've always wondered: *How can you take a barn from a person and drag it from one place to another intact? It's not like it's a matchbox.* Many years later, people would walk around the grounds of collective farms throughout Ukraine, pointing: "That was my barn." "And that one was mine.") The wealthier villagers were deported to Siberia in train wagons; others simply disappeared, and no one asked what had happened to them.

Bomchyk obediently handed over everything that was demanded of him. During the day, he cleaned out the collective-farm stables, and in the evenings and on weekends, he built his own home for his future family, just across the street from the home he had grown up in.

One night, the insurgent friends came by to ask for some food and clothes. They were whispering to him from outside, urging him to join them, insisting that the liberation cause wasn't dead yet, but Bomchyk was fast asleep, a chicken-down comforter pulled up past his ears, and didn't hear anything. He'd tell me later, "Sparrows would sometimes fly over to chirp under the eaves, but whoever followed their song was as good as dead."

The friends stopped coming by. Till the end, Grandpa Bomchyk was convinced that he had done the right thing. Between a slavish existence and a heroic death, he chose the former, and only thanks to this choice did I become possible.

The NKVD, the People's Commissariat for Internal Affairs infamous for terrorizing the local population, discovered the insurgents' bunker a few days before the Pentecost holiday in late spring. After a short shoot-out, which everyone in the village heard, the bloody bodies of the insurgents were piled onto a cart next to the dairy and kept in plain sight for two weeks—as a lesson to others. The local women, as they carried their still-warm, freshly drawn milk to the dairy before dawn, hung their heads low and, holding their breath, quickly scurried past. Among those women was Bomchyk's future wife. If she had had more courage, if she had admitted that her uncle was lying on the cart, if she had gone up to wipe the blood off his brow and close his eyes, I wouldn't exist.

I'm the offspring of meekness in the face of power and fear in the face of death.

And the price that had been paid to survive fell on my shoulders. Through the generations, considerable interest had accrued. Little by little, I had to start paying off my debts.

MY DESIRE TO EAT was overwhelming. I calculated the distance to the nearest grocery store—five hundred meters. That distance could be covered in a matter of minutes. I just needed to leave my apartment, and then the building, walk along the sidewalk, then cross a little road and a little public garden with fruit trees (who plants apple and cherry trees in a city, and why?), and then I'd be there. I'd slip into the supermarket's refrigerated coolness, past the artificially selected Spanish tomatoes and frozen chicken thighs, buy some bread and oatcakes, buy pasta, buy anything and everything, then go back home the same way.

"Come on, you can do it," I told myself.

I got dressed and ran out of the apartment. Then out of the building. I even took a few brave steps on the sidewalk, until my heart began to leap out of its nest in my chest and my head started spinning. The blue sky dangled beneath my feet. I pressed my back against the concrete wall and squatted down on the sidewalk. I covered my face with my hands to avoid seeing the passersby gawking in my direction. Inhale–exhale. I let out a loud laugh. What I was feeling was shame and powerlessness. The same things that were hiding behind Bomchyk's laughter. The same things my father was trying to distract himself from by practicing kung fu. The battle was lost the moment the decision was made to never engage in it. That's why I couldn't even call this defeat; it was something more humiliating than that. It was dishonor.

I'd stand up, take two steps, then squat, huddling against the wall to wait out the fear, which felt violent and insurmountable. My first visit to the store—five hundred meters—took up an entire day. I also needed to squat in the store a number of times. But I stocked up on everything. It was the middle of August. When I finally got back home, it was dusking. I ate and laughed, and ate and laughed.

XVII.

DAYS LIKE TEARS

(Him)

"ON THE DUNG HEAPS of Europe, we wriggle like worms," wrote the poet Oles (private address: Singerstraße 1, 1st District), whom the Ukrainian community knew only as the poet Oles, even though that wasn't his real name. "The poet Oles arrived in Vienna recently," Ukrainian newspapers reported when he moved there in 1920, as if informing about some minister or general. The poet Oles was a star of Ukrainian literature, and the fact that he had spent his entire preceding life working in a slaughterhouse on the outskirts of Kyiv in no way tarnished his reputation. Days amid meat and blood, and evenings amid friends, strolling in an elegant white suit. He wrote poetry in the impressionistic style, typically on amorous and patriotic topics.

While living in Vienna, the poet Oles was one of the creators of the Union of Ukrainian Journalists and Writers, which, in turn, initiated the establishment of the Ukrainian Free University in January 1921. For the first winter semester, over seven hundred students enrolled, including forty-two women. The poet Oles also published the literary periodical *Na Perelomi* (*On the Cusp*). He could be found most often sitting at the parliamentary café.

"HAVE YOU HEARD?" the poet Oles asked Andrii Zhuk, whose wife, together with the Ukrainian Women's Union, had founded a Ukrainian elementary school in Vienna at Josefstädter Straße 79.

"Have I heard what?" responded the short and sprightly Andrii Zhuk, an earnest socialist and close friend of Lypynskyi's, whom the latter never did manage to "unconvince" of his leftist ideas. "There's so much information these days that a man feels like a crayfish on ice. There's no knowing who to believe."

"The English press is writing that in one of the central governorates of Russia, the local Council of Deputies has approved the erection of a monument to Judas Iscariot. The monument is meant to show that any and all prejudices are alien to the Bolsheviks."

They sat in silence for a moment.

"And I heard," Zhuk piped up, "that the Bolsheviks will hang on in Ukraine for at most another year or two. The peasants despise them and are revolting en masse. In a year or two, there'll be a new attempt to establish a Ukrainian state. No one has any doubts about that."

"Under whose leadership?" asked Osyp Nazaruk, pulling up a chair. A skilled and cunning lawyer from Halychyna, Nazaruk described himself as "a brute made of inlay," supported himself in exile by writing, and most feared dying of hunger, hence why he always ate a lot and with gusto. "Who is capable of heading a new Ukrainian state right now? Petliura discredited himself once and for all with his alliance with Poland. The people of Halychyna will never forgive him that; they refer to him as nothing other than Warsaw trash."

"And the people of Halychyna can be called the mud of Moscow themselves. After all, they didn't see anything disgraceful in crossing to the side of Denikin's Russian Volunteer Army to restore Russia's 'prison of nations,' as Lenin put it.'" The burly and influential Yevhen Chykalenko had come for the day from Baden in Lower Austria, where he and his young wife had of late been making ends meet on one thousand kronen a day. All of his property, money, and sway had been left behind in Kyiv.

"Lypynskyi," Chykalenko shared excitedly, "has thought up this repugnant scheme with Hetman Skoropadskyi, who has now settled down in Berlin. They want to restore the monarchy in Ukraine. They founded a Union of Agrarian-Statists and are publishing some little monarchist newspaper. Pshaw! Filth and scum!"

Chykalenko spit on the ground in disgust, the bitterness of his saliva reminding him of his growing health problems. "I once considered Lypynskyi the most intelligent man in Ukraine, but I see that I was wrong. Prudence doesn't protect against folly. At a time when embittered people the world over are toppling monarchs, how is it possible to wish a monarch for Ukraine? And Skoropadskyi, that degenerate, disgraced himself completely when he was in power. There were barely any Ukrainians in his government. His Hetmanate was chock-full of Russian-speakers and Tsarists."

"Weren't you, Yevhen Kharlampiovych, offered a ministerial position?"

"I was even offered the hetmanship but declined because I value my reputation."

"Allow me to treat the esteemed company to some white wine!" Osyp Nazaruk interjected, already holding a half-liter carafe of Grüner Veltliner in his hands. As he poured the beverage into glasses, he threw in, almost as an aside, "The government of Halychyna, with my assistance, commissioned Lypynskyi to write a short history of Ukraine for schools. The honorarium's already been paid. Lypynskyi was very much in need of it because he's sending every kopiyka to his wife and daughter in Kraków. That's why, rumor has it, he drinks so much."

The heads of those present looked up with interest. Nazaruk paused for a moment, relishing the attention he had gleaned, then continued solemnly: "There's even a joke going around: when Lypynskyi drinks, at first he sticks to being Ukrainian, then he presents himself as a Russian officer, and when he gets fully drunk, he cries loudly in Polish, 'I'm an honorable member of the *szlachta*!' "

A bashful chuckle rolled round the table. Nazaruk concluded: "I'm telling you this, and it's the truth, but if you name me as the source, I'll swear that I never said such a thing."

Yevhen Chykalenko *hmph*ed and turned away. In reality, he couldn't stand this unprincipled featherbrain. Nazaruk had managed to work for all the Ukrainian governments and was now planning to move to America, where he would no doubt swindle money out of the Ukrainians there for the liberation of Halychyna.

"The Poles in Halychyna are being ferocious," Zhuk remarked in order to change the topic of conversation. "In Stanislaviv, anyone who leaves the house without a Polish cockade gets beaten in the streets. A pregnant woman was shot in the leg for it by a soldier. The poor woman was brought to a hospital, where the doctors amputated that leg, which then caused the woman to give birth. She shrieked nonstop through the whole ordeal."

"You're telling horror stories," the poet Oles said with a dismissive wave. He was sensitive to gory images. "How does Baden suit you, Yevhen Kharlampiovych?"

"We're staying in a hotel without heating and can't find another place to live, that's how. And it stinks of sulfur there because it's a health resort. Food is very difficult to come by, and you can only buy milk with a doctor's prescription. We're looking to move somewhere else."

"They say that Czechia is the most comfortable right now."

"Who says that? I just came from there. Austria is the cheapest—cheaper than Prague or Berlin."

They sat in silence for a moment.

"Please don't tell Pisniachevskyi or any of his people that I was here," Chykalenko began to speak in a lowered voice. "Or he'll write in his weekly paper again, 'The old Ukrainian intellectual Chykalenko, my teacher in life, came to visit us once more.' He advertises his closeness to me everywhere, even though I never considered him close during our *Rada* days and even described him as a dangerous and dubious man. Pisniachevskyi once tried to demonstrate the worthlessness of the Ukrainian national movement in a Russian newspaper by describing it as a dumpling-and-hearth movement. Even now he's defaming everyone left and right in *Volia*, that newspaper of his. For him, everyone's a corrupt thief, whether justified or not."

"It's clear that Pisniachevskyi is a doctor by profession," the poet Oles said with a laugh. "He cuts open the abscess of our citizenry with a pen, as if with a scalpel. And when an abscess is cut open, it always reeks, isn't that right? All of our embassies and missions have stolen as much government money as they could. Without any benefit at all for the Ukrainian state."

Chykalenko sighed: "God gave us a great moment but didn't give us any great people. Our intelligentsia has displayed all kinds of nastiness and analphabetism, which attests to its political infancy. A new generation must grow up."

"Pisniachevskyi," Nazaruk chimed in, somewhat belatedly because he was just swallowing a last bite of breaded zucchini, "more than once attacked Mr. Vasylko, an authorized representative of the UPR's government-in-exile, in his weekly, alleging that he was using his own funds to finance Ukrainian institutions abroad on credit, in hopes of profiting from it in the future. Vasylko, in response, placed a biting communiqué in the journal *Trybuna*, in which he wrote that Pisniachevskyi had on more than one occasion solicited such funding himself but had been unsuccessful. And that's why he was kicking up a storm in his newspaper. When he read that, Pisniachevskyi got so angry that he showed up at the embassy and beat Mr. Vasylko with a cane."

"We've lived to see the day!" Zhuk and Chykalenko exclaimed in unison. "Before, editors would get beaten, and now an editor is the one doing the beating."

Nazaruk repeated his warning, just in case: "If you name me as the source, I'll swear . . ." The plate with the zucchini had emptied, and he was looking over at the waiter, deciding whether to order another portion. "Here in Austria, they'll bread and fry anything. Whether it's zucchini or a severed hand . . . Off into the oil! And it tastes good too!"

Chykalenko rose up from the table; the last train to Baden was leaving in an hour. He reached for his wallet, but the poet Oles stopped him. "Leave it, we'll pay for everything, Yevhen Kharlam-piovych. You've paid enough in your life."

Chykalenko thanked him and walked out of the parliamentary café into the street. It was cold. He buttoned up his jacket so that no one would see that there was another, thinner jacket underneath it. Chykalenko was spending his second emigrant winter already like that, wearing two jackets. It's good that the winters were mild here and he had been able to sell his father's mink coat with the beaver collar. He got two hundred fifty thousand for it. Chykalenko was hoping to live off this money for the coming year.

"RUSSIAN BOLSHEVISM," CHYKALENKO wrote in his diaries, "is supernatural and won't be able to adapt to life, which is why it will fail. But it will be replaced by some other Moscow power, and to us they're all the same . . . A slave nation will never liberate itself unless someone foreign forces it to do so, some German or English prince with an army."

And when he had to undergo surgery, he wrote, "For some reason, they didn't cut out my stomach ulcer, just made a new egress. I fear that they tortured me needlessly on the operating table for four hours. I heard everything, felt everything, even though I was under a light anesthetic, and I kept begging them to let me die because I didn't have the strength to endure it. It wasn't until toward the end that they put a mask with chloroform on me."

Chykalenko kept diaries scrupulously ever since learning to write. Right before fleeing Kyiv, he stashed several thick notebooks in a hiding place and was now very much regretting it because there was no news from home ("It seems as though even a bird won't be able to fly over to us from that land of blood, death, violence, and horror"), but he was afraid to reach out himself so as not to expose his sons, who had refused to emigrate, to danger. It was unknown whether those notebooks had been burned already, whether the house on Mariinsko-Blahovishchenska Street had been ransacked, whether his sons were still alive. Right then the notebooks would have come in handy for Chykalenko, for the Ukrainian newspaper *Svoboda* in America had commissioned his memoirs and promised a large fee.

"IF THEY DON'T swindle me and actually pay, it'll be enough for a few years," Chykalenko bragged to the two men who had come to visit him at the Rudolf Hospital at Boerhaavegasse 8 in Vienna at the exact same time, without having planned to.

It was December 1922.

One man was Lypynskyi; the other was Pisniachevskyi, the editor of *Volia*.

Chykalenko would later write in his diary: "Lypynskyi has lost even more weight; his eyes are sunken and have acquired a strange expression. If I had run into him on the street, I wouldn't have recognized him, all the more so because he's grown a beard."

"Where have you been hiding, dear Viacheslav?" Chykalenko barely whispered, sprawled out on his bed. Tubes were sticking out of his body in all directions, one of them out of a particularly humiliating spot. "Everyone keeps asking, where did Lypynskyi disappear to?"

"I've withdrawn, Yevhen Kharlampiovych, because I fundamentally disagree with what's taking place. I live in Reichenau—an hour and a half from Vienna by express train. It's a mountainous area. Once you're better, be sure to come and visit."

"You see that they've cut me up like a pig. First they found an ulcer in my stomach, and then they had to operate on my urinary tract. A growth blocked urine from exiting my bladder, and they had to cut me open to scrape it out. And worst of all, I'll have to lie like this for a month longer with a tube in my bladder until it grows back together inside. What a disaster! And Pisniachevskyi, look, is sitting and rubbing his hands because he already knows what he'll write about in his little newspaper!"

Pisniachevskyi was indeed rubbing his hands, whether from cold or nervous excitement.

"You don't like me, Yevhen Kharlampiovych, even though I respect you the most out of today's intelligentsia and generally regard you as my teacher in life."

Chykalenko grunted in displeasure and flopped over in his bed.

"I don't even have anywhere to write for anymore," Pisniachevskyi added, crushed. "I had to shut down *Volia* because the print shop sued me for debts. I barely settled up with my employees. I think I'll go back to my medical practice."

The entire time, his eyes kept darting in different directions; Pisniachevskyi was continuously looking around as if afraid that someone would burst into the hospital room any second and shoot everyone who happened to be there. He kept his head low, ready to jump under the bed to hide if need be. At his feet he had a small valise, the kind used to travel out of the city for a few days' rest.

Chykalenko said, "And I kept looking for an opportunity to quarrel with you, Lypynskyi, because you did a very foolish thing with your new political views. The hetmanship, Skoropadskyi— why are you embarrassing yourself like that? That political idea is dead and will be of no benefit to anyone."

Lypynskyi tensed up. In December of the preceding year, he had formed the Ukrainian Union of Agrarian-Statists with a few like-minded colleagues in his own home, which was supposed to unite the dispersed Ukrainian monarchists and proclaim Pavlo Skoropadskyi the hetman of Ukraine again. Lypynskyi himself became the chairman of the Council of Jurors. He began to print his theory of monarchy in the pro-hetman volume *Khliborobska Ukraina* (*Agrarian Ukraine*) under the sentimental title *Letters to My Agrarian Brethren*, where he outlined the main reasons for the defeat of the liberation movement and a strategy for the future fight. Ukrainians had lost because they lacked "an idea of, a belief in, and a legend about a single free and independent Ukraine that unified all Ukrainians." Prone to a revolutionary impulse, they were always fighting *against* something (against Poland, Russia, landowners, Bolsheviks, Hetmanites), and not *for* something. They were driven by hatred toward their enemies, and not by love of their own land and a desire to build an independent state on it. They lacked a "unifying" idea. By using traditional Ukrainian statehood—of which the Cossack Hetmanate of the seventeenth and eighteenth centuries was the only example in the history of the Ukrainian people—as a theoretical basis, such an idea could be created. Accordingly, the candidacy of Pavlo Skoropadskyi, the only living descendant of a hetman, was self-evident for Lypynskyi.

"I read your attack on me, Yevhen Kharlampiovych." As he spoke, Lypynskyi glanced distrustfully at the journalist opposite him, whose presence next to the patient's bedside he, like the patient himself, didn't like much. "But I think that the main difference in our views lies not in Hetman Skoropadskyi but in our understanding of Ukraine's future. You don't believe in current leaders, in Petliura or Skoropadskyi, and are positive that the current generation has already done what it can and isn't worth anything more; someday better ones will come and do everything. But I don't believe in that because I don't see the preconditions for succeeding generations to produce better Petliury or Skoropadski. An honest and intelligent Ukrainian can only be someone who doesn't engage in politics. Therefore, it is understood that everyone who's honest and intelligent must withdraw from it. But can a Ukrainian nation and a Ukrainian state be created by thrill seekers and tricksters alone? I doubt it! That's why I decided to work with those who were available, making use of the lessons learned by previous generations. I don't know if the path I've chosen is the right one. Maybe it would've been better to swap out politics for archaeology earlier in my career. At least then I would have been able to die peacefully, not covered in spit and the butt of jokes for Pisniachevskyi-types . . ."

Lypynskyi bit his tongue, but Pisniachevskyi, it seemed, hadn't heard the last sentence. "I'll be back in a second," the journalist said, then jumped to his feet and ran out into the hallway.

Apart from the uncommunicative patients recovering from recent operations on the neighboring beds, Chykalenko and Lypynskyi were left alone in the room. Lypynskyi was all aglow, riled by the unanticipated speech. For a long time now, he hadn't participated in live discussions and had relegated communication with the outside world to the plane of written correspondence. He lived in Reichenau as a recluse, barely ever venturing to Vienna.

But Chykalenko, instead of saying something in response, kept persistently glancing at the valise that Pisniachevskyi had come with.

"Go ahead and open it," he enjoined Lypynskyi, who didn't at first understand what was being asked of him.

"Don't be scared, open it. We aren't strangers. That valise under the chair over there. Open it."

"What for? What if he comes back?"

"Open it!"

Lypynskyi timidly snapped open the latch. The valise opened just enough for its contents to be visible. A passport and some official documents tied with a ribbon, a few issues of *Volia*, some clean men's undergarments, toothpaste powder, and spare shoes.

"I knew it," Chykalenko groaned. "This one's gone mad too. He's getting ready to flee because he thinks the Bolsheviks are looking for him and want to kill him. I'd been told as much, but I didn't believe that such a sharp mind could be clouded by the fear of persecution."

Lypynskyi shut the suitcase.

They sat in silence for a moment.

"You must be sorry about your possessions, Yevhen Kharlampiovych. You've lost so much. My estate also got burned down and sometimes, to be honest, I take great offense at all the people who let themselves be duped so easily. They naïvely believed that the Bolsheviks would confiscate the property of us landowners and just hand it over to them. Far from it. They say that there's a terrible famine in the southern governorates."

"My dear Viacheslav, I lived in the Russian Empire through old age, and in those sixty years, I got to know it so intimately and grew to hate it so much that I'd rather not have any property there, even if that means never setting foot again in my dear Ukraine. I lived in that cursed empire like in a prison, and I don't want to anymore. These days, I work on my memoirs and chop wood. I haven't lost anyone close to me, I haven't yet lost my sanity, and that's enough."

INDEED, CHYKALENKO'S SANITY would remain with him until the end of his emigrant days, in 1929, though he would first end up losing his young wife and his favorite son, one after another. He would admit to Lypynskyi that, till then, there had never been a happier man than him: he had safely survived the war and ten years of revolution, while many of his acquaintances were losing their children. It was only now that misfortune after misfortune was finally crashing down on him. "Petro died on the way to exile, and Ivashko appears to have been arrested as well. And my bladder refuses to function properly; I have to relieve myself all the time."

"Enough!" Chykalenko would write in his final letter to Lypynskyi. "I've had my fill of suffering as an émigré, both physically and emotionally. I'm terrified to go on living. When I go to bed, every day I ask God for death . . . From the bottom of my heart, dear Viacheslav, I wish that you outlive me."

That wish would come true.

And Pisniachevskyi would go down into the ground in Bratislava, forgotten by everyone, even the Bolsheviks, though he never would part with the valise prepared in the event of a sudden escape.

"This name hasn't been heard in some ten years," his former rivals from *Svoboda* would write in a 1933 obituary. "Even the older generation has begun to forget him, and the younger one doesn't know of him at all. That notwithstanding, Viktor Pisniachevskyi was, after Yevhen Chykalenko, the most notable Ukrainian news editor."

Around that time, the poet Oles would begin his next poem with the line, "In exile, days flow like tears."

XVIII.

THE KNIGHT OF DARKNESS

(Me)

AS YEARS PASSED, I seemed to have less and less innate freedom left. I had been born with a big orb inside me, filled with freedom, like gas, but gradually my inborn supply of freedom leaked out, seeping into the surrounding expanse, and the orb began to deflate and pucker. It was impossible to replenish its contents anymore, just as it's impossible to reinflate bouncy balls that have been accidentally punctured by a splinter on the road. Over the years, I slowly transformed into a living prison, one where nothing is allowed and everything is forbidden. One sleepless night, I even jotted down in a blank document the following sentence: "Like through an interminable prison, I walk through myself." I don't know where it came from.

THE ODDEST THING was that I didn't let myself indulge in completely innocent things—like, for instance, having long hair. I would let my hair grow out to my shoulders at most, but more often than not it was very short, barely covering my ears. Twice, I shaved my head completely, and even though friends would hint that baldness doesn't suit me, for some reason I felt incredibly attractive. I would eagerly wait for the hair to grow back enough so that I could get rid of it again. My attitude toward my hair was overall disdainful. The only thing that concerned me was that it remain clean.

I also didn't let myself have pierced ears and made fun of women who wore earrings.

I didn't let myself uncork a bottle of wine just for myself. I'd open a bottle only if one of my golden-haired men was also interested in relaxing for a bit with a glass. Or if guests were coming.

I didn't let myself enjoy heights, even though as a child I had had an incredible love of heights and would often climb up to the very top of the walnut tree Grandpa Bomchyk used to smoke under. I felt at home on top of the walnut tree and knew that even if I were to fall, nothing horrible would happen. The trunk of a walnut is completely different from that of other trees. It somehow resembles the body of a massive water boa—greenish, shiny and smooth, and cool to the touch. I remember climbing up barefoot, gradually conquering its height. First I would content myself with the lowest thick branch, then I would find the courage to pull myself up to the second "story," and eventually the third. From the third branch, I could already see Grandpa's yard. From the fourth, I could see the village road, the neighboring houses, and the church on the little hill in the shade of the cemetery's pear trees. Someone had once planted a bunch of them there, and ever since the trees matured, the villagers had been forced to dig graves for their loved ones among the sprawling root systems. They would inscribe death into a pear orchard. In early autumn, the graves would grow covered in a densely woven sackcloth of little seedlings. The pears would rot, and above them clouds of wasps and bees would swarm. As a child, I knew that the cemetery-orchard was dangerous; pear trees are the worst for climbing.

———

I BARRICADED THE DOORS to our apartment's balcony with a couch, to lessen the temptation to go out onto it. The balcony doors elicited as much unease and uncertainty in me as did the front door of the apartment. I recall when I had voiced this aloud to my third golden-haired man when he was still living with me: "Balconies are actually very dangerous because no one checks them. There's no guarantee that ours won't fall when I set foot on it."

By deciding the balcony was too dangerous, I cordoned off another one of my pleasures, narrowed the expanse of my existence even more. Once upon a time, I used to love balconies very much.

"So, what, you're not going to go out on the balcony anymore?" the man asked in response.

"No."

"And what if I go out and call to you?"

"Why would you do that?"

We both knew why. The man, who had always generously shared his own internal orb of freedom with me, suddenly wanted to know what he'd receive in return. Was my love for him greater than my fear of everything else? I didn't respond, but he must have guessed my answer, since he ended up leaving.

With him gone, my typical day began with a safety check. First, before even opening my eyes, I would listen attentively through the silence for, God forbid, any extraneous noises, soft furtive footsteps, creaking of the parquet, or someone else's breathing. Next, I'd visually plunge myself into reality and survey the room, checking how firmly the windows were closed, and looking for shadows behind doors or items that had been displaced even a little. After that, I would carefully walk around my realm, peeking into nooks and crannies where some unknown person could hide, and trying the latches on the entryway and balcony doors to convince myself that they were still locked. Only then was I able to relax somewhat, even though I never really relaxed at that time. New habits kept popping up—for example, washing my hands with soap every time I touched something. At first I resisted this habit because I was aware that total loonies did things like that, but after touching a book or some other surface, my fingertips would burn with a hellish fire until I rinsed them off with water. Water became a fetish. Every evening, I'd climb into a bath for a full, final cleanse, though, before long, I'd find myself climbing back out to inspect the suspicious noises floating in from outside and conduct another safety check.

"I SPOKE WITH NINA," my mom reported over the phone one day. "And Nina's of the opinion that if you can sleep, then it's worth waiting on the pills."

Nina was that nurse at the regional psychiatric hospital and mom's neighbor.

"Nina recommended going to see a therapist. She gave the number of a friend of hers. She says that she's very good. Her name's Olia."

I wrote down the phone number but had no intention of calling. I didn't trust women named Olia and planned on becoming my own therapist. That's how one evening, while missing the golden-haired man, I convinced myself to move the couch and open the balcony doors. As I did so, I imagined telling the good news to my lost love: "I stepped out on the balcony! I did it! Now you can come back!"

My foot timorously crossed the threshold of the balcony and trembled in the air. The floor was covered in pigeon droppings, trash, and a thick layer of dust.

I'll have to wash the soles of my feet with soap later, was all I could think as I stepped into the danger zone with my bare feet. *No, it's better that I bathe entirely. It's very dirty all over here.*

I grabbed on to the railing because my head had begun to spin.

Somewhat automatically, I glanced down at the courtyard packed with cars, ballparking the distance down. My entire body turned to jelly, becoming unwieldy and resistant to my will.

Ten meters down to the ground, swept through my head. *Two seconds of flying.*

I jumped back into the apartment, horrified at my own thought (or wish?). I locked up the balcony, pushed back the couch, and only then dialed the number on the slip of paper. Olia answered immediately.

"Nina gave me your number," I said. "She works as a nurse at the regional psychiatric hospital."

"Yes."

"You offer therapy sessions?"

"Yes."

"I'd very much like to meet with you, but I'm trying to avoid leaving the house right now . . ."

"Trying to avoid or can't?"

"Can't, I guess."

"Then let's Skype."

THE RIDICULOUS THING was that Olia's office was very close to my apartment, a few minutes' walk away. Nonetheless, I never saw her in real life, only through my computer screen. She was a young pretty blonde, as I had imagined. Our meetings took place regularly, twice a week.

"So, what do you two do?" my mom would prod. "She probably gives you some sort of tests?"

"Well, last time I spent an hour crying."

"Why?" My mother's face turned steely and hostile, which was typical when she took offense.

"Because I was such a bad mother, right? Oh, what a bad mother I was. And you were all such angels."

Actually, she hadn't been a bad mother; therein lay the biggest problem. Thinking ill of her was yet another thing that I never allowed myself. When there were reasons for it and I had the urge to think negatively of her, pangs of remorse that destroyed me more than anger instantly subsumed me. If I dared to voice my disappointment in her, my mother would immediately have heart pain, and my guilt would increase even more. It was impossible to bear. I'd cry, and Olia, from what I recall, would say the following: "Tears are anger at someone else that you're scared to verbalize to them and, instead, turn on yourself."

I'd wipe my eyes and punch at the air, attempting to look aggressive.

Sometimes Olia would tell me stories about other clients of hers. This must be a generally accepted trick of pastors of the church of psychotherapy: to cheer someone up, they offer examples of souls that are even more lost. Names, obviously, aren't disclosed. Olia could've shared my own story with others roughly like this: panic attacks, doesn't leave the house, her man left her, has broken off any and all social contact. In lieu of commas, Olia would probably insert one or two words of empathy because she was overall an empathetic type. Initially, her empathy annoyed me—until I learned to relish it.

ONE OF OLIA'S PATIENTS, X, lived in a remote Carpathian village and hadn't left her little one-story wooden house for a full decade. X had no idea what was wrong with her. When she'd try to go out, she'd have a "heart attack." Paramedics showed up a few times in an ambulance, tried persuading her that she was healthy, and then eventually put the woman's telephone number on a black list and stopped answering her calls. Relatives and neighbors would make fun of her. "Why are you being such a drama queen?" they'd ask. Then those close to her grew ashamed and started viewing her not just as an embarrassment, but as some sort of curse that had been brought on the family. They beat her. They asked the priest to try to talk some sense into her. No one even thought of helping the woman, because in the part of the world she and I come from, the human head has one purpose—to eat. The head is assumed incapable of anything noteworthy beyond food consumption.

When internet was installed in the village, X, by some miracle, found Olia. Thanks to Skype, they were able to have regular therapy sessions. The woman slowly began to leave her house, and with time the radius she was capable of distancing herself from it grew. Like a dog having its leash slacked meter by meter.

"Now," Olia would tell me, "she can travel thirty kilometers from home, to the bazaar in the neighboring village. There are seventy kilometers between me and X. We need to do a little more work to be able to meet in person."

WITH THE EXAMPLE of the woman X, Olia wanted to demonstrate that the leash around my neck would be slackened too someday. That is, that I would slacken it myself. But the leash wasn't what troubled me the most. If push came to shove, I could force myself out for therapy sessions the way I forced myself to the store for groceries. It's just that making it to Olia's in my current state would take an inordinately long time. What truly frightened me was the irreversibility of brain processes. When the opportunity presented itself, I asked Olia if she was sure that she would be able to identify if, and the moment when, I truly lost my mind. Olia assured me that she would. She said that people like me don't lose their minds.

Her optimism and empathy did yield certain results. For example, with time, I covered the five-minute distance from my home to the grocery store in two and a half hours, as opposed to three. I began washing my hands not a thousand times a day, but nine hundred and ninety, occasionally even without soap. I washed the floor less and less often—not every day, but three or four times a week. I returned to writing and wrote a few stories, mostly about fear and funny human lunacies, for instance, about this one woman who decides to eat only potatoes because that made life simpler.

All of the stories I wrote invariably began with the words "This one woman...," "This one man...," and again "This one woman...," as if singularity and uniqueness had suddenly become exceedingly important. It no longer mattered what happened next in the story. That's probably how I personally transitioned from the "everyone" that humans conventionally subscribe to (to be a part of everyone, to be like everyone) to the extreme of "one" (I am one, how singular I am, how unique, how unknown, a one and only one).

I felt terribly lonely in my singularity. I would tell Olia about Lypynskyi, but she didn't want to listen: "Are we discussing you or some historical figure from the last century?"

"Well, this historical figure didn't have the opportunity for therapy..."

Olia treated my enthusiasm for history as an "intellectualization" of an internal conflict—namely, that I was hiding in my mind in order to not feel something strong and shameful. What, precisely, she never did say.

IT WAS JULY, I think, when I found the courage to resort to a desperate measure—to travel to Volyn Oblast to visit the Lipiński's estate in Zaturtsi. By then I already felt calmer out in the street; I was only washing the floors in my apartment once a week, like a normal person. But public transportation still scared me, all the more so since the trip to Volyn by train (trains, to be more precise) would take up an entire day. That's why I decided to travel by shared car, thinking that it would be calmer and safer with a living person. And faster, of course. I wrote to some driver through the online service BlaBlaCar. He was driving to Lutsk and called as soon as my message came in: "Not a problem, I have room, we're leaving tomorrow morning at six." I packed my backpack and spent the whole night sitting awake on the couch; I was so anxious about venturing out that far that I wouldn't have been able to sleep anyway. At exactly the appointed hour, I was waiting at the crossroads in front of my building. The day was breaking. A black car pulled up a minute later.

"I'm going to ask you to not drive too fast." That was the first thing that I declared as I climbed into the front seat next to the driver. I didn't look at the driver himself. Some young couple were already settled in back.

"So, what's fast for you?" the driver asked.

"When it's scary."

We drove, and the bright light of the morning sun flooded the car to the very brim. Hilly tracts of fields and plantation forests stretched on both sides of the road. Tiny villages, as if out of a movie, and cottages, beautiful but sometimes abandoned, flickered in the company of gardens, some well-tended but others not. The lush greenery screened the poverty. I caught myself thinking that, preoccupied with my own fears, I had forgotten how soothing and inspiring ordinary contemplation of the world around you could be. The couple in back were kissing. The driver turned on soft music.

"What's your name?" he asked.

"What does it matter?"

"I'm Oleksandr," he said, obviously wanting to chat, then fell silent and pulled on dark sunglasses. He was wearing all black and had long, thick black hair tied in a ponytail. Equally thick black eyebrows with gray streaks stuck out from above his glasses. Some sort of knight of darkness, I thought.

We made it to Lutsk, the city closest to the Lipiński family estate, without incident. I paid him without saying a word and exited in front of Hotel Ukraine. I pictured how Lypynskyi's brother

Wlodzimierz once proudly drove down this street in the city's first automobile. The residents likely flanked the road to watch.

. *Well, here I am*, I thought, *alone in a completely foreign place, who knows why and what I am hoping to find here.* The ground lurched under my feet, and, to keep it from swinging all the way up, I poked into a pizzeria for some lunch. From there, I called a taxi and finally set off for Zaturtsi, a little village thirty kilometers outside the city, where the actual manor was. My heart was pounding wildly, but not out of anxiety; maybe it pounded out of excitement at seeing and experiencing something new. Until then, I had researched Lypynskyi's life only through texts written by him and other people. We were bound together solely by words and my imagination. Now the story was becoming three-dimensional and could shatter against the real image. My excitement battled my trepidation.

THE MIDDAY SUN was intolerable. The fields and plantation forests that had seemed to radiate life early in the morning now looked parched and yellowed, covered in a blanket of dust kicked up from the road. There wasn't a single living soul around. The village languished in what felt like an unnatural silence. I got out next to a sign for the Viacheslav Lypynskyi Memorial Museum on the main road because I wanted to walk the rest of the way. I followed the sign down another road, this one straight and narrow, which was supposed to end at the estate. I imagined how, a hundred years ago, Lypynskyi had walked here just like me, or maybe ridden a horse, and the locals, busy with housework, had peered out of their yards to see who it was. Now there was no one peering; only piles of fresh cow dung attested to an inevitable human presence somewhere close by. The smell of manure had never disgusted me.

The closer I got to it, the more distinct the features of the manor house became. The home had been destroyed three times—in 1915,

1918, and 1920. The porch, supported by four columns that rose majestically above me, had fortunately remained intact each time.

First I circled around the building (you could see that it had recently been restored), then I walked inside. The large wooden door creaked ominously. A villager by the name of Petro squeezed my hand with his rough, callused palm.

"So, why are you interested in Lypynskyi?" he asked skeptically after an hour-long conversation. "For an average tourist, you know too much."

"So, tourists visit?"

"Sometimes. They come from abroad. He died elsewhere."

"But his body was later transported and buried here in Zaturtsi, no?"

Petro hesitated a bit.

"Well, yes, but the grave itself is gone. He was buried in the family vault at the Polish cemetery, over there, next to the pond, along the main road. There used to be a Polish church there once too. When the Soviets came, the church was demolished. And then a tractor driver from the collective farm—he passed away a while ago—razed the cemetery to the ground in exchange for some moonshine. The grave slabs got repurposed as flooring in the collective farm's pigsties. Until not long ago, the home we're standing in also housed animals."

"They hold animals in high regard in your village," I said for some reason. Petro seemed to catch the irony of my comment—only in the Soviet Union could pig accommodations be deemed more important than history and graves—then added something else about people who simply didn't understand "the value of that sort of thing."

"Lypynskyi was a great man," Petro continued, almost with tears in his eyes. "I have this one photograph, will you give it a look? Since you know so much, maybe you can tell me who it is."

The photograph hung on a wall in the exhibition hall. It was taken at his sister's wedding: Kazimierz and Klara Lipiński are still alive, and Uncle Rokicki, his mustache curled up, his gaze mad, is standing to the left of the happy bride. Lypynskyi himself was still at military training at the time.

"This one over here—do you know who he is?" Petro pointed at a stately bald-headed man in an overcoat with a white collar, sitting in the first row of wedding guests. He looked like a government official. But I didn't know.

Instead, another photograph caught my attention. In it, Lypynskyi, older, is sitting with his brother Stanisław on a bench in a garden or park, a hat on his head, a cane in his hands. Two women are seated on either side of the brothers. The one next to Lypynskyi is in a beret; a scarf or shawl hangs down from her shoulders untied; her hands rest demurely in her lap. The woman is looking into the lens; Lypynskyi is as well. Nonetheless, you can feel that the two of them are barely stomaching the situation in which they've found themselves. The woman's expression is impenetrable, demonstratively indifferent—her jaw clenched, her lips pursed. She's no beauty at all.

"This is Kazimiera, right?" I hadn't come across pictures of her anywhere before.

Petro nodded. "I think that they're separating here. It's sometime after the war."

I WANDERED AROUND a bit in the grove surrounding the house (Petro explained that part of the Lipiński orchard had managed to be preserved), then, cutting across a sun-scorched pasture, I walked out onto the main road to catch the bus back to Lutsk. The absence of Lypynskyi's grave affected my perception in a strange way. It seemed as though his death had permeated the air. Sharp and stifling, it could be smelled, even tasted, bitter and unjust, full of distress, reproach, and blame. Deprived of a grave, his death had willfully inscribed itself into the landscape. His bones, plowed through by a tractor in exchange for a bottle of moonshine, stirred underfoot, making the ground itself frightening. How do you tread on such ground?

I waited for an hour, but no bus came. No cars stopped either. I had an overwhelming urge to run from there, to not see and not feel whatever would happen after the end of the story. I had always thought that the end meant a big nothing, a reign of black matter, deafness and blindness, a mathematical zero. But it turned out that the end can pass by imperceptibly to those of us in the story. Most of us will keep imitating life for a long time still, not realizing that what we call life is just a branch growing green on a withered tree: the tree's roots have been long dead and replaced by disparaged bones.

I started to cry and reminded myself that tears are unverbalized anger at someone else. But at whom? At the tractor driver who was merely obeying an order he had received from someone at the collective farm? At the peasants who just stood and watched, not understanding "the value of that sort of thing"? At the party members who gave the instructions, adhering to the Soviet policy of destroying harmful history, the policy of lobotomizing memory? Or, perhaps, at my own grandfathers and grandmothers, great-grandfathers and great-grandmothers, who proved too weak to resist this lobotomy? Who was to blame? Who should I be angry at?

In desperation, I dialed the most recent number in my phone. A harsh male voice responded, and, swallowing tears, I unloaded everything in one fell swoop: "Oleksandr, I'm the one that drove to Lutsk with you this morning. I'm sorry that I didn't introduce myself. It was so stupid of me. It's just that I'm broken, you see, something's off with my head, I'm very scared of everything, and I've gotten stuck here on the main road in this village. If you're still in the area, come and pick me up, please. I'll pay whatever you ask. Just come and pick me up."

I think I kept rattling on, but I remember that when I stopped, there was an exhausting silence on the phone. It lasted for an eternity. I even thought that the man had hung up as soon as he realized who it was. But he finally spoke up: "Fine, I'll come. But you calm down, okay? Go sit in a coffee shop . . ."

"There are no coffee shops here."

"Then breathe. Inhale through one nostril, then exhale through the other."

"Those kinds of gimmicks don't help me."

"Then just lie down on the ground and relax."

"The ground here is frightening, I'll stand."

"Okay, then, stand."

I don't know why he agreed to come. But the knowledge of an impending rescue made me feel better. I wiped my tears and hid in the shade beneath the willows so as not to get sunburned. The knight of darkness rescued me from there half an hour later—in his black car, with his black hair, in his black sunglasses and T-shirt. After the predominance of light blue and gold colors in my life, he was soothing. For the first time, I didn't recognize my own likeness in the person facing me.

"Thank you for saving me," I said, settling into the front seat.

The driver shrugged and accelerated. We drove very fast, but it wasn't scary.

XIX.

THE SANS DIET

(Him)

"THIS IS THE REGIMEN: you *can't* consume salt, all manner of canned goods, sausage, *salo*, vinegar, Maggi seasoning, or vodka.

"You *can* consume, but in limited quantities, meat (at most three hundred grams per week), fresh fish, black pepper, beer, coffee, and tea (with just enough milk to color it, no more).

"You *can* consume milk (up to one and a half liters per day) and all other dairy products, provided they're unsalted. Eat as much produce as possible too. All baked goods must be without salt, including bread. Eggs, sugar, and honey are allowed.

"In lieu of salt, use garlic, onions, mint, bay leaves, horseradishes, lemons, marjoram, parsley, and other root herbs."

This "sans diet" distracted and protected Lypynskyi from his memories. Solitude became his everyday norm; illnesses became his escape from the life that had dealt him a crushing defeat. Being ill meant being preoccupied, which, in turn, meant feeling less. The pain his body suffered soothed his incorporeal pain—the one that was a hundredfold harder to endure.

Lypynskyi went into hiding in the foothills of the Alps, in the resort town of Reichenau, where he survived on the twenty dollars that his brother sent him monthly from Zaturtsi. Mountains were the favorite domicile of tubercular consumptives. Sometimes the payments were delayed because Stanisław didn't have enough for himself or the harvest was poor. Then Lypynskyi would tighten his belt even more and feverishly work on his *Letters to My Agrarian Brethren*, viewing writing as the only means by which he could potentially earn money. Physical work was no longer an option for him.

CONTRARY TO POPULAR HOPES, Bolshevism persisted in Ukraine and had no intention of caving; the much-awaited "breathing space" that its demise would have brought was a long time in coming. Meanwhile, Eastern Halychyna was definitively subsumed by Poland. Those who had once been great became nobodies. Conversations died out, plans were wrecked, money ran out, and newspapers shut down. Of the Viennese newspapers, the socialist *Nova Hromada* (*New Community*), which the Bolsheviks continued to finance through 1925 for propaganda purposes, survived the longest. But there was no one left to read it. Through the irony of fate, the newspaper's enthusiastic publisher, the ardent communist Semen Vityk, would eventually become a victim of Stalinist repressions himself, dying in a gulag labor camp.

Otaman Petliura, the military commander and former head of the UPR's Directorate, moved to Paris. There he rented a secret apartment without a kitchen in the Latin Quarter. He subsisted on eggplants and coffee, the cheapest diet he could come up with. On May 25, 1926, at 14:10, he paused next to a bookstore on the corner of Rue Racine and Boulevard Saint-Michel to look at a window display and received seven bullets from the revolver of emigrant Sholom Schwartzbard, ostensibly out of revenge for the Jewish pogroms committed by the army of the Ukrainian People's Republic. A great epoch was ending, leaving behind no traces.

The regulars' tables of Ukrainian refugees in Vienna broke up, and former ministers and military commanders scattered throughout European cities or headed overseas to North or South America. Correspondence between old friends revived only on Christmas or Easter, dying away before long for once and for all. The most courageous—or the most naïve—returned home, to the now Ukrainian SSR, which had joined the new Soviet Union as one of its original four republics in 1922. They returned home fearfully and at their own risk, and were soon shot dead by Soviet authorities for alleged membership in nonexistent counter-revolutionary organizations.

Lypynskyi had no intention of returning to Ukraine. His estate, inherited from Uncle Rokicki, had been nationalized and was no longer his, and in 1925 his uncle had also been forced to flee headlong with his wife. The Bolsheviks had swiftly confiscated his uncle's jumping horses for the needs of the revolution and were supposed to come back any day to confiscate the man himself. The only thing that is known for certain is that the Rokicki forded the Zbruch River—the border waterway between Poland and the newly formed Soviet Union—but never resurfaced abroad. The couple simply vanished. Yet another tragedy with which Lypynskyi was forced to live. His family was being rooted out, and he too was turning from a flowering plant into an unneeded weed.

EVEN THOUGH LYPYNSKYI'S manner of thought was more than rational, he transferred the question of his own purpose and the pain of political defeat onto a religious and spiritual plane, in order to save himself from self-destructive despair. He wrote in his little breast-pocket notebook that he hadn't come upon the idea of Ukrainianness himself, that it had come to him on its own, it had come from God, and if God had designated him to do this work, that meant it was necessary to his design. It wasn't for Lypynskyi's intellect to question God's design.

His daughter, who was growing up in Kraków, thought otherwise. Like Kazimiera, she couldn't forgive her father for his decision to prioritize Ukraine's independence above all else, and refused all contact with him.

"It's Kazimiera instigating her," Lypynskyi would complain to his housekeeper Fin Yulí, so enraged he trembled. Again and again, his letters to his daughter returned unopened.

Again and again, Lypynskyi's body temperature rose sharply, and he would find himself sending postcards to cancel acquaintances' visits or his own outings to Vienna, then take to his bed for several days, sometimes several weeks. Like that, lying in bed, he'd scribble off letters to some of the other four hundred people with whom he routinely corresponded.

The written correspondence of "the monarchist in Reichenau," as Lypynskyi was known now among colleagues, reached an immense scale. Barely traveling anywhere, he coordinated the entire Hetmanate movement from the foothills of the Alps. Under the influence of Lypynskyi's theoretical texts, this movement was gaining considerable popularity, particularly among Ukrainian émigrés. Supporters of the movement (the "like-minded members," as he called them) bombarded him with questions, and Lypynskyi obligingly replied to each in detail, explaining the most minute nuances of a rather complex ideological system. For as long as his secretary Tsyprianovych was able to still decipher his chicken scratch, he typed out the letters on his typewriter. These impassioned missives later passed from hand to hand or were read aloud like true sacred writings at evening gatherings of

Ukrainian émigrés as far away as Canada's Hafford or as close by as Poděbrady in Czechia.

In some respects, Lypynskyi really did behave like the leader of a new faith, demanding from his disciples obedience, self-discipline, and a complete inner rebirth. Lypynskyi ventured so far as to offer instructions in areas that were none of his business: what a hetman-follower should read, who he should be friends with, how he should dress, and what he should dream about. What made him lose his composure the most was receiving questions from hetman-supporters in envelopes bearing addresses written with mistakes. When someone forgot a diacritical marker in the name of a little-known Czech town, Lypynskyi would explode in an angry tirade, saying that those kinds of mistakes only evoke irreverence toward the person who makes them. In his responses, Lypynskyi didn't hesitate to seek pity for his health:

"Forgive my illegible writing, but I'm working lying down."

"Someday I'll ask Tsyprianovych to take a photograph of me as I'm writing a letter to you. That'll give you an idea of how I take care of my correspondence now."

"This spring [this winter/this autumn/this swelter] is simply killing me."

A BRIEF MEDICAL history of Lypynskyi would be as follows:

In 1920, he had an ocular ulceration and some sort of pleural effusion. In addition to that, he suffered from chronic fever and insomnia. He routinely broke out in sweats.

In January 1922, he fell ill with a severe flu.

In 1923, he had fits of "old age and neurasthenia." He began treatment for tuberculosis with the drugs Elmizen, produced by Dr. Wojnowski in Warsaw, and Mineralogen, from a pharmacy in Berlin. He ordered five little bottles of each in syrup form by mail, which he sedulously drank every morning on an empty stomach.

But it helped little. Lypynskyi closely monitored the latest medical discoveries and always maintained confidence that tuberculosis would be managed just like diabetes. Two Canadian doctors had just received the Nobel Prize for their discovery of insulin. But Lypynskyi wouldn't live to see the discovery of the first antibiotic effective against tuberculosis. Only in 1952 would the American Selman Waksman, an emigrant from the Kyiv area, receive the Nobel Prize for streptomycin.

Some of Lypynskyi's associates tried to intimate to the patient that his illnesses were psychological in nature. Osyp Nazaruk, the lawyer and journalist from Halychyna, who had suddenly become his closest pen pal, wrote from the United States that people like Lypynskyi were now referred to as "hypochondriacs" and were being successfully treated by means of autosuggestion. This required repeating sentences like, "I am healthy," "The disease is diminishing," and "Soon I will be completely well," throughout the day.

"Those are pretty sentences," Lypynskyi retorted exasperatedly, "but when there's a hole in your lungs right above your heart that's the size of a fist and another one on the other side that's a little bit smaller, then repeat whatever you want, it won't make the holes close up." Then, as was typical of him, he immediately apologized: "It's the illness that's made me so sharp-tongued . . . Tell me whether or not you read what I write. If not, I'll write less, but will do so more clearly."

IN 1925, LYPYNSKYI stayed at the Wienerwald Sanatorium under the care of Hugo Kraus, a pulmonologist known throughout Europe, who confirmed that Lypynskyi's lungs were very damaged, but reassured him that the tubercular process itself was *langsam*, that is, slow, and not acute, as the patient had previously thought. Lypynskyi spent all day long lying in the open air, quit all mental work, and was reviving well. It was then that an experimental method of treatment was tested on him: air was pumped into his lungs.

Lypynskyi put on three kilograms, though the intensive work on the preface to the full edition of his *Letters* quickly undid the small gains. Lypynskyi knew that this edition was his final battle, that with his personal war lost and his health steeply declining, he wouldn't be able to write anymore; perhaps that's why he pushed himself in the end. Progressive Ukrainian society was eagerly awaiting the publication of the book, in order to, famished, pounce at the expansive preface (the letters themselves had appeared earlier in periodicals), gulp it down in a matter of minutes, and, after swallowing it, hold their breath, unable to speak, and lie in wait with the presentiment of the incredible scandal that would inevitably erupt.

That same year, in 1926, another well-known book was published, namely, *Nationalism* by Dmytro Dontsov, Lypynskyi's greatest opponent since their first meeting in the Polish town of Zakopane. A historic battle took place on the pages of these two publications, *Letters to My Agrarian Brethren* and *Nationalism*—between Lypynskyi, a champion of state slogans that would unite all residents of Ukraine in the interest of their common land, and Dontsov, editor of the Lviv-based *Literary-Scientific Bulletin*, who had suddenly gone from being an extreme leftist to an extreme rightist and become an ideologue of integral Ukrainian nationalism.

Despite Lypynskyi's impassioned warnings, despite all his counterarguments and insults (in his preface he called Dontsov a skunk supreme who "sprays his internal fetid seepage on everything that stands in the way of taking advantage of Ukraine's destruction"), it would be Dontsov's book, and not Lypynskyi's, that would become the bible for the next generation of Ukrainian youth, who would flail between socialist and nationalist ideologies like between the banks of a swift mountain river onto which few manage to clamber alive.

In his *Letters*, Lypynskyi's admonishments were unsparing:

"In the foreboding that, after the destruction, the youth would turn to lofty idealism and political engagement, I begged all of you that we remain united and strong, to seize the ideological wave that approaches. This wave came, but to the detriment of Ukraine, it's being seized by nationalists because those of us who hold truth in our hands are too rotten and too individualistic to seize this wave."

"Without honor, discipline, idealism, and nobleness, which only monarchies can uphold, there's no need to even dream about an independent Ukraine. Only on the axis of the Hetmanate can Ukrainians turn away from Poland and not swing back to Moscow. Without the Hetmanate, Ukraine can only remain a thick fog. Powerless, the fog will sometimes drift east, sometimes west, depending on who's blowing on it, and you alone, the 'Ukrainians' of chaos and everlasting night, will feel comfortable in this fog."

"Don't worry, I don't belong to the same 'Ukrainian nation' as you, and I won't challenge your places in your cutthroat rivalries and pantheons."

IN 1926, LYPYNSKYI lost eleven pounds all at once. At Skoropadskyi's insistence, he relocated to Berlin, where the hetman had been living in exile for a number of years already, and accepted a position as a lecturer on the political history of Ukraine at the new Ukrainian Scientific Institute at 28 Französischen Strasse. The hetman wanted to have his maker within reach. But dealing with the maker was becoming increasingly difficult. Lypynskyi had become categorical, demanded an almost utopian morality from the Hetmanites and the hetman himself, rejected all compromises, and displayed enormous willpower, against which everyone else seemed like pusillanimous good-for-nothings. Evidently, theory was easier for the hetman-maker than practice.

People traveled just to have a look at Lypynskyi. Everyone had read his books, but few had seen him in real life. He would come out to meet his guests, "smiling amicably and nonchalantly, a man of medium height, attractive, with dark hair combed back, elegantly dressed, with military bearing," as one of his visitors described him. His eyes gleamed feverishly; his cheeks were flushed. The guests didn't believe that Lypynskyi was as sick as was said about him. They'd declare from the outset: "Your retinue, Mr. Lypynskyi, must love and value you very much if they exaggerate the poor state of your health so much."

Lypynskyi would remain silent, a grimace frozen on his face. After each such visit, he wouldn't get out of bed for several days. For Lypynskyi, displaying physical infirmity in front of strangers was unbefitting of a true Hetmanite. His secretary Tsyprianovych knew this opinion of Lypynskyi's well but was by nature indecisive and taciturn. As such, he failed to forewarn Lypynskyi's colleagues from the institute of this preference when they were organizing a lecture for him and, knowing about the tuberculosis, decided to cleverly facilitate his ascent up the stairs. The assembly hall where the lecture was to be held was located on the fourth floor. Everyone was already gathered and waiting for the speaker.

Lypynskyi was just walking up to the main door when four students holding a wheelchair ran out to meet him. Just like that, on a wheelchair, like some pharaoh on a golden throne, they were supposed to transport Lypynskyi upstairs.

He froze. His chest once again tightened and crackled, as it had back when he had fallen off his horse at his uncle's racetrack. The feebleness of his body suddenly became both an insurmountable burden and a source of shame. A curse. A prison from which he couldn't break free. Lypynskyi turned around and walked away. The lecture was canceled.

———

IN 1928, LYPYNSKYI began to refer to himself as a cripple, occasionally describing himself as a cripple lost in a desert. His Berlin doctors urged him to return to the mountains, and the patient, barely alive, left for Austria. His little house in Reichenau was already occupied by someone else ("My moving from there was a big mistake," he would later write), and another one couldn't be found in the area at an affordable price. He ended up having to look in Styria, which was cheaper. The search lasted several months, over the course of which Lypynskyi experienced an acute crisis and became convinced that now, at long last, he was at death's door. Fin Yulí held his hand and wiped the sweat from his brow, as Kazimiera once had, while his loyal dog Tsyprianovych read aloud old letters from his closest friends. For instance, from Osyp Nazaruk, who had returned to Lviv and become the editor-in-chief of the religious newspaper *Nova Zoria* (*New Star*).

"You, esteemed and dear Mr. Envoy," Tsyprianovych read, "completely underestimate the power of the 'propaganda' with which Moscow has felled our statehood for a second time now, meanwhile the billionaire Wrigley has accustomed an entire nation—a hundred million people—to chew gum in America! These are facts that need to be reckoned with."

Lypynskyi smiled through his feverish daze and bade the secretary to send a postcard with his greetings to Lviv. He had been dissuaded from a friendship with Nazaruk on more than one occasion, but Lypynskyi liked those kinds of people—energetic and insufferably candid, just like him.

Finally, with a donation from a wealthy philanthropist from Canada and additional help from his brothers, he acquired a dilapidated cottage in a remote area near Graz, naming it *das Sterbe-*

haus, the "death house." Out of all his medications, Dicodid alone helped—an opium-derivative drug that was significantly stronger than morphine.

"My brothers, Stanisław and Włodzimierz, who consider themselves Poles, bought me, a Ukrainian who was robbed by Ukrainians, this little house so that, living in a strange land, I would at least not have to die in a stranger's house ... To reach me, you must first travel from Vienna to Graz, and then take the train to the Lieboch station. Mr. Tsyprianovych will meet you there and help you get to the house. Please let me know if you enjoy walking and are able to do so: the walk from the station to my house in Badegg is about two kilometers. Otherwise, we'll send a wagon because this place is a backwater with no carriages for hire."

The cottage was single-story, with a small terrace that the housekeeper bestrewed with potted flowers. Lypynskyi occupied one wing—a room that served simultaneously as a bedroom and an office. In the middle stood a desk, which increasingly served the household as a dinner table. In the other wing, Fin Yulí occupied a smaller room, while the guest room, which was even more tiny, was occupied by Tsyprianovych. When guests visited, the secretary would relocate to the barn if it was warm or, if it was cold, to Fin Yulí's room. The kitchen was located in the corridor between the two wings.

Lypynskyi would wake up very early, drink tea that he prepared himself—whenever he was able to—in an electric kettle gifted by Tsyprianovych for his forty-fifth birthday, then sit down to write. No one had the right to disturb him. He talked to himself while drafting letters. Sometimes he'd shout something in a spurt of anger; other times he'd become annoyed because he understood more and more what the world should be like and how people should live in it, but the world and its people—for some reason, as if on purpose—did everything contrariwise.

———

OSYP NAZARUK, LYPYNSKYI'S favorite "pupil," was the most resistant to Lypynskyi's didactic ways. He'd publish articles in the newspaper he edited by people who, in his teacher's opinion, were utterly undeserving. In one of his biting letters to Nazaruk, Lypynskyi suggested snidely that such behavior could be explained solely by material gain. On more than one occasion he had heard talk that Nazaruk was fond of easy money because he was very afraid of dying of hunger.

Once sweetly adulatory toward Lypynskyi and perfectly capable of managing his mentor's brash communication style, in 1929 Nazaruk unexpectedly bared his teeth and bit down hard. Everyone was shocked.

"By accusing me of graft," he said to certain people, who relayed everything verbatim to Lypynskyi, "the honorable envoy forgets that he himself received close to two hundred dollars many years ago from the government of Halychyna through my hands but never did write the history of Ukraine for schools as promised. I'm telling you this, and it's the truth. You can quote me."

It was a punch in the gut: Lypynskyi no longer had the strength to straighten himself up again. For him, who had sacrificed everything—even his family—for the sake of the Ukrainian idea, the accusation of misappropriating government funds was the greatest possible insult. He had accepted the financial assistance in the form of an honorarium for a school textbook only at the insistence of Nazaruk himself, and later tried to give back the money many times, but Nazaruk wouldn't allow it, assuring him that Lypynskyi had long since paid off any debts to Ukrainians with his *Letters*.

The conflict detonated Lypynskyi and Nazaruk's longtime friendship like an explosive. Outsiders watched its developments with curiosity and gaping mouths, some even getting dragged into it personally, but not a single soul stood up for Lypynskyi, not even his closest associates. In long letters to him, they offered evasive excuses, hinting that perhaps Lypynskyi really was a bit too harsh, perhaps it wasn't worth being so categorical. To which Lypynskyi responded: "Wouldn't it have been simpler to write, 'Dear Viacheslav Kazymyrovych, I love you very much, but getting involved in a fight on your behalf is awkward for me'? The result was this: no one defended me, and I, an active Ukrainian statesman, am entering history as some sort of swashbuckling rogue who makes money off ideas or, as Nazaruk put it, misappropriates government funds. Meanwhile, the ones who were passive and spineless will be lauded as Ukrainian patriots, even though they never actually did anything and didn't even know what they should have been doing, and instead allowed themselves to be suppressed by noxious Muscovites and Poles."

Only thanks to intermediaries was a court rigmarole between the two avoided. Lypynskyi sent Nazaruk a few more harsh letters, enclosing in the final one a handkerchief spattered in coughed-up blood.

Nazaruk reacted haughtily: "My pen itches to mock you caustically, but I'll spare you that mockery. I'm responding because I have a habit of responding to even my greatest enemy . . . It's clear that you were mistaken in thinking that I'd allow myself to be terrorized, because that sort of thing isn't possible with a character like mine. You've calmed your demeanor through harsh discipline, so it's difficult to discern what immeasurable pride, in the sense of the first cardinal sin, and what indignation are hiding behind it."

Here, Nazaruk hit the bull's-eye. Indignation and pride were all that Lypynskyi had left. He was prone to ranting and raving. In the final years of his life, he had become an angel of vengeance.

———

HIS FORMER COMRADE-IN-ARMS Serhii Shemet, now Hetman Skoropadskyi's secretary in exile, undermined the authority of Lypynskyi's ideology with increasing frequency, considering it individualistic scholasticism infected by religious mysticism. In truth, the goal was to curb the inflexible Lypynskyi's power in the party and reduce his influence over the Hetmanate movement as a whole.

"The aspiration to make a Mohammad out of Lypynskyi and his *Letters* into a Qur'an is an exaggeration," Shemet wrote in a party bulletin. "Such an exaggeration only pushes the realistically attuned Ukrainians, who are seeking political know-how, not political faith, away from us. For such Ukrainians, among which I count myself as well, the *Letters* remain a textbook, not a Qur'an."

After several proposals at compromise, the indignant Lypynskyi decided to act in the most radical way possible. He disavowed the hetman and all his former fellow party members, those "damned, blind, deaf, and dumb, yet simultaneously pleasant and likable Shemets," those "slaves, scoundrels, political tricksters, cowards, and doltish fame-seekers, unfit for government work." Lypynskyi liquidated the Union of Agrarian-Statists as the chairman of its Council of Jurors, publishing a biting communiqué with detailed explanations in the Lviv-based *Dilo*.

"I most definitively opposed the gossip from the hetman's house and, with the hetman's knowledge, protested against ideological and organizational chaos, and even more adamantly against this 'Smerdyakov-ness' [from Pavel Smerdyakov, a protagonist in Dostoyevsky's *The Brothers Karamazov*], which stifles any and all enthusiasm, any and all advances, any and all desire for creative polemics and further work. Because how am I to convince anyone that I'm not vying to become a Mohammad and to have my *Letters* be a Qur'an? How do I defend against Smerdyakov-ish scoffing of that which is holy for me, that to which I've devoted my whole self, my peace, my health, my life? Over my long years of public service to Ukraine, I've seen enough of the devastation spread by Smerdyakov-ness. It's the only thing killing supporters of Ukrainianness with the tragic question: Is this sort of thing really worth dying for? Smerdyakov-ness is a contagion a hundredfold more dangerous than the entirety of communism. Because in the fight against communism, this anti-Christian idea, the idea of Christ can revive. But Smerdyakov-ness is a putrid poison that brings forth only decay, rot, and death."

In response, the Hetmanites pronounced Lypynskyi a mentally and spiritually enfeebled incendiary, who was destroying his life's work with his own hands: "The sun of a great mind has begun to dim. Lypynskyi has gone mad."

With a supply of obituaries, they waited, like Komodo dragons, close by for the bitten antelope to collapse from their venomous bite.

"Don't you dare," Lypynskyi warned them, "quote my works as mottos for your bulletins. Don't you dare refer to me as your ideologist, because I'm not your ideologist. And should you not comply with these demands, I'll find a way to put an end to your political infamies . . . I will not be engaging in any more polemics with you."

His Ukraine had died. All that Lypynskyi had left was pride and indignation. And his Orpington chickens.

XX.

RATIONAL CHICKEN BREEDING

(Us)

THE LAST PHOTOGRAPH of him dates from October 1930. Lypynskyi is sitting on a stool in front of his "death house," dressed not in his usual dressing gown, but as if expecting a visitor. Trousers and a light topcoat, with a slightly oversized canvas cap on his head. Everything on Lypynskyi is a little oversized because there's very little left of his body, and before long it will vanish completely.

Based on the angle at which the shadows are falling in the photograph—it was a very sunny day—one can assume that it's around five or six in the evening. Lypynskyi's head is lowered. He's fully absorbed in his own business and isn't paying any attention to Tsyprianovych's photography experiments. Around his chair, a dozen chickens tranquilly peck at the grass. (The photograph is black-and-white, but I know that Orpington chickens are black and bright orange.) One chicken had jumped up onto her master's lap. Lypynskyi is feeding her from his palm. A flash.

Behind him is a tall porch with a terrace, where a woman in

a white blouse is standing, her elbows leaned against the railing. Her sleeves are rolled up, and her face is hard to make out. Maybe it's the housekeeper Fin Yulí. For some reason, it seems like she's smiling. Maybe she's even saying something to Lypynskyi, but I can't hear. Not a single sound will break through the tightly sealed hatches to here, where I am—on the other bank of memory.

Is it possible to kill time? To destroy it? To wipe it out of existence? Is it possible to shade over time with charcoal so that, God forbid, not a single face can poke out of the gloom of the past? To dig up the graveyards and pretend no one had ever been buried there? To cut the frames you want and like out of the film reel that is the past and simply glue them edge to edge, as if what had existed in between had never been?

When my parents and I would drive to the village to visit Grandpa Bomchyk or Grandma Sonia—when I was little, they lived very close to one another—along the way we always passed a bizarre metal structure enclosed by wire fencing, mounted with warning signs of painted skulls. There were satellite dishes affixed on the very top of the structure, from which antennas stuck out, pointing in various directions. For some reason, I thought that this was a space station and that, with its assistance, humanity was preparing to receive greetings from distant galaxies. I was very proud of the fact that a notable event would take place at the entrance to our family's village. Until my father explained that the purpose of the "dishes" was to ensure tropospheric government communication in the event of nuclear war. In peacetime, they were supposed to jam enemy radio waves. So that it would be impossible to inadvertently catch the foreign radio stations banned by the Soviets. So that the time excised from our nation's filmstrip wouldn't slip back in the form of sound and, gaining a voice, come to life again.

LYPYNSKYI HAD A NICE TENOR. When something was going awry, he could at times break into shrieking, but would quickly regain control of himself. Even though there were no grains left in his palm, the chicken had nonetheless remained in his lap. She raised her flat head just barely—not really upward, but sideways, the way chickens do—and with one eye was tracking every movement of her master. Her gaze was grim: impending death could have looked at Lypynskyi like that.

He could tell each of his chickens apart by their appearance; he knew how much each one weighed and how well she laid eggs. Lypynskyi had found no other way to earn money. His political and writing activities had stopped, his correspondence had become limited to a few names, and news made it to him only through newspaper columns.

The economic crisis in the United States had just reached its peak:

"Thousands of stray cats and dogs have been kicked out of their homes by people who have nothing to eat themselves, and are now roaming the streets."

Mass repressions had begun in the Soviet Union:

"In Kharkiv, the Bolsheviks have been conducting arrests among the Ukrainians, with over a hundred arrests in recent days alone. The arrestees are being charged with conspiracy to proclaim an independent Ukraine with the help of disaffected units of the Red Army in Ukraine."

In Poland, police attacks on the Ukrainian population of Halychyna grew rampant, in what some were calling "pacification" and others were calling "the Polish atrocities":

"They're beating people like savages—primarily, more politically conscious Ukrainians, members of village establishments and community councils, and high school and university students."

"Prisons are overflowing with Ukrainians."

"After the beatings, many people are left with broken bones, legs, and arms, or are fighting for their lives."

"One man, for example, had his hands tied to his knees and a pole inserted between his arms and stomach. Then the bound man was rolled across the ground and whipped with a chain until his body was a lump of flesh."

"In one of the villages of the Lviv District, a peasant was tied to a wagon and had to run behind it for about three miles, all the way to the city."

Lypynskyi carefully monitored the events but kept his thoughts to himself.

"When I was healthier," he'd tell Tsyprianovych, "I carried on my work patiently. But then I grew exhausted: I lost my equilibrium and verbally chastised everyone for two years straight. And then that too passed. These days, I'm slowly growing calmer."

Raising Orpington chickens was a melancholy conclusion to a blustery career. Heavy and stumpy, they alighted with difficulty and lay a maximum of one hundred and eighty eggs a year each. Orpington roosters could rival royal peacocks in their beauty, but Lypynskyi hadn't acquired any roosters yet.

"Have you written to Ms. Arnim, the breeder, Tsyprianovych?"

The secretary was readying the camera, attempting to catch the last rays of the sun in the lens.

"I did, as you instructed me to. I ordered two roosters. They'll arrive by mail in a few weeks."

MY GRANDPA BOMCHYK had similar chickens, though, granted, he didn't know what Orpingtons were, or that they had first been bred in the late nineteenth century by the Englishman William Cook, who named the breed after his native suburb of London. My Grandpa Bomchyk probably didn't even know that there was a city named London. He knew Chelyabinsk in west-central Russia, had heard about Kolyma and Kamchatka in the Russian Far East from his neighbors, and had traveled once to either Rostov or Tula, both in the direction of Moscow, to sell apples. The east spread out welcomingly before him, but he had never been to the other border, the western one, and only had a very vague idea of what went on there, even though you could reach it on foot from his village.

At dawn, while I was still sleeping, Grandpa Bomchyk would open up the chicken coop. Next, he would go to the storeroom attached to his house and grab two fistfuls of wheat or barley from the sacks next to the attic ladder in order to feed his poultry. The hens would wait outside the storeroom, the most impatient ones perched on the threshold. With a deft sweeping motion polished over decades, Grandpa Bomchyk would scatter the grain so skillfully that the hens wouldn't have to clamber over one another to peck at it. Then he would shut the storeroom door and turn a large, rusted key in the lock.

I often imagined what was going on in there behind the closed door. (The storeroom had no windows; it must have been dark.) Items rested on shelves, just as they had in the light when the door was open, and hunks of cold baked pork hung on iron hooks from the opposite wall. Grandpa Bomchyk kept the baked pork till late summer, when his closest relatives would gather in the house he had built with his bare hands to celebrate the summer harvest. The lard was stored in aluminum pails on the ground. Over time, it would grow covered in a thin layer of mold, which we would scrape off with a knife and throw away. Individual cracklings would settle at the very bottom of the pail, and as we ate the last of it, the snow-white lard resembled a fancy Italian dessert of white cream speckled with bits of sponge cake. But Grandpa Bomchyk didn't know where Italy was, nor did he know what dessert was. For him, ordinary sugar was a dessert. When he had a craving for something sweet, he would simply dust fresh bread with sugar, after first sprinkling it with a little water or spreading some sour cream on it. Or he'd go to the storeroom and fetch some plum butter out of a yellow clay jug. The plum butter would also sometimes be covered in a layer of mold. In general, mold felt very much at home in my grandpa's storeroom. The place smelled of dampness, earth (there was no floor), mice, jerked meat, and wheat. Once I was a little older, I finally ventured to climb up the attic ladder; at the top rung, you needed to hoist yourself up by your arms, resting your stomach on a board, and from there plunge into the ominous hole in the ceiling. When I first managed to pull off this acrobatic trick, Grandpa Bomchyk was celebrating the summer harvest. Guests were gathered around the table in his house. His younger brother, an ardent Communist who worked in some ideological capacity, had come from the city.

"The commies have destroyed the village," Grandpa Bomchyk said scornfully to his brother after his third tumbler of moonshine.

The brother was reclining on the couch and inhaling chestfuls of air as if he were gearing up to blow everything in front of him off the face of the earth. "The village is a breeding ground for nationalism. It needs to be destroyed," he responded.

"And why have the commies forgotten about me?" Bomchyk asked.

I don't know if I made out the whole conversation correctly because I was still in the attic. That's where Grandpa Bomchyk hid all the things that he couldn't bring himself to throw away—his past. Spare chipped or cracked milk jugs, and embroidered sheepskin coats, so eaten to a pulp by moths that my parents had to burn them after Grandpa Bomchyk's death. Corncobs were drying on burlap mats. Sacks of various sizes stored white beans from the preceding year, the year before that, and the year before that.

I groped my way around the attic. There were also two chests, one large and one small. The large one I was unable to open; in the small one lay ancient matches as long as my whole palm. Beneath my feet, books rustled. They were lying around, opened, amid dust, nails, and broken glass, like perished soldiers after a bloody battle: a physics textbook for fifth grade (my father's, from 1963), an astronomy textbook (also his, from 1966), a class reader (from 1911, I don't know whose) published back during the Austro-Hungarian period. I moved through the darkness like a sleepwalker. Through a tiny hole in the tin roofing, a single ray of light made its way in, and I raised everything to it that I wanted to examine more closely. The guests in the room below must have heard my steps above their heads, but they were engrossed in what had become a heated argument.

At the end of it, Grandpa Bomchyk exclaimed, "I don't know why I put up with a commie like you in my own house!"

His brother snarled back, "You should thank me that this house hasn't been taken away from you."

Between them, on the table, there were little plates of sliced herring layered with disks of onion, and of meat jelly and *tsvikli* (grated beets with horseradish), a large plate of cold cuts (cold baked pork and sausage, most likely the Moskovska that my parents used to bring from town), and a large plate of fresh vegetables (cucumbers and tomatoes).

After I climbed down from the attic, I joined the table. I was given a small cup of fruit compote and a fork with a broken prong, with which I immediately reached for the meat jelly, then generously poured vinegar over it. As was the case every time, my grandpa's brother bounced up and down on the couch agitatedly before finally leaving, offended. By then Grandpa Bomchyk was completely drunk. As usual, my mom surreptitiously hid the bottle of moonshine out of his line of sight, while he muttered, reminiscing drunkenly, "Sparrows would sometimes fly over to chirp under the eaves, but whoever followed their song was as good as dead."

Grandpa Bomchyk grew to be very fat, and when he died at age eighty-seven, the table at the memorial service collapsed under the weight of his body. My parents sold his last cow. His dog, thank God, had already died a natural death the day before. The chickens ended up having to be slaughtered all in one go. My mother did so while my father hid out at the neighbor's house.

For some reason, I've always thought that, out of everyone, I remembered Grandpa Bomchyk the best. But when I start sifting through the memories themselves, I discover that there actually aren't that many of them. And that the ones that do exist aren't related to one another and don't say much about either my grandfather or the time he lived in. It's as if inside of me, in that part of my brain that's responsible for memory, someone's also installed an antenna for tropospheric scatter, and it jams, jams, and jams radio signals to keep me from remembering my own past. I don't even know (and there's no one left who would know) what Grandpa Bomchyk's parents' names were. Their surname was Okhrym, but they took their first names with them to their graves, the locations of which I will no longer be able to uncover either.

IN A LETTER to Andrii Zhuk, Lypynskyi wrote disappointedly, "You and I, we'll both die here in a foreign land. Meanwhile, all sorts of scum will return home to Ukraine, get cured of their myriad illnesses, procreate, and enjoy the remainder of their lives. Such is the law of Ukrainian nature."

Do these harsh words apply to me as well?

Zhuk would die forgotten by everyone in Vienna's Josefstädter Straße in 1968; he'd live the longest out of that entire mighty first wave of emigrants. There would be many more waves to come.

When Volyn would be captured by Soviet troops in 1939, Lypynskyi's brother would leave everything behind and flee from Zaturtsi to Poland. In exile, he'd finally gain fame as a selective breeder. His best-known potato variety would be called Voltman Zaturetskyi, and his best-known wheat variety Displaced.

FINALLY, THE WOMAN in the photograph—the one who was leaning with her elbows against the terrace railing—straightened up. You could see that her face was very young and didn't resemble the housekeeper's. What's more, Fin Yulí had short hair, and hers was long. She began to speak in Polish: "Father, these chickens seem to really like you."

"Yes—yes," Lypynskyi replied, I can hear his voice quite clearly, "chickens have always thought I was one of their own. When Kaz... your mother and I visited the Rokicki's farm—the farm, incidentally, was called Kurnyky, 'Chicken Coops'—the chickens immediately surrounded me and wouldn't let me pass. I don't know if you remember."

"How can I remember if I hadn't been born yet?"

"Ah, indeed. And you've never even been to Ukraine."

They walked into the house, and the housekeeper quickly set the table. Lypynskyi's daughter Ewa was given the privilege of choosing where to sit first.

"I don't use salt because it's very bad for your health, but you can salt your food if you like. Fin Yulí doesn't listen to me either and always salts her plate on the sly."

Lypynskyi sat down next to Ewa. He wanted to stay as close as possible to his daughter, to touch her, to see how she moved and what she did, to be the first to hear what she said.

"How is your grandma?" He didn't have the courage to ask how Kazimiera was doing.

"She took the earthquake in New Zealand last year very badly. That's all she could talk about."

"I heard about it too, I think," Tsyprianovych remarked, ladling pea soup into bowls. "Apparently an entire city, along with all its inhabitants, was swallowed up by the earth."

"You believe all sorts of nonsense, Tsyprianovych."

Ewa reached for the salt, then glanced at her father and changed her mind.

"Father"—Lypynskyi started every time he heard this word from her lips—"I've always wanted to ask you something. What you devoted your whole life to . . . none of it worked out for you, right? I don't mean to judge you, I've grown up, you mustn't think . . . I just want to know."

Lypynskyi's entire body collapsed on itself. Tsyprianovych stopped eating and inconspicuously placed his spoon in his bowl; chewing at a moment like this seemed inappropriate. Lypynskyi exhaled softly from the depths of his tubercular lungs: "I came to the conclusion that Ukrainians aren't fit for life as a polity. It's an anarchic nation."

Ewa cut him short: "I'm not sure I want to know more. But I want to see where you were born, where Grandma and Grandpa lived. I don't even have photographs of them."

"I had some somewhere. Tsyprianovych will show you."

"I wrote to Uncle Stanisław in Zaturtsi that I'd like to visit them. He and his wife seem like good people."

Ewa's bright voice resonates across the whole room. I can hear it very clearly, just as I can hear how the gigantic blue whale is slapping its tail against the surface of the sea somewhere not too far away. Very soon, it will open its mouth and begin to suck in everything and everyone: Lypyskyi, Ewa, Tsyprianovych, Fin Yulí, the Orpington chickens bred in a henhouse, the little house in Badegg that would be bequeathed to the secretary and housekeeper to use till their deaths, the letters and notes that, per Lypynskyi's wishes, wouldn't be allowed to be published for at least ten years and, even then, no one would really want to publish. The blue whale will suck it all away: everything that Lypynskyi fought for and lost, his pain and his hatred, everything that he saw and felt, his body, all his illnesses, his memories, his Ukraine.

IN JUNE 1931, the newspaper *Svoboda* would print in bold black letters on its front page the headline "**VIACHESLAV LYPIN-SKYI DEAD**," and I would read it at some point in the future and not know who it was referring to. That's when time would conquer me. The blue whale would shut its mouth and swim on.

The blue whale of forgottenness.